WATCHTOWER

THE CHRONICLES OF TORNOR
Book 1

ELIZABETH A. LYNN

ibooks
new york
www.ibooks.net

DISTRIBUTED BY SIMON & SCHUSTER, INC.

A NOTE FROM THE AUTHOR

The land of Arun is a fictional place, and its people, culture, and customs bear only inadvertent resemblance to people and histories of our world, with one exception. The art of the chearis, as it is described, resembles in some aspects the Japanese martial art aikido, created by Master Morihei Uyeshiba. This imitation is deliberate. Writers must write what they know. In gratitude for that knowledge, the author respectfully wishes to thank her teachers.

A Publication of ibooks, inc.

An ibooks, inc. Book

Distributed by Simon & Schuster, Inc.
1230 Avenue of the Americas, New York, NY 10020

ibooks, inc.
24 West 25th Street
New York, NY 10010

The ibooks World Wide Web Site Address is:
www.ibooks.net

ISBN 0-7434-9809-7
First ibooks, inc. printing December 2004
10 9 8 7 6 5 4 3 2 1

Cover art copyright © 2004 Scott Grimando
Cover design by Mat Postawa

Printed in the U.S.A.

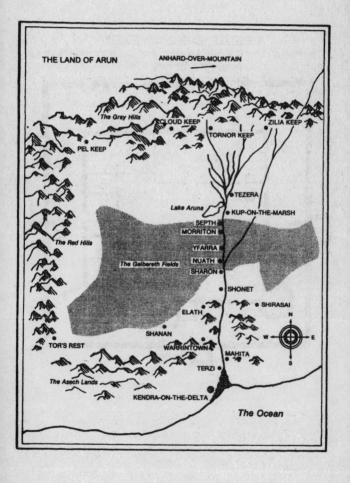

THE LAND OF ARUN

ANHARD-OVER-MOUNTAIN

The Gray Hills

CLOUD KEEP

ZILIA KEEP

TORNOR KEEP

PEL KEEP

TEZERA

Lake Aruna

KUP-ON-THE-MARSH

SEPTH

MORRITON

The Red Hills

YFARRA

NUATH

The Galbareth Fields

SHARON

SHONET

SHIRASAI

ELATH

N

SHANAN

W   E

TOR'S REST

WARRINTOWN

MAHITA

S

TERZI

The Asech Lands

KENDRA-ON-THE-DELTA

The Ocean

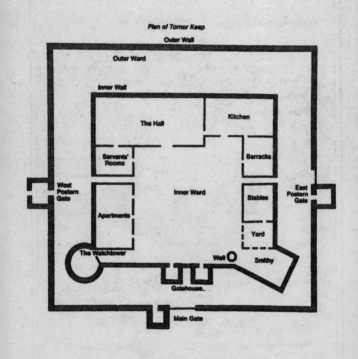

Plan of Tornor Keep

Outer Wall

Outer Ward

Inner Wall

The Hall

Kitchen

Servants' Rooms

Barracks

West Postern Gate

Inner Ward

East Postern Gate

Apartments

Stables

Yard

The Watchtower

Well

Smithy

Gatehouse

Main Gate

o n e

Tornor Keep was dead and burning.

Ryke's face was soot-stained, and his wrists were skinned raw where he had torn them twisting in his chains. His head ached. He was not sure of what he'd seen and not seen happen. He lay in the inner courtyard. He could see a plume of smoke from the outer wall, where Col Istor's sappers had breached it and pulled it down. He smelled the smoke of a nearer burning. Behind him, in the great hall, something was in flames.

Athor, lord of the Keep, was dead, long beard bloody from the wounds he'd taken. Ryke had seen him fall, and in the haze of the fight had expected Tornor castle and tower and walls to waver and fall with him in the shock . . . But it had not happened. The walls were still there. All the men of Ryke's watch were dead. They lay outside the gates they had died defending, frozen into the uncaring

1

snow. Ryke pictured the women from the village coming in spring to dig the bodies of their husbands and sons from the loosening ground.

He was light-headed. He curled into the stone, wondering how many other men of Tornor were still alive, and what Col Istor planned to do with them—with him. He had expected to die with the men of his watch. He still expected to die. He did not want to, but it was hard to summon up a will to live with Athor dead, with the balance broken, the order of things spoiled. He wondered if Col Istor had had him dragged inside and chained in order to make an example of him. The stone was rough beneath his cheek. He shivered. From somewhere in the great square Keep he heard the sound of chickens cackling, and the voices of the women rounding them up. The winter had just begun, two weeks back, and he was not yet cold-hardened. The second big snow had ceased that night. No, he thought muzzily, the snow stopped two nights ago . . .

Fitfully, between shivers, he slept. He woke trying to roll away. Someone had kicked him in the side.

He looked up. Framed against the blue winter sky, Col Istor stood over him: black hair, black beard, a fat swarthy southerner's face.

"We just got the fire out," he said to Ryke casually, as if he were talking to a friend, not a chained and defeated enemy. "Those crazed people set the kitchen on fire rather than surrender." He squatted. He wore mail and a long-sword. His iron helmet looked like an old pot. He smelled of ash. "You warm enough?"

"Too close!" said someone sharply from behind him.

"Shut up." He was thick-shouldered, a bulky man. His dark eyes inspected Ryke as if the watch commander were a goat marked for slaughter. "You fight well," he said. "You're not really hurt, are you? No wounds except that head knock. It saved your life. No broken bones. You're young. You're better off than your lord."

Slowly Ryke sat up. He considered hitting the man with the chain around his hands, but he did not have the strength left in his arms to swing the heavy iron cuffs. "Athor's dead."

Col Istor chuckled. "I don't mean the old one," he said. "I mean the young one, the prince."

"Errel?" Ryke blinked. The smoke stung his eyes. He had not slept in two days, his head was thick. He scooped up a handful of snow and rubbed his face, trying to think. Errel, Athor's only son and heir, had been out hunting when Col and his soldiers appeared at the Keep five days ago. He had not come back. Athor and the commanders had assumed him safe. Ryke had hoped so, very much. "He's out of your reach."

"He's among us," said Col Istor. Standing, he beckoned to the man at his back. "Get him on his feet."

That man stepped forward and dragged Ryke up. He had big ungentle hands. Ryke leaned against the wall until his legs stopped shaking. Col watched him with detached interest. The man did not look like a warlord. Everyone knew that war came from the north. It was born in rock, and it toughened in the constant strife, now at truce, between Arun and the country yet farther north, Anhard-over-mountain. Athor of Tornor, watchful for signs of the Anhard raiders, had paid no heed to the rumors that reached the Keep through the southern traders, about a mercenary chieftain rising out of the peaceful farms of Arun, the shining golden grainfields, the Galbareth. Yet this man had warred on wartrained Tornor in winter, and won.

"Bring him," Col ordered.

They walked across the inner ward to the gate. Ryke had trouble in the slippery snow. The cold wind half revived him. Col's army was all around in the bright sunlight, cleaning up the castle. There was a line of corpses stacked against a wall. Most wore battle gear, but one still wore a leather cook's apron. There was no way to tell which of the cooks it was.

Once Ryke fell. They waited until he struggled up, and went on.

They went through the inner gatehouse, under the iron teeth of the portcullis. Guards stood at attention. Several of them wore spoil marked with the fire-emblem of Zilia Keep, the easternmost of the Keeps, three days ride from Tornor. Ryke did not know what had happened to Ocel, lord of that castle, and to his family. He had a big family. Probably they were dead. More guards swarmed in the outer ward, between the walls. One carried an armful of spent arrows. He held them by the quill end, spoiling the set of the fletch. Southerners knew naught of shooting. Ryke wondered if the Keep could have held out longer with more arrows. The Keep's fletchers had kept the castle supplied with hunting shafts. But since the making of the truce they had more or less ceased crafting war arrows.

He decided it would not have mattered.

Over the wall, Athor's banners snapped in the wind, a red eight-pointed star on a white-field. As Ryke watched, a small dark figure wormed up the pole and cut the banner down. Ryke looked away, aware that Col was watching him. The cuffs dragged painfully at his wrists. They walked along the south wall. The dog cage sat in the sun at the foot of the watchtower. It was a small stockade with a linen awning shading it. Athor had built it for his wolfhound bitch and her pups. There were no dogs in it now. Errel lay sprawled across the dung-spattered stone, covered by a filthy blanket. His face was blue with cold and cut up about the mouth. His eyes were closed. Only the steady rise and fall of his chest told Ryke that he was living.

"He doesn't look like much," said the man whose name Ryke didn't know.

Col Istor said, "My men found him on the west road, heading toward Cloud Keep. He killed four of them with that long bow of his. But he's whipped now."

Ryke wanted to wrap both hands around Col's thick neck. "What do you want?" he asked.

Col Istor teetered, heel to toe, smiling, cheerful. He wore patterned leather and over it a linked mail vest. Beneath the leather the linen tails of his tunic flapped. The mail looked light and strong, as good as anything made by a northern smith. "I could kill him," he said. "Or make him a servant. A pigherd. Or I could keep him alive in chains."

"What do you want, thief?" Ryke said.

The other man backhanded him across the face. The blow sent Ryke into the wall. His head spun, shot through with lights like arrows. He swallowed back sickness and stayed on his feet.

"Held, let be," said Col Istor. The man so named stepped back obediently. Col glanced at the sky. "It's clear now," he said. "Is it going to snow later?"

First they had been talking about Errel, now they were talking about the weather: it made no sense. "What—"

"Just answer me," said the war chief. He laid his left hand on his scabbard, not in threat, but lightly, as if the feel of the sword in its sheath gave him comfort. The leather scabbard was metal-worked. The sword was probably of Tezeran steel, the best there was.

"In another four or five days. Sooner if the wind veers east."

"We'll have to get food from the village, but I don't want to starve people to feed the army. What kind of stores did Athor keep?"

"The storerooms are filled with grain and salted beef," said Ryke. He sucked at his cheek, tasting blood. Held's blow had cut it. "It may not be sufficient. Athor counted on being able to feed two hundred men, plus staff. There are more of you." He tried to keep his tone expressionless but did not quite succeed.

"It galls, doesn't it," said Col. On the wall, the men were raising his standard: a red sword on black. Held wore the device on the right breast of his outershirt. "Look at me, Ryke."

Ryke met his eyes. The man had force.

"That's better. The army can eat light if it has to. How good is the river water?" He referred to the Rurian, the river that fell down the mountains west of the Keep. Joined by smaller streams, it broadened as it hurried south, and Ryke had heard that it flowed unbroken to the sea. It curved by Tornor almost close enough to brush the castle wall: it was the Keep's principal water source.

"It's snow water; it's pure," Ryke said. "What is this?"

"You asked me what I wanted," said Col Istor. "I want you. You know the Keep, the villages, the weather, the needs of the country. I want your service. In exchange for your loyalty, your princeling there stays alive and fed." Both men turned to look at Errel through the spacing of the wooden palisade.

Ryke tried to ask himself what Athor would do. But Athor was dead as mutton and could not speak. "Suppose I say no," he said.

Col Istor smiled. "You can watch while Held breaks his hands."

He said it in a normal tone, loud enough for Errel to hear if he could hear at all. The prince did not move. Ryke watched the lift and fall of his chest. He too must have been hit on the head. A man can die from a head blow. A man can die from cold. "How many watch commanders do you have?" he asked.

"Three," said Col.

"Make it four."

Col tugged at his beard. "Four," he said slowly. Beside him, Held stirred but did not speak.

Ryke said, "Get Errel out of the cage."

Col nodded at Held. The man unfastened the cage door. Seizing Errel by the feet, he dragged the long body out. Ryke went down on one knee. He almost fell; he steadied himself and held out both hands. A few soldiers, black-bearded, curious, stopped their work to watch. Col reached out and enclosed Ryke's hands in his own. Ryke licked his lips. He would not swear to Col Istor the oath he had sown at fifteen to Tornor's rightful lord. "I'll serve you," he said, "with loyalty, as long as Errel's left alone and unharmed."

It sufficed. Col stepped back to let him stand. "Good," he said. He swung toward Held. "Have him carried to the surgeon." Held pointed at two of the watching soldiers. They came forward: one took Errel's shoulders, the other his limp feet. "Tell Gam and Onran to choose out men to make a fourth watch. You too." Held nodded with reluctance. Col ignored it. He turned back to Ryke. "Come on," he said. "We'll get the smith to strike those chains."

When Ryke walked out of the smithy, Col was waiting for him. They strolled toward the barracks. Col said, "Your watch is like the other: that'll bring all of them down to just under a hundred men."

"How many did you come with?"

"Five hundred. We left fifty to hold Zilia Keep, and lost fifty in the fight." Ryke stifled his pleasure at the news that Tornor had accounted for the loss of fifty of Col's men. He would have to keep such thoughts from his mind: he was Col's man now. "I'll announce a new guard schedule tonight at dinner. You'll have to keep the men working and in trim. In one or two months, after the worst of the snows, we'll send out parties to harass Cloud Keep. It won't stand when the time comes to fight.''

Cloud Keep was ruled by Berent One-Eye, who'd lost his eye to a stone kicked up by a running horse in the last of the Anhard wars, nine years ago. Ryke wondered how Col knew that Cloud Keep was weak. He might have northerners—*traitors*, said his mind, and he forced the thought back—among his troops who would be able to tell him such things.

"And after Cloud Keep, Pel Keep?" he asked.

"Yes. That will be hardest. Harder than this was. Sironen's no fool. He'll be expecting me."

They passed the Yard. Despite the snow, there were men practicing, with knives and swords and axes: Col's men now. Every Keep on the mountain passes, every large village, every southern city down the Rurian to Kendra-on-the-Delta had a Yard. Every boy, from the time he reached thirteen, went through its gates each day to practice. Without this training Arun would long ago have been overrun by Anhard. Since the truce, Ryke had heard, the training in the southern Yards had grown lax. It was easy for the farmers to slacken. It was the Keeps that took the brunt of war.

They slowed to watch the men circling in combat. Once every Yard had had a Yardmaster, a man whose skill at war was unquestioned, whose responsibility it was to teach the boys and oversee practice. The custom had lapsed in Tornor. Col scanned the Yard from one side to the other. His bright eyes missed nothing. The two men nearest them swung at each other with wooden swords. "His guard's clumsy," Col muttered. He shouted at the nearer man, who yelled back without turning and held his shield higher.

Col glanced back at the smith. "I did that," he said.

"You were smith?"

"Yes. So was my father, and his father before him. We lived in Iste village. Have you heard of it?" Ryke shook his head. "It's a pinprick, near Lake Aruna on the Great South Road. I used to watch the lords of the Keeps ride back and forth between the mountains and Kendra-on-the-Delta, wanting to be with them, jealous of every horseboy on the line. I borrowed my name from it. That and my father's old battle-axe were the two things I took when I left home.'' He stuck his thumbs in his belt. ''The men may give you trouble, you being a northerner, and so late an enemy. Do what you must to keep them in order.'' And I'll be watching to see how you handle them, his tone implied. He sauntered toward the great stone barracks. ''They should be gathered by now.'' Ryke, who had lived ten years in the building and knew every crack in its walls, followed.

A hundred men lounged in the southwest corner of the barracks: the cold corner, farthest from the kitchen chimneys. They rose as their chief entered. The smell of roast ham filled the room, leaking from the kitchen. Ryke's mouth watered. He felt himself the stranger. Fair-haired, fair-skinned, taller than the men, he stood out among them like a red fox in the snow. They eyed him warily. He wondered what Held had told them.

Col Istor said, ''This is Ryke, late a commander of this Keep. He'll command this watch. His authority is equal to that of any other commander's.'' He teetered, gazing at the silent soldiers. ''Is that clear?'' There was a grumbling assent. ''That's all.'' He turned toward the stairs. As he left, he flashed a yellow grin at Ryke.

Ryke folded his arms. The men were waiting for him to speak. Sunlight patterned the faded wall hangings. Grease from the sconced candles made the scenes of men at war almost unrecognizable. On the nearest panel, archers aimed their arrows at Anhard raiders. A sword slash marked where, in a silly drunken stupor, some soldier of the Keep had hacked at the Anhard warriors on the wall. Under the peaked shape of their helmets, the faces were pale blobs. Ryke surveyed the living soldiers standing in front of the painted ones. They had so recently been his foes . . . Scattered through the swarthy faces he saw northerners. He did not know them: they were, he guessed, men of Zilia Keep who Col had bought or threatened or enticed to his service. No doubt one of them had told Col who Ryke was.

He walked down the row of pallets till he came to the innermost one. "I'll sleep here," he said, and nudged the bundle of gear that lay on it to the floor. A rangy redhead stepped from the ranks. "What's your name?" said Ryke. This was the unofficial leader of the group.

"Vargo," said the redhead. He had freckles on his face and on the backs of his hands. He wore an empty axe sheath on his left hip. He faced Ryke squarely. "That's my bed you took."

Ryke pointed to the pallet next to it. "No, that's yours. You're watch second."

A murmur of interest and surprise came from the observing soldiers. Vargo licked his lips, clearly puzzled, having suddenly been stripped of a cause to fight.

"Col will announce a new watch schedule at dinner. Assemble here before then for weapons inspection. You have the afternoon to polish your gear. I'll see what I can do to get us some extra blankets. Vargo, you stay; the rest of you are dismissed." Slowly they dispersed out the door or to their pallets, moving in clumps to talk. He sat on the pallet. Vargo did the same. "You know them. Tell me about them: which are the slackers, and which cause trouble."

Before dinner, Ryke had Vargo line the men up outside the barracks, in the courtyard. Scullions peered curiously through the kitchen windows. The men at the inner gatehouse turned to watch. Ryke walked slowly along the column, looking at weapons and at the men's eyes. One man slouched, leathers greasy, sword hilt untouched. His name was Ephrem; Vargo had warned Ryke that he might make trouble. He stared at Ryke. He was broad-shouldered and dark-eyed, squat as an ox. Ryke said, "You were in the barracks with the others. You heard the order."

The man glanced from side to side. "I was busy." His stance challenged Ryke to react.

Ryke took a backward step. Ephrem relaxed. His shoulders slumped. Ryke pivoted and hit him crosswise on the left side of his jaw. Beneath his glove he gripped a smooth iron bolt, taken from the smithy. Ephrem's head snapped back. He slid two arm's lengths and landed, limp as a worm, on the cold courtyard floor.

Ryke went on. It took him a little time to complete his inspection. Ephrem was still out cold. "You and you." Ryke pointed at random. "Take him to a bed." The men jumped to drag Ephrem out of line. The scullions jeered at the unconscious man. The others stood. Ryke let them wait, feeling their temper as a man might feel the temper of a newly broken horse. A few turned to watch Ephrem being lugged into the barracks. He waited for them to face him. It grew very silent. A dog barked somewhere within the walls, a lonely cry. Ryke wondered if it was one of Athor's wolfhounds, looking for its master and not finding him. "Dismissed," he said.

Col announced the watches before the start of the meal.

Ryke shared the table with Col and the other commanders. Their table sat below the space, now bare, on which Athor's war banner had hung. The men were seated at long tables, three of them, which reached outward from the small head table like the three tines of a kitchen fork. Ryke's men had morning watch, sunrise till noon. The soldiers were hot with victory. Col had said the army could eat lean but he was not making them fast this night, their first in the castle they had labored to take. Kitchenboys staggered from the serving windows under great platters of food: slabs of bacon, goat, two whole sheep taken from the village, bread, cheese, sauces, potatoes, wine. The men toasted Col, the commanders, each other. They drank to their dead. They did not speak of Athor's two hundred dead, buried now in shallow pits outside the outer walls.

Ryke did not drink to the toasts.

The other commanders watched him: Onran stealthily, old Gam, the horse commander, with amusement, Held with grim mistrust. If Col saw it, he said nothing. At the foot of the hall, over the serving windows, hung pikes, axes, javelins, swords, helmets, shields with patterns of silver and gold, spoils taken over the years from the Anhard raiders who had come over the mountains to loot and had found themselves looted. Some of them were dark with rust. Ryke remembered the raid, nine years ago, in which Athor of Tornor had killed the chief of the raiders. It had happened the summer of his eighteenth year. Ryke carried a souvenir of that war, an Anhard skinning-knife. He had taken it off the body of a man he'd killed. He wore it in a sheath in his right boot.

Along the hall's side walls hung tapestries depicting the building of the Keep. They showed masons and master carpenters with their tools, men carting stone from a quarry, workmen digging the foundation pit, yet more stones on a raft floating downriver, down the snow-swollen Rurian. Ryke looked at the faded hangings so that he would not have to watch the southerners in their triumph. The room was hot and smoky. As the platters grew bare, Col rose. The men cheered him. He roared them to silence.

"You fight well and I'm proud of you," he said. They pounded the tables. "Enough! Twenty-five men of each watch will return to Zilia Keep, to hold that Keep against rebellion. You'll leave tomorrow. Take what provisions you need from the kitchens here; you'll leave the villages alone as you travel. Those left here will dig in for the winter. I understand there are two or three months of cold yet due to this misbegotten country. We'll stay warm sweeping out the snow and raiding at Cloud Keep's border." The men shouted. "Shut up. We'll not grow soft because we're stuck indoors. But we'll not grow bored, either. We'll live like lords. We'll bring women from the village." They liked this, too. "They tell me there's a whole set of rooms for women in the apartments in the west wing, so you can stop fighting over the kitchen maids. And, just like the great houses in Kendra-on-the-Delta, Tornor Keep will have a *cheari*." Ryke frowned. It was a word he did not know, out of the old southern tongue. "He's new to the game but he'll learn fast."

Ryke leaned to Gam. "What's a cheari?"

"It means jester, a fool," said the horsemaster. Ryke nodded. It was southern custom, especially in the great city houses, he had heard, to dress a boy in paint and feathers and set him to tumbling for his supper. He leaned back in his chair. He was very tired, and the smoke and noise were starting to make his head ache. From beneath the table, a warm head pressed against his knee. He felt a sleek coat and silky ears. The dog nosed into his palm. He thought it was one of Athor's wolfhounds. He fed the beast tidbits from his plate.

Preoccupied, he barely noticed when the tumbler came from the kitchen doorway and began to do cartwheels at the foot of the tables. The tumbler was tall for a boy, and clumsy. They had dressed him in leggings trimmed with red velvet, but his chest and feet were bare. Someone tossed him a marrowbone. Pretending to be a dog, he held it in his teeth and ran around on hands and feet. "Good boy!" said Col. The tumbler barked. Laughing, the men tossed scraps. The youth gathered them up. Trotting like an animal, waving a willow switch like a tail, he came toward the high table. Ryke saw that he was no boy, but a man, muscled, lean, and bruised. His face was painted blue. The man passed him at a dogtrot, and Ryke saw that it was Errel. He did not believe it. He looked at Col Istor. The war chief was smiling, as at a well-played jest. Trembling, Ryke rose.

Col stood. So did Held. "Your oath, commander," said Col. "He's alive and unharmed. Sit down." Around them the noise continued unabated. None of the revellers had yet noticed that something was wrong. Col Istor's eyes were hard. "Sit down!" Ryke sat. He could not breathe. His head roiled with pain. He waited for the granite walls to shiver, to crack, but they did not. . . . Col's lips moved. Ryke stared at the woven figures on the walls. The taste of the food was like ash in his mouth. He heard nothing through the roaring in his skull.

t w o

Four months after Athor's death, the north (excepting Pel Keep) lay solidly within Col Istor's grip and in the grip of winter.

Ryke was riding from the Keep to the village in which he had been born. Every third week or so he made this trip, acting as Col's agent and emissary. He wore his furred riding cloak and fur-lined boots over leather breeches and woolen hose. The ground was covered with old snow. It was crusty; the horse's hooves cut cleanly through it. Between the Keep and the town lay a stony, unfarmed waste. In summer grass grew between the boulders, and the children from the Keep brought the castle's herd of milk-goats there to graze, while they picked petals off the blue daisies. At one time the town had filled the space, attached to the Keep by stone walls, but the town had grown. The walls were broken down for building. Now only remnants remained of the original houses. Seen from the castle, the field seemed to have a grain, a pattern where the ancient streets once ran. But up close the pattern melted into a random jumble.

Athor's stores proved not to be enough to feed three hundred men, not counting the servants, the women, and the horses. Col had to requisition food from the village. He kept his word, not to starve the village to feed the army, but by law and custom, a percentage of the village harvest and herds belonged to the Keep and could be claimed by the lord of the Keep at any time. Ryke carried the tallies on his belt: so many hogs, so many sheep, so much grain, to be delivered to Tornor within a week, assuming the weather permitted it. In return for this, the men of the Keep hunted the wild goats and kept the flocks safe from badger, wolf, fox, and cat. Southerners hunted with pikes and slings, not bows. A week back the men of Gam's watch had followed a boar trail south, but they had lost it, to the chief cook's disappointment. He was a southerner, and had never had a chance to prepare boar.

The tallies, graven with signs (a sickle for grain, a horn for goats) and notched to indicate the number of bushels and beasts needed, clacked at Ryke's hip. Col had made the carvings himself. He had Ryke bring the message to the townsfolk that Errel lived. "Tell them his good health depends on their cooperation," he said. "I don't want them to do anything stupid, like plan a rebellion." He teetered, smiling, rocking heel to toe. Ryke had not bothered to point out that a village of mostly old men, striplings, children, and women would not plan rebellion in midwinter.

He entered the narrow familiar streets. They went up and down, following the contours of the land. From the hill he glimpsed the river. There were women in wool cloaks and hoods crouched at the banks, fishing through holes in the ice. He rode to the house of Sterret, the headman, to leave the tallies. As he entered the village proper, the dogs massed to bark at him. A woman's voice screeched them to silence. They were ribbed and lean as wolves. He rushed his horse at them to make them scatter. Athor's wolfhound bitch, which had somewhat adopted him, had followed him to the postern gate whining to go with him, but he had told the guards to keep her back. He was glad now that he had done so: the village dogs would have scented her a stranger and torn her to pieces.

Sterret was a wheelwright; his sons had learned the trade from him. (One of them had traveled south to Kendra-on-the-Delta; the old man heard from him once a year, in summer.) Their house was larger than some others, built of grey stone with a real chimney and ovens and a tile roof. Icicles hung from the protruding edges of the tile. It sat in the center of the town, adjacent to the market. Children, undeterred by the cold, ran in the streets ahead of Ryke's horse, clear voices calling, all the way to Sterret's gate. Ryke recalled playing the hiding game in and out the doorways of the houses till his cheeks numbed and his toes in their sheepskin boots turned stiff and blue.

Sterret came to his gate to receive the notched sticks, accompanied by his youngest son. He walked with a cane; he had served in the Anhard wars and been wounded in the hip. The metal tip of the cane drilled precise holes in the ground, as if a carpenter made them with an auger. He ran his thumb down the markings. "It will be done," he said. "How is the prince?" A shutter opened. The smell of spiced sausage wafted from the kitchen. A woman looked out.

"Errel is well," said Ryke.

"Tell him we do not forget," said the boy, hot-eyed.

"I will tell him."

"Come," said Sterret, to the younger of the two sons left to him. He had had six. He laid a hand on the boy's shoulder. Using the child as support, the wheelwright limped inside his house. The shutter closed.

The houses grew smaller and poorer toward the edges of the village. Fewer had chimneys. Instead of tile, they were roofed with sod. Ryke dismounted outside a plain stone cottage. Smoke rose through a roofhole. He tied his reins around an iron ring set in a stone. The door opened. His mother, wrapped in wool, stood in the doorway. He bent to kiss her cheek. His youngest sister peeped from behind the door. He smelled oat mash. Shaking his cloak free of snow, Ryke waited for his mother to invite him in.

She sat him at the table and fed him: barley cake, sour beer. She walked from firepit to table to firepit, stooping, with the slow gait of a woman who has borne twelve children and lost seven of them. Four of them had died before Ryke was born. He stretched his feet to the fire. The snow ran off his boots and hissed into the flames. "Art thou well?" she asked.

"Yes. And thou?"

She gave the little girl a barley cake, pretending not to hear him. Her hair was grey, thick, and long, and she wore it braided, as befitted a married woman. The braid fell down her back beneath the brown cloth of her hood. He knew her age, vaguely; she was somewhere between forty-five and fifty. She looked older than a man of her years might. Women in the mountains aged faster than men.

"She has a cough," said the girl-child. She kept a tight hand on her mother's apron.

"It's naught," said his mother. "I caught a chill."

Ryke frowned. His father had died of a chill caught in summer after swimming in the river, an ill way for a fighting man to die. He had been one of Athor's watch seconds, and lived within the Keep much of the year. "Have you been to the healer?"

She pursed her lips, in the way that told him she would not speak more of it. Stubborn as winter, his father once said of her. She reached for her knitting. "Kepi will be prenticed to the healer in the spring."

Kepi was his middle sister. "How old is she now?"

"Nine."

"That's good." Mountain villages valued their healers. The current village healer was an old woman named Otha. She had had a prentice, some eight years back, but the girl had run away, and she had refused to take another, causing the village a deal of worry. "How's Evion?" Evion was, excepting Ryke himself, the oldest boy. He was thirteen. In a happier time he would be in Tornor under the wing of his older brother, as kitchen or smith or stableboy.

"He's well. He spends his days with the men. I see little of him." Her lips moved; she was counting. He waited for her to finish her row.

"And Becke?" Becke was the oldest sister, nineteen. She had

two children. Her man had died under the wall of Tornor, his head split by a southern axe like a piece of dry kindling. She had lost the third babe out of the womb. His mother said nothing. Twice he had tried to talk with Becke, but she had kept within her house and refused to see him. "And thou, little one?" he teased, tugging his youngest sister's braids. She shrieked and, giggling, ran to the safety of the skirts. She was seven.

As he remounted he saw a cluster of boys eyeing him from the shelter of the carter's broad doorway. They turned their heads when they saw him looking. He did not know any of them. They wore thick sheepskin, turned inward against the cold. He wondered if they hated him because he was alive. He was alive for Errel's sake, for Tornor's sake. He gathered the reins in his gloved hands, and waved to the boys. It was not his fault that their fathers and brothers were dead.

Stony-eyed as the figures in the tapestries, they stared through him. One of them threw a rock—not at Ryke but up. It spiraled into the sky and fell slowly back. Landing on a roof, it clattered on the ice-sheathed tiles. The boys ran. Ryke urged the horse toward Tornor. Backed into the whitened hills, the village houses leaned into each other as if for warmth. The dogs barked. The oath to Athor and the oath he'd sworn to Col Istor gnawed at Ryke's heart.

Four days after that visit to the village, he found out what it was that his mother had not wanted to tell him about his sister.

His men had the late watch, noon to sunset. Ryke was making the rounds of their posts. The courtyard rang to the sound of hammers: the men were building another table and two more benches. Wood shavings skittered over the stones. The sky was light, but the sun had fallen behind the walls, and the inner wall lay in shadow. Two boys ran into the great hall, one carrying a load of loose sticks, the other a sticky armful of torches, heads tarred. Lost in thought—a dream, of a summer when he had ridden with his father to the farm of a cousin at the very edge of the Galbareth; he remembered the hum of the wind over the flat land; his father had lifted him to his shoulders so that the child Ryke could see the ocean of grain, purpling in sunset—he came to the watchtower stairs and nearly knocked a woman down. Hastily he caught her, hand under her elbow, muttering apology. She wore her hair pinned on top of her head with a fishbone comb, southern fashion, but the way she moved and stood was familiar. She wore a gown of blue wool. The line of her jaw was his own. She averted her eyes and began to move around him. He put a hand on her shoulder. "Becke?"

She answered flatly out of the gloom. "It's me."

She was not dressed like a serving girl. "What are you—"

"I'm Keep's woman now," she said defiantly.

"How long have you been here?"

"Three weeks." She shifted under his hand. He let her go. He could just see her eyes, like sparks in the twilight: light brown, hazel, like his.

"Where are the children?"

"With Ana." Ana was her neighbor. Ana's husband was the carter.

He did not know what to say to her. He did not know her very well. She had been eight when he left the village to live at the Keep, and from then on he saw her only in the summer and at the harvest. She had been a wild child. Sometimes they had been friends; more often they had fought. He wanted to say: *What would Jebe think?* But Jebe was her man who was dead, and of course if Jebe were alive she would not be here.

There was no shame to being Keep's woman, especially not for a widow, especially not in wartime when there were few men in the towns. If she bore a child, the child would be fostered in the village until it was old enough for the Keep to claim it back. Errel's mother had been Keep's woman.

Becke was young yet, clear-skinned and lovely. "Why didn't you tell me you were here?" he said.

"I didn't want to see you," she said. Her tone was cold. She smelled of honeysuckle. Ryke guessed she had a ribbon or a sachet of the dried flowers woven into her hair. In the watchtower someone

struck a light. "Let me by, brother. I'm waited for." He moved to
let her pass. Her skirts rustled against his legs. She went up the watchtower stair. He bowed his head. It shamed him to think of his sister
in Col's bed. He wondered why Col had not taunted him with it. It
could only be because he did not know. He could not even be angry.
Women had to survive. Becke served the southerners, just as he did.
He would have to put it from his mind, as he had learned to put so
many things.

He and Errel had arranged a way to meet; signaling to each other
by means of a token, which passed from one to the other of them as
if it were a love sign, carried by a friendly kitchenmaid.

They met on the wall of the Keep, above the great hall, standing
shoulder to shoulder like two men on watch, bundled and hunched
against the swirling snow. Errel asked how the village fared. Ryke
told him. The prince's face was thin and hungry. He asked the questions Athor would have asked. Ryke remembered Errel the hunter,
Errel the bowman, Errel watching at Athor's back, young and grave,
as Ryke knelt and swore his father fealty . . . Now he ate what he
could scrounge from the table scraps and the cooks. Ryke leaned his
elbows on the wall. Deep inside, where he hid it, rage burned. It
warmed him. He spoke in measured tones of sheep and pigs, visioning
for himself that privileged instant in which he closed his hands around
Col Istor's throat.

"Sterret asks for you always. The villagers do not forget to whom
they owe their first allegiance."

Errel's cheeks reddened. "For their own sake, I hope they offer
Col no contest," he said.

"They do not."

"I am glad to hear it. Do Col's men keep the hunting covenant?"

"Three of Onran's men brought a wolf in yesterday."

"That's good," said Tornor's lord.

He wore an ancient fur-lined cape, stained boots too big for him,
and no gloves. He did not look like a soldier. Col had made it clear

to Ryke that he did not want them to meet, and this was the fourth such meeting in as many months that Ryke had dared to plan. "Are you fit, my prince?" Ryke said.

Errel chuckled. "Need you ask? I am fit enough to tumble for my dinner in the hall each night. Fit for what?"

"Would Col let you work in the stables—play stableboy—if you begged it of him?"

"He would like that, to have me beg him. But I doubt he would consent to let me trade my Jester's willow for a currycomb. He likes this jest too well."

Ryke could not understand how the prince could laugh. He wondered what Athor would think if he knew his son still lived, playing for his supper and his life like a dog trained to sit and speak. Athor would have raged. Athor's rages were famous. But Athor was dead. Errel pulled the cloak tighter around his shoulders. His face was beardless, scraped clean for the paint Col made him wear. "I had a thought—" Ryke said.

"Tell it."

Ryke checked the length of the wall as far as the veiling snow permitted him to see it. No one was on it. Beneath them in the inner ward a shivering light-haired girl ran in haste toward the kitchen. She carried a brass bowl. Her bare feet left scant marks in the filmy snow. Ryke said, "I hid a pack with travel furs in a corner of the stable where not even old Gam could find it. If you can get there..."

Errel stared west into the stormy twilight, hands flat on the chilly stone of the embrasure. "That's not the way," he said.

"Do you mean you don't want to escape?" The words rang loudly on the battlement.

"Softly," Errel said. "The wind might drop." They listened. No one came. The prince said, "I dream of escape. But though I play the fool, I have not turned into one. That's not the way to do it. That would leave you here, to face Col's fury. I will not agree to any plan that puts you at risk."

"One man moves quicker than two—"

"No. I don't want to hear any more about it." He turned from a gust of wind to stare hard at Ryke, eyes like blue ice. "Oaths are binding in two directions, Ryke."

Ryke bowed his head. "Yes, prince."

The wind died. In the lull they heard the sound of steps coming their way. It was the guard. They flattened to the stone, and he walked by swathed in furs without seeing them. Tyke waited to speak until he could not hear the footsteps. "Do the Cards tell you aught, prince?" At Errel's request, he had thieved from the prince's old apartments his pack of the Cards of Fortune. Magic made Ryke unhappy. He did not like to believe that the future existed in little, in symbol, within a double handful of painted pictures. But Errel had skill with the Cards.

Errel said, "Suppose I said yes. You have no faith in the Cards."

"For a way out of here," Ryke said, "I will trust every kind of magic there is, even the Cards."

They walked south. A light streamed from the window of the watchtower, dim through the falling snow. Col was there. Ryke's bitterness rose. Errel said, "Out of their presence it is not wise to speak of the Cards. They are old and powerful, and like many oldsters, they resent being talked about where they themselves cannot hear it."

Over the blow of the wind, they heard a powerful voice shouting in anger. "Held making rounds," Ryke said.

Errel said, "Do you know what they call him in the kitchen? Col's dog."

Ryke wondered what Col Istor would make of the Cards. "He calls for you a lot lately," he said, worrying at the source of bitterness as a dog worries a sore.

"It takes the men's minds off the scanty rations."

"Sironen will stop him," Ryke said. "Sironen will stop him when he goes to take Pel Keep."

"Maiou."

The sound made Ryke jump like a nervous horse. Poking out of the fur of Errel's cloak was the tawny orange head of a kitten. "What—"

"I found her freezing on the stair. I'll take her to the kitchen, she can be kitchen cat."

"Maiou," said the kitten. It began to purr tempestuously. As if in answer to the minute noise, a growling screech lifted from beyond the castle wall. It wailed and fumed.

"Wildcat," said Errel, with the interest of a hunter. "They don't often come this close."

"She must be hungry." They both craned westward as the cat began to mourn again.

"Look." Errel pointed. It was a rider, two riders, coming from between the grey rocks that hid the mouth of the west road. That road led to Cloud Keep, to Pel Keep, and followed to its end, to the Great Mountains that marked Arun's western border. There were no Keeps in the shadow of those peaks. None were needed. They rose ice-tipped, dark and sheer as a wall.

"Messengers," said Ryke.

"I see them," said Errel. "That's strange. It's unusual for one of the green clan to travel so far north. The last time they did so was to help make the Anhard peace."

"They follow war," Ryke said. Squinting into the grey distance, he could just make out the flag the riders carried. A green one was for heralds, messengers, or truce. Under the wall, a voice shouted. Men gathered at the postern gate.

"Yes." The kitten mewed again, and the Jester stroked it absently, eyes fixed on the small figures riding toward the castle.

"I must go," Ryke said. "They'll be looking for me."

"Yes. You go."

Ryke frowned. By Col's order, his cheari was forbidden the walls. It would go ill with Errel if the guard found him. "You shouldn't stay here," he said.

"I know," said Errel. "I'll take the north staircase. You go ahead."

Ryke left him. He wondered what message could be traveling to Tornor in the winter, and from where. It would not be a threat, one did not send warning of war. It could be an offer, an alliance (from Cloud Keep?) a request . . .

Into his mind came a picture off one of the Cards, as he had seen them sliding through Errel's long fingers: a cloaked and hooded figure, in green, riding under a dark blue sky on a sorrel horse. The name of the Card was the messenger. His boots echoed on the slippery stone. He came to the north stair and hurried down it into the smoky warmth of the great hall. He heard his name. "I'm here," he said. "Who wants me?"

"Col's calling for you," said Vargo. "What's it all about?"

"I don't know."

His men crowded him. He could smell the ale on their breath. "Are we raiding Cloud Keep again?"

"I don't know." He shook the snow from his cloak. Fastening it back, he stepped out of the hall into the inner ward. The wind was dropping. He pulled the hood around his face and strode toward the spiral staircase of the watchtower.

Tornor Keep was a mole's warren of stairs and corridors. The original castle, like the line of the lords of Tornor, went back two hundred years, and the outer and inner walls, the barracks, and the great hall were still of the old stone, dark, rough granite out of the mountains. But the apartments, the storerooms, stable, Yard, smithy, the mill and the kitchen had been added to so many times that one could only guess at the original dimensions of the inner court. Morven, Athor's father, had added a laundry to the apartments, and Athor had repaired and enlarged the mill which straddled the Rurian just below the Keep. The apartments stood empty now, save for Col's living space and the comings and goings of the Keep's women. The men slept in the barracks, the servants slept in the kitchen, the cooks in tiny sleeping rooms in the storerooms. Ryke did not know which of Tornor's lords had built the watchtower. Legend said that he had ordered it built "so that he might see the Anhard raiders before their kings give the order to attack." It was true that the windows only looked north.

East, west, and south the tower was blind. Perhaps because of that, perhaps for other reasons, it had fallen into disuse. Athor had talked about having it boarded up, or even torn down.

But Col liked it. He had decided to hold all of his councils there, and had ordered it scoured clean, whitewashed, and rewindowed. Each of the new yellow panes had an iron frame that could be singly opened. Ryke climbed slowly. The long stair was ill-lit and wearisome. At last he neared the top of the stairway. He heard voices; chiefest in them, Col's. The man was pleased with something. The aura of his pleasure flowed down the stair like a brisk wind. A page, outside the door, bowed and pushed it open. Ryke stepped into the chamber of the tower.

The three other commanders were already there. Ryke nodded to them, and bowed to Col. "Ryke," said the chief. "My fourth watch commander." He showed teeth through his black beard. In honor to the visitors, he was wearing a tunic of fine purple wool and a sash of blue velvet in place of his usual leather and linen. He waved a hand at the messengers. They were dressed in thick travel furs. They stood with their backs to the fire. The wool lining of the furs gleamed green, the mark of their position and their neutrality. "Norres. Sorren."

Ryke nodded. Two slender beardless faces gazed at him assessingly. They're boys, he thought, and then looked more closely at their height and weight and at the way they stood, Norres' left shoulder brushing Sorren's right, and at the way they wore the long daggers on their hips, ready to hand. They were not boys. Memory nudged him. A dark-skinned southern trader in the summer, following the river with a load of silks and spices, had stopped at Tornor and stayed up late, dicing with the watch, long after Athor retired to his bed. The trader had told stories. (They had not done him much good. He lost three rounds of dice and paid with a length of silk and a dozen peacock feathers before giving up the contest in disgust.) He told stories about the famous captain Ewain Med, and the tale of the outlawing of Raven Batto.

When he could not awe his listeners with stories of the city, he talked about the messengers. The green clan, he called them. They carried documents that no one else could be entrusted with. They couldn't be bribed. They wouldn't spy. The northerners, smiling, assured him that they knew all about the messenger folk. It had been they who carried the truce words between Anhard and Arun. Piqued, the trader whispered a tale of a man who sought to bribe two messengers to carry a lie. They skinned him, and nailed the skin to his front door. Pushed, he said their names. They were, Ryke thought, very like *Norres* and *Sorren*. He recalled another thing about the messengers in the trader's tale. They had been *ghyas*. The word was southern; it meant something like hermaphrodite. A ghya was half man, half woman, or else neither man nor woman, but a third thing. If you did not know, Ryke thought, such a one might look like a youth. He glanced away as he realized that he had been staring at the messengers. They did not seem to notice. He decided they were used to stares.

Col said, "They bring a truce offer from Berent One-Eye."

Berent One-Eye ruled Cloud Keep. Col had been sending raiding parties up to the wall of his castle for a month. The chief was smiling. Ryke guessed that he had expected the offer, perhaps counted on it.

"He'll send me a hostage, a younger son, to arrive within three weeks of my acceptance of truce."

Held rasped, "He's less a fool than I thought. He knows he'd lose a war with you."

It was truth. But Ryke pitied Berent, offering a son to stave off the army whose vanguard he expected to see at his front gate any day. He pulled at the ties of his cloak. The octagonal room was hot. Col had had the walls whitewashed with lime and covered with ancient tapestries from the apartments. On one wall, a man with a gilt-thread beard rallied his men. Ryke could almost hear him shout. Under the grime, his face reminded Ryke of Athor.

Onran said, "What if it's a trick? He might be lying."

"No," said the messenger on the right, Norres. "He is not lying." The ghya sounded amused.

"How can you be sure—" began Onran.

Col cut him off. "Onran jests," he said. "Will you have some wine?" He tilted wine from a jug into two glasses. The messengers picked up the yellow crystal goblets and drank. Sorren's hood fell back, revealing shoulder length hair tied with a green ribbon and a skin as pale as any northerner's. Norres lifted a hand to his/her hood. They were both pale. Sorren had a puckered scar under the left eye.

Norres said, "I have never seen a room like this before."

Col said proudly, "You should see it in daylight." He tapped the table on which the wine jug stood. "When we first came the windows were bare, the chimney blocked, the stairs so slimed that one could not climb them without peril." He tugged on his beard. "One day I hope to see this Keep as fine as any of the great houses of the south."

You will not have that chance, Ryke thought. Sironen will stop you. He unclenched his fingers, which had bunched. Col went on talking. Ryke had rarely heard him so quick-tongued. "You'll join us for dinner. After the ride from Cloud Keep you must be hungry. There's not much luxury here but there'll be food enough, and wine, and entertainment."

"You are hospitable," said Norres.

"I know what is due to messengers," said Col. "Light!" The page scurried forward. "Show our guests to their rooms."

Norres said, "May we first visit the stable? It is our custom always to look after our horses."

"My horsemaster himself will take you there," Col said. Gam bridled, momentarily annoyed at thus being assigned page duty.

"Thank you," said Norres. The ghyas lifted their hoods over their heads and followed Gam. The page backed away, lantern swinging wildly. Col motioned to the child to shut the door.

When it closed, he turned on Onran. "Spare me your comments, boy, until these two are safely gone. It is ill luck to doubt the word of a messenger, and those two are more dangerous than most. I have had some experience with the green clan. I want no quarrels with them."

Onran muttered apology. He was the youngest of the commanders, twenty-two, brash, quick, well-liked by his men. "They give me the shudders," he said. He reached for the wine jug.

Col twitched it from his grasp. "Keep it to yourself. And warn the men. I want no stupid jests tonight. We will discuss this later. You are dismissed." There seemed nothing more to say. Onran's face was red. He stamped down the stairs. Ryke followed him into the cold, more slowly.

The steepness of the stair made talk impossible till they reached the courtyard. At the bottom tread they bunched together behind the page's lamp. Onran's face was stiff and sullen. "Give me that," he said, grabbing for the light, but the boy eluded him and scampered back up the stair. He cursed.

Behind him, Held said sardonically, "Is your mouth cold?" Onran swore at him. Three abreast, they walked toward the barracks.

Onran said, "I was jesting. They took no offense."

"Lucky for you," said Held. "If they wished to, they could skin you, and no one here could stop them. Privilege of the clan. It happened once, to some southern lord."

"What did he do?" Onran said.

"He tried to bribe a messenger to lie." Held jerked a gloved thumb at the apartments. "I've heard, too, that it was those very ones."

"What do you know of them?" asked Onran, with a child's facination.

"What everyone knows."

"They've no sex."

"I've heard that."

"And they fight like wolves of hell."

"And it costs the earth to hire them," said Held. "That's how Col can be sure that Berent One-Eye means no trick by this truce. If he wanted to lie, he would send his own herald, not a messenger." It was odd to get this much speech from Held. Ryke decided that pleasure at Onran's discomfiture had loosened the dour southerner's tongue.

Onran kicked at the flagstones. "I still think it could be a trick," he muttered.

Ryke said, more to shake Held than because he thought it was true, "Perhaps he's subtler than you judge him." Held cast him a venomous look.

Onran grinned. "Perhaps he owns a secret treasure."

"All these mountain Keeps are poor," grated Held. "This thrice-damned winter sees to that."

All three glanced at the sky. The snow had stopped; clouds raced across the star patterns, pushed by a brisk west wind. Ryke said, "If you will stay here, Held, you must learn to like the winter."

"In a pig's ass," said Held.

Onran changed the subject. "Col's pleased to have company."

Held's face smoothed, as it always did at the mention of his chief. "We'll feast tonight. I heard him giving orders to the cooks." They had fallen into step with one another. The beat of their wooden boot soles echoed over the stone. Ryke thought with distaste of the dinner. He would have to be there. Col liked him to sit through Errel's foolery; it was his way of tightening the chain. There was no way for Ryke to turn traitor, to think traitor, with Errel prancing like a puppet to Col Istor's least whim.

Onran chuckled. "My men tell me Ryke's got a girl in the kitchen." He poked Ryke's side with his elbow.

"Oh," said Held, "surely a man of commander's rank can do better than the bed of some sluttish kitchen-maid."

It was meant to anger. But Ryke thought of Errel, and shrugged off the insult. "Till dinner," he said to Onran, and strode ahead of the other men like a man on an errand. The servants were lighting the torches in the great hall.

three

Three hundred people crowding the great hall made for heat and a rowdy evening.

The men of three watches faced off down the long sides of the four tables. Over their heads the torches in their wrought-iron sconces smoked and dripped ash on the floor. Col, his commanders, and his guests sat at the head table. The servers rushed between the serving window and the tables. The wood groaned with the weight of platters of hams, mutton, geese, pots of fresh eels drawn from the river, sauces, fruit preserves—the cooks had outdone themselves. Dogs prowled the benches, hoping for morsels. The room looked much as it had when Athor called for a feast—except that the men wore badges of red and black, and their faces were not the faces of the men Ryke had known since childhood, learned from, fought beside.

As a special treat, Col had invited the women from the apartments to join the meal. They sat on the benches with the soldiers. Ryke had watched them come into the hall; he did not think Becke was among them, but could not be certain. They had dressed for the occasion. They wore velvet and soft cotton and fine woolens and the glinting shimmer of silk. The finery made rough contrast to the soldiers' homespun.

Ryke filled his plate with eels in wine, a dish he loved. But after the first few bites he had to push the laden bowl away. His stomach hurt. Against the dark wall of his inner vision he saw Errel's thin and hungry face. A worried serving girl bent over him. "Is it spoiled?" Her bright face reminded him of his sister Kepi. He smiled at her concern.

"No, it's fine. Just bring me a slice of ham, and a clean plate."

Ryke's men had the night watch, midnight to dawn. Keeping one ear cocked toward the conversation at the head table, he worked on setting up the watch order in his head. Col was in a good mood. He tossed pork bones to the dogs, teased the serving women, talked strategy with Onran (who blushed to be thus singled out by his chief, but managed not to make a fool of himself) and horsebreeding with Gam. He argued that the horses of the Asech tribes were stronger than the northern mountain breed. Gam contradicted him. He made sure both guests had enough to eat. Norres spoke for both the messengers throughout the meal.

When the wine grew low, Col ordered a cask of sweet wine to be brought from the cellar. "And bring the silver dishes," he added. The wine steward bowed and brought three bowls full of sweet red wine. Col lifted his dish. On it in low relief was the figure of a goat running from an archer. "Fine work," he said, running one finger along the chasing. "As good as any southern smith could make." He touched the white silver as if it were alive, and Ryke remembered that he had been a smith's son.

At the close of the meal, the men pushed the benches back to stretch their legs. The women wiped their greasy hands on linens made steamy in the kitchen. Ryke looked for Becke, but did not see her. Col waited till the meat carcasses had been taken from the table, and then called for a second cask of sweet wine, and for desserts. The servers brought dishes filled with cream, honey, and ice.

"Where's my Fool?" said Col.

They brought the whole cask this time, dragging it into the hall on a wheeled cart. Errel was riding it. "You interrupted me," he said haughtily to Col. He hopped off the cask, did a handstand, and whirled upright.

"What were you doing?"

"Pissing." He leered, ducking the bread crust Col threw at him. He went round the tables flourishing his wand, tapping the men on the shoulder. "You, you, you, you, you . . ." As he slid by Ryke, he grimaced. Under the blue and white painted stripes, his face was taut and intense. He was wound as a spring. His bare feet made no sound on the stone. He cartwheeled into the lane between two tables and gestured, as if making a spell. "Yah!"

Ryke noticed with private amusement that not a few of the men leaned superstitiously away from the tapping willow stick. "What's this?" demanded Col. He had not been tapped.

"Ye shall all be unpricked," intoned Errel.

Every head turned to the high table. The two ghyas smiled. The men at table roared with embarrassment and relief. The tapped men jeered or flushed.

"My cheari," said Col to the messengers. "A southern custom." His face was red. Ryke wondered what he would have done if the messengers had been offended. "He means no harm. Come here!" he called to Errel.

Errel leaped on the table. Moving with delicate steps, he walked between the mugs and plates, slashing with the willow wand at hands that reached to trip him. One man seized his ankle. The Jester tipped a bowl of ice into his lap. He reached the head table. He bowed to the messengers, and sank to a frog-crouch, arms dangling, in front of Col.

Ryke had to look away for a moment. He heard Held laugh meanly, and turned back. Col leaned both elbows on the table. For the occasion, Errel was wearing a ruffle round his neck. "You know Berent One-Eye," said Col.

"Certainly," said the Jester.

"Would he learn from me, and attack in winter?"

"Never," said Errel, shaking his head till the bells rung on his cap. Ryke saw the men nearest the high table cock their heads to listen.

"How can you be sure?" said Col.

Errel said gravely, "Only the man with the soul of a wolf makes war in winter."

Col caught the ruff. "I make war in winter," he said.

Errel seemed unperturbed by the big hand at his throat. "Berent One-Eye is a man of peace and honor." He paused. "As a general, he'd make a better dogboy."

Col chuckled, and pushed. Errel leaped nimbly backward and landed on the floor. He disappeared. Suddenly a man in the middle of one of the tables yelled. "Goddamn it, he bit my foot!" The soldier howled. Errel popped up at another table, shaking his capped and belled head in a mime of injured innocence. Col grinned. Errel's tricks ranged from the merely silly to the near-insolent. The men sometimes swiped at him, but Col had given strict orders that no one could discipline his cheari save himself.

Glancing down the table, Ryke saw one of the women sitting frozen to the bench, lips pressed tight together, hands clasped in her lap. He knew her: name was Madi, and she came from the village. Her outrage gladdened his heart. He looked at the messengers in their green tunics and high boots, wondering if they knew who Errel was, and what they thought (if they did know) of the humiliating and dangerous charade he played. He wondered what they really were and if they were truly sexless. Maybe they were geldings. He had heard of such things happening to men in war. But there was no softness to them, such as one would expect to meet in a eunuch. They had the hard subtlety of marble.

Dessert eaten, the women retired to their chambers. The drinking began in earnest. Ryke watched his men. By Col's rule, the squad next on watch did not drink. In a lane between two tables, two men were wrestling. Dogs barked around them. Col shifted with irritation.

One of the men, the more drunken, tripped and fell on his ass. He swore, and the men threw spoons at him.

Ryke stood. He went round the end of the table and booted the two drunks aside. "Clear me a bench," he said. Freeing a bench, the men pushed it toward him. He sat cross-legged on the floor. "Arm wrestle," he suggested, rolling up his right sleeve.

The men quieted. They loved contests. One of Onran's men swaggered forward. He was big in the belly. Onran called, "A jug says Scavat wins!"

"Two on Ryke!" called Vargo. Ryke grinned. He clasped the man's hand and tipped him over easily. Onran groaned.

"Next?" He took on two or three more. His reach and clear head gave him the advantage. His knuckles started to ache. He was ready to quit when a heavy hand fell on his shoulder. Col walked around the bench to sit opposite him. Ryke said, "My arm's tired."

"You've done no work," said Col. "Anyone half sober could take those drunks." He rolled up his right sleeve. "A fair fight, Ryke."

Silently the men gathered to watch, their eyes gleaming. "A fair fight," Ryke repeated. He flexed his fingers a few times to ease the cramp, and set his elbow on the bench.

He still had reach, but Col had strength of shoulder. The man was broad as a bull. They clasped hands. Held counted for them. "Go!"

The muscles jumped in Col's arm as he drove Ryke's hand down. Ryke set his teeth against the grip and held his arm still, tipped but steady, unbending against Col's force. His only hope was to let the chief wear himself out. Sweat popped on his neck and forehead. It stung his eyes. Col had big hands. His dark eyes glittered. His lips pulled back from his teeth, giving him for a moment the look of the winter wolf. Ryke's neck ached. Col moved his arm a fraction. Ryke groaned and bent both hands back to where they'd been. He felt they had been hours at it. His fingers were being crushed. Col pushed. Ryke's arm angled slowly back.

Than the strength went from him. His knuckles hit the bench. He rolled against the floor. He lay and panted till his head cleared. He could hear Col panting too.

"A fair fight," he said hoarsely.

The men cheered. Col flexed his right arm, and then rolled up his left sleeve. "Next?" he said, as had Ryke. Nobody moved. Ryke stood up. His men made a place for him on a bench. "Bunch of weaklings," teased Col. "Bunch of women." His soldiers laughed and agreed. They punched each other's shoulders and would not move.

Col glanced around. "Where's my cheari?" A bell sound answered him. He pointed to the stone. "Errel! Can you arm wrestle?"

Errel skipped into the U, bowed, lay down on his back and hoisted a leg.

"Sit up," said Col.

The Jester rolled upright.

Col put his right arm on the bench. "My tired side," he said. "Come play, Fool." There was teasing cruelty in his tone.

Ryke leaned for a wine carafe. He poured himself a mug, heedless of rules, and tossed the sweet liquid back. It stung his throat. His sweat stank. He wiped his forehead. At least there could be no pretense that this was an honest fight.

Errel rolled up his sleeve. He was not a weak man, but his arm was thin beside Col's. They clasped hands. Col growled and thrust. Errel held him, muscles ridged. The men murmured surprise. "He's tired," said Held of Col. The seconds beat out. Neither hand moved. Ryke knew Errel would not last. Col's lips thinned. He swore. Errel went over hard. Col smashed his hand against the floor. Ryke saw the prince's face twist at the impact. Col let him go. He tumbled backward and came up onto his knees, cradling his right hand in his left.

Col rose. "Wine."

Half a dozen hands reached to him. He took the nearest mug, drank, and tossed the dregs over Errel. "Not bad, princeling," he said. "We'll try again sometime." Then he wearied of the game. "It's growing late. Clear this out. Commanders, we meet in the watch-

tower.'' He faced the two ghyas, sitting silent at the high table.
''Guests, you are no doubt anxious to fulfill your errand. Please re-
main with us a little while longer, while we deliberate. I shall have
an answer for you to take to Berent One-Eye within three days.''

Even in four months, some traditions had arisen phoenix-like out of
the ashes of the old ones. The men dispersed under the eyes of the
watch seconds; the watch commanders waited in the courtyard while
the page with his bobbing lantern lighted Col up the tower stair. Held
paced, restless. His men had the watch. Ryke leaned on the wall. His
right arm ached. The muscles twitched. He heard the mutter of conversation as the soldiers strolled to the barracks. The lucky ones in
the two day watches went to the women's apartments. A few walked
arm and arm, content with each other. Southerners were more lax
about such affections than northerners were wont to be, Ryke thought.
Comradely devotion was all very well, but wars were fought with
men, and it was the responsibility of a man to take a woman to bear
him sons. In the hall the servants worked, scrubbing down the tables.
In the kitchen, the cooks shouted at the scullions.

Ryke closed his eyes. With only a little work he could imagine
himself thirteen again, brought to the Keep by his father. He had been
awed and solemn in the face of all these giant men. He had been
kitchenboy for a while. He cleaned his share of pots with soaps, sand,
and vinegar, rubbing his hands raw, and after a few months, when
they let him serve at table, he scuffled with the other boys for the
privilege of serving the lord of the Keep. He wondered if the kitchenboys battled in the corners for the right to serve Col Istor.

He opened his eyes. Mocking memory, southern voices called
across the courtyard. The page waved his light from the bottom step.
In a line, Held first, slow Gam last, the commanders tramped to the
tower. The page held the door for them. The room smelled of pine.
Col stood by the fire. He wore brown wool over the purple tunic. An
edge of purple showed at his throat. He was holding one of the crystal
goblets in his hand. He turned it. It sparkled with the firelight as if

made of diamond. The eight-sided chamber lit with tiny dancing points.

Reflections gleamed palely in the black windows, curving and changing in the places where the glass itself was runneled and streaked. Col put the goblet on the table. It became a cup of yellow glass, no more. He swung toward Gam. "Well, old man, what do you think I should do with this truce?"

Gam tugged at his grey beard. His men swore he clipped it short, like a horse's mane. Unmoved by the challenge, he said, "Take it. Berent will know you do not mean to keep it."

"What do you think?" Col said to Ryke.

Ryke looked at the man in the tapestry. He did look like Athor. "You would have heard if Berent had been hiring men. He hasn't. He has only a small army now."

"I can eat any army he has," Col said. "But can I trust Berent's truce?" He laughed. "More to the point, is he fool enough to trust mine? Even Berent's not that stupid. He thinks to hold me off while he gathers men. What kind of an army can he hire and train in two months?"

"Is that when we take him?" said Onran eagerly.

Col shrugged. "Perhaps three months." There was a block of cheese on the table, yellow as the goblet. He drew his knife from his belt and cut a strip from it. "Here," he said, extending it to Ryke. Ryke took a bite. It was hard on the outside and smooth inside. His stomach contracted, reminding him he had had little dinner. It was cow's cheese, not the more familiar goat cheese. It was tasty. Col must have had it brought from the storeroom. Col cut another strip.

They ate the cheese. Finally Ryke said, "Berent's no fighter. Out of all the four Keeps, he was strongest to make the Anhard truce. Athor used to say—" he hesitated.

"Go on," said Col.

"Athor said that Berent lost his heart when he lost his eye."

Col said, "I'll wager that, if he has the gold to pay the messengers a second fee, he sends them west."

"To Sironen?" said Onran.

"He makes a truce with me and at the same time he makes alliance with Pel Keep against the time I break that truce. He knows I will. He'd love to have Sironen do his fighting for him."

"Would he send north?" said Held.

"Ask aid of Anhard? I don't know," said Col. "Would he, Ryke?"

It was the sort of scheme Held would think of, Ryke thought. He did not bother to hide the disgust in his voice. "Berent's a northerner; his line's held Cloud Keep for generations. He'd never ally with Anhard."

Held looked skeptical. But Col said, "You're one of them, you should know."

He lifted the goblet again. "Some trader brought this all the way from Kendra-on-the-Delta." He looked at the dark windows. "Does spring never come to this land?"

You were not invited, Ryke thought. He bit his lip to hold the words back. Col grinned, as if he had guessed the thought. "It comes," said Ryke. "Two months. Perhaps three months."

Held said something obscene about the quality of life of the north. Col looked at him. "I find such comments tiresome," he said. Held stiffened as if the chief had struck him. "What do you think of them?" he went on, pointing down toward the apartments where the messengers were quartered.

Ryke shrugged. Gam said, "I liked it that they went to see their horses."

"Yes. They take pains. An admirable trait."

"You think they fuck boys?" Onran said to Held.

Held said, "I don't care if they fuck pigs." Onran sniggered.

Col picked up a candle in a silver sconce. Leaning to the fire, he touched the wick to a coal. When he turned back he was smiling. "Maybe they do. I've heard of such." The candle flame reflected in the window glass like the moon in the still water of a lake. He put the light on the table. "Differences make me curious. That's the difference between you and me." He was speaking to all of them, speaking softly into the dark. "You should care. You should care."

*   *   *

The Keep slept in the night watch.

Ryke moved methodically through the castle, making rounds. In his belt pouch he had tucked a piece of clean linen from the surgeon's stores. He walked along the outer walls, the inner walls, to the smithy, the barracks, the stable, the hall. He looked into the gatehouses. His men waved, muttered greetings. At the western gate they offered him a chance at dice, which he declined. Southerners played different rules; he did not know them. None were asleep. He had not thought they would be; in the cold it was harder to fall asleep on watch.

The night was moonless. He felt strange, fey. He crossed the courtyard a second time. Ghosts seemed to walk in his head: Athor's ghost, his father's ghost. He was ridden by his memories of men now dead. He was glad the moon was not full. At the full moon, the old tales said, spirits of the unquiet dead could rise and walk. For the first time in months Ryke wished for a woman, not in lust but in the need for comfort. He wondered what the women in the apartments would do if he went to them for comfort. Probably they thought him a traitor. Men were supposed to have more choice than women. He thought of Becke and then of Madi. He wondered if she, if they, would listen to him if he tried to explain how it was not always so.

The wind blew. Like some night creature caught in a trap, Col Istor's banner flapped on its pole. Ryke wondered where his wolfhound was. Sheltering, he hoped, in some warm and windless corner. He thrust his hands beneath his armpits to warm them. He entered the kitchen, nodding at the guard who stood there, and went toward the scullery. The kitchenboys huddled together in sleep like dogs in front of the ovens. He stepped over their legs. The iron pots on the walls vibrated softly.

The scullery smelled of grease and soap. With the connivance of the cooks, Errel turned it at night into a tiny rude bedchamber, with a straw pallet and a crate for a table. Ryke looked over the wooden barrier. Errel was awake. By the light of a stubby candle, he had laid out the Cards on the crate. They made a pattern. Ryke could see some of them. He knew their names: Death, the Wheel of Chance, the Dancer, the Stargazer.

He stepped over the barrier. On the wall, his shadow imitated him, grotesquely tall. He sat on the pallet. There was barely room for two of them in the cell. "Let me see your hand."

Errel held out his right hand. The middle finger was black and hugely swollen. It stuck out at an angle. "It's broken," said the prince calmly.

"Can you move it at all?"

"No."

"It needs to be splinted." Ryke peered around the littered scullery for a stray piece of wood.

"No," said Errel. "If Col sees it splinted he might wonder who did it. He notices things like that. He has teased the cooks about feeding me too well: only teasing, but he means it. Suppose he asks who splinted the hand, whom shall I betray? He won't believe I could do it for myself."

"At least let me bandage it." Ryke dug the clean linen from his pouch. "He can hardly object to that." He took Errel's wrist between his knees. He wrapped the third finger to the ones on either side of it. Errel hissed with the pain.

"You—shouldn't—be—here," he said.

"My men have the watch. I'm making rounds." Ryke tied the last knot. "Is that too tight?"

"No." Errel panted for a moment. "It's easier," he said. With his left hand, he reached into a shadowy niche. He brought out a hunk of bread. He tore a piece from it and handed the rest to Ryke. "The last of my dinner. Have some. I ate like a lord tonight."

Col's brutality had not stripped the irony from his voice. Ryke bit into the bread. It was crusty and still warm. He heard the gurgle of liquid. Errel passed him a mug of wine.

Abruptly the prince said, "What are the messengers here for, Ryke?"

"They carry a truce offer from Berent One-Eye. In exchange for peace, he offers Col a younger son."

Errel turned his head to look at the pattern on the table. Ryke did not know what it told him. "I suppose he feels he has no choice," said Errel. "But truce or no, Col will need to take Cloud Keep in the spring, before the men grow bored and stale." One-handed, he swept the Cards into a pile. "Did you meet the messengers? Did you speak with them?"

"We met. We didn't talk. I learned their names."

"I know their names," said Errel. "Norres and Sorren. The scullions have done naught all night but gossip about them. What did you think of them?"

Ryke shrugged, as he had when Col asked. "I hardly spoke with them. Only one of them talks. They seem much as other men."

Errel laughed, a soft sound, swiftly silenced. "Do they," he said. He rose from the pallet. The candlelight showed dabs of paint still on his face. "Ryke, get up."

Ryke rose. Errel knelt. Lifting the pallet, he held it up with his shoulder and knee, reaching for something beneath it. The coarse dust made Ryke want to sneeze. He pinched his nose ferociously to halt the reflex. Errel drew a pouch from the floor. He let the pallet drop, and struggled to unknot the strings that closed the pouch, using his left hand and his teeth.

Ryke took it from him. "Prince, let me." He held the pouch close to the candle. Through the soft skin—pigskin by the feel of it—he touched the distinctive shape of a ring. At last, the knots came loose. He thrust a finger into the bag's mouth. The ring rolled onto his knuckle. He withdrew it. It was a thick gold band crowned by a flat square ruby. The gem was carved with the eight-pointed star, the crest of the line of Tornor. Ryke had last seen it on Athor's hand. This is another, he thought, stupid in surprise. Athor lies under earth, and the ring he wore is buried with him.

But he knew that there was only one. The touch of the gold made him shudder.

Errel said, "Before they buried him they brought me to see his body. I took it from his hand. It was always loose, and after death a man shrivels . . ." Ryke held it out to him. "No, you take it."

Ryke did not want it. "Where?"

"To the messengers. Can you get to their rooms without being seen?"

"Of course."

"Show them the ring. They will know it. Tell them who you are. Ask them if they will help get us out of here."

"Why should they?"

"I knew them once. Sorren and Norres. I helped them. It's a chance, and they have horses. Ask them. Go to them." The words whispered in the dark cell. They seemed to come out of the very stone itself. Ryke felt feverish. He closed his palm over the ring and dropped it into his breast pocket.

In the kitchen a sleeper whined. Ryke wondered if perhaps he and Errel and the whole great Keep were not together dreaming a fever dream, like the stories his mother told to quiet him when he was sick . . . He said, "Prince, I'm gone."

f o u r

As he left the scullery and
stepped into the inner ward, the night cold, like a grave wind, clawed
at his shirt. Hand to his throat, he walked quickly across the court to
the door that opened into the center of the apartments. The fever left
him there. He leaned against the wood. The hard surface was stead-
ying. He rested in the shadow, waiting to see if anyone had noticed
him. A dog barked sleepily, not at him. Dust blew across the courtyard. He heard the sound of a blow—no, it was the noise of something falling. He imagined the guard on the wall above him fumbling
in the darkness, his hands so chill that even in his felt-lined leather
gloves he could not feel to grip a pike.

He looked up. The sky was clear. The mountains loomed to the
north beyond the outer wall, lightless, impenetrable, and black. Over
his head burned the two stars that men called the Eyes. Radiating out
from them was the Tail, a sinuous starry track. The stories never said
what creature, human, animal, or demonic, lived in the sky. Ryke

43

thought it was a fish with silver spotted scales and teeth like a wolf. He had heard that in the south people read the future in the star patterns as Errel read it in the Cards. He wondered what names they gave the star pictures. Turning from the night, he ran his hand along the door, feeling for the bolt. He gasped as he stubbed his fingers on it. He drew it back. The door creaked. He slipped within and found the inside bolt. It stuck. Ryke forced it, afraid that someone would notice the door swinging free. Grudgingly it gave, easing into the rusty socket with a sound like a man with toothache. Again he waited to see if anyone had heard. No one came to look. He was invisible, a shadow roaming through a castle filled with ghosts. He laughed. The fever returned, flaring through his veins, persuasive as lust.

Col lived in the rooms that had been Athor's, closest to the hall: by tradition, those rooms were kept for the lord of the Keep. The women's rooms were in the south end of the apartments. The messengers had been given rooms midway in the corridor, where the traffic of men visiting the women would not disturb them. As he felt his way along the hallway lined with empty rooms, Ryke heard an occasional distant muffled laugh or yelp from out of the women's quarters. Doors swung disconsolately. The floorboards creaked. When Athor was alive he had filled even the unused chambers with life. Ryke looked into one room to see the leaping starlit body of a rat. He wished for a torch. The white-washed walls were icy cold. Here more than anywhere, ghosts shambled at his heels. He walked by memory and starlight.

Candlelight reflecting from a wall warned him he had found the visitors' chambers. A page slumped on the floor outside the door, sleeping despite the chill. The door was ajar. Ryke leaned his weight on it slowly. It opened with a faint moan. The page did not wake. Ryke stepped past the sleeping child. Save for the red shimmer of coals in a brazier, the bedchamber was dark. He drew a breath to speak, and silently a hand leaped out of the night to catch him by the hair. It jerked his head back. He kept his balance with an effort. If he fell, the page might hear the noise and wake. "Friend!" he whispered.

He felt the cold caress of a knife on his throat.

"Don't move," said a low voice. A candle lit, blinding him. "It's the commander Ryke."

He located himself. The speaking one stood in front of him, holding the candle: that was Norres. Beside him, then, holding his hair and the knife, was Sorren. He strained to see past the candle. "Look in the pocket over my heart." Norres' hand, deft as a pickpocket's, took the ring. It caught the light. The fingers in his hair jerked.

"How did you get this?" said Norres.

His eyes swam with involuntary tears. He struggled to keep his footing. "Errel sent me," he said. "The prince."

Sorren released him. He leaned on the wall with the flat of one hand. He smoothed his hair. The messengers looked at each other. Norres stepped back from him, leaning to put the candle in a sconce. The light illumined, in fitful shivers, a bed, a chest with brass locks, the sleek edged point of an Anhard javelin in brackets on the wall. "We thought you were Col Istor's man," said Norres.

"I serve him: I must. But I made oath first to Athor, lord of Tornor. My service was the price Col put on Errel's life." They exchanged looks again. Except for that pale thin hair like northern grass, Ryke saw that they were not really lookalikes.

"How do we know Col Istor did not send you?" said Norres.

"Why would Col send me?"

"It has happened before," said the ghya, "that a fool sought to trap a messenger into betraying neutrality."

Ryke said, "Col Istor is no fool. And I am not a trap. Errel sent me."

"What does the prince ask of us?"

"He asks if you will help us—him and me, the both—escape from Tornor."

There was no way back from here now that he had said it. He laced his hands together. Sorren sucked breath. "Damn." The word rang oddly to his ears. It was melodic and high, a womanly voice, his mind told him. He squinted. Beneath the soft wool undertunic he saw the unmistakable curves of hip and breast. He was looking at a woman.

Norres said, "Don't stare, watch commander."

Sorren brushed a strand of hair off her face. The tunic's dull blue reflected the paler hue of her eyes. Norres' eyes were grey as twilight. Sorren folded her arms across her breasts. "Let be, Norres," she said. "We can take you with us when we leave," she said to Ryke, "if you can get outside the walls."

Ryke was disconcerted. He had not expected her to continue talking. Now that he saw she was a woman, he could see nothing else. "You'll do it?"

Norres said, "We'll take you with us when we go. But we cannot take you far. The terms of our service demand that we return at once to Cloud Keep. We'll take you there."

Sorren brushed her hair back again. She wore the dagger on her right hip, like a short sword. He wondered if she had gotten the scar beneath her eye in battle. He had never met a woman who knew how to fight. "Who are you?" he said.

Norres said, "We're messengers, commander."

"But Errel said he knew you. Are you northeners?"

Norres frowned. Sorren answered. "We were northerners." Her accent wavered between north and south so that he could not place it. The belt around her hips was worked in silver in the style of the mountain smiths. He could not see the dagger sheath.

"From Tornor?"

Norres said, "We have been here before." The tone of the response warned Ryke that more questions were unwelcome. "We agree to what you ask. Leave us now. Be under the shadow of the watchtower the morning we depart, outside the outer wall, and when we ride from the Keep on the west road we will take you up behind us."

"Bring food if you can," said Sorren. "The hunting is poor on the road. And travel furs; it will be cold in the pass." Norres handed Ryke the ring. Sorren bent to the candle and blew it cold, to let him leave in darkness. The fire coals glowed like a red eye. A firm hand—

Ryke did not know whose—guided him to the door. Head spinning with plans, he stepped over the soundly sleeping page. He had to go to the stable and get the travel pack he'd hidden. He weaved from side to side in the darkness. A rat chittered at him. He had not really expected them to say yes.

He was not able to get back to speak with Errel until his third set of rounds.

It was an hour before dawn. There was an edge of light on the eastern sky, and the stars sank toward it, paling into sleep. His men were wakeful at their posts, grumbling at the cold. Ryke went to the stables. Digging the travel pack from its hiding place under a loose board, he took it with him. The guards paid no attention. The stableboys snored in the loft. The horses shifted in their stalls. He went to the kitchen. From the apartment in the storeroom light gleamed. The chief cook was awake and yelling at his assistant. Kitchen-boys and dogs lay in stupor under the warm mouths of the great brick ovens. Ryke tiptoed into the scullery. Errel sat up. "Ryke."

"It's me."

The prince's jaw glinted with golden stubble. His eyes were hollow; he looked as if he hadn't slept. "What did they say?" he asked.

"They said yes," said Ryke. He held out the ring. "I'm sorry it took me so long to return." He let the travel pack fall.

"No matter," said Errel, automatically courteous. He reached his right hand for the ring, remembered, and held out his left. He looked over Ryke's shoulder, eyes unfocused. Ryke wondered what he was seeing. His lean face softened in relief and brimmed into a smile. His eyes were luminous. "I thought they would not refuse," he said, stretching loose-armed to the growing day. "Thank you, Ryke. You did well." Ryke did not know what to say. "How long before Col sends them back to Berent?"

"In three days, or less," Ryke said.

"That is well," said the prince. He glanced out the vertical slit that was the scullery window, as if the extremity of his longing could hasten the coming of the light.

Ryke said, "Did you know that one of them's a woman?"

Errel slanted a look up at him. He knelt to hide the ring beneath the bed. "I knew them as children," he said. He laid the pallet down again. It was narrow as a plank, a servant's mat, coarsely covered with a piece of linen sacking.

"They lived in the Keep?"

"Sorren did. Norres did not."

"Why don't I remember them?"

"They left. It's a long story." He sat on the pallet, bandaged hand resting in the palm of his good one. "How are we to meet them? I see you brought a travel pack."

Ryke explained.

"In the tower's shadow. Aye. Col will feast them in the hall before he sends them back. I'll hang about the kitchen while they eat. The cooks are used to it. I will find a way to get to the western gate when the horses are brought from the stable."

"I will meet you."

"I wish I had my bow." Errel looked wistfully at his hand. "I doubt I could hold it now."

"I can try to get it," said Ryke. "Col has it in the tower."

Errel smiled grimly. "Could I draw it, it might help to keep the pursuit from coming too close to us, if we are pursued. I almost wish we might be."

"Don't say that." Ryke made the sign to avert ill luck.

Errel said, his voice rock certain, "If we once leave the walls, we shall not be caught again. I know."

The reference to the Cards made Ryke nervous. He glanced around the tiny space, but they were hidden wherever Errel kept them, in his shirt or under the bed.

The roosters were crowing from the corners of the outer walls. Dogs barked. It would soon be change of watch. In the kitchen, the scullions stirred. Ryke did not want them to see him. "Prince, I'd better go."

"Yes," said Errel. He lay down in the bed and wrapped himself in the thin blanket. His eyelashes trembled. He looked tired, as he was, and very young.

The next day, Ryke joined his men in the Yard.

When he was Athor's watch commander, Ryke had trained two hours a day, three days out of every week, enough to keep his breath steady and his belly flat. Being a big man, his strength and length of arm had given him some natural superiority, and he had learned to make good use of these gifts. He had never been able to call up the killing rage that substituted for skill in battle in other men. In Col's service, his training had grown infrequent. As he walked into the fenced-off fighting square, he felt puffy and tired.

The space echoed with the crack of wooden swords hitting each other. Ryke sifted through the pile of swords till he buckled on the stained leather leggings and breastplate. He did not bother to wear a helmet, but as he strode onto the court he noticed that most of the training men were wearing them. A head blow from a wooden blade could kill. He saw Vargo leaning on the fence and went to him. The freckled man was rubbing his right elbow. A wooden sword lay at his feet. Ryke picked it up, thinking it had been damaged and then put back, but it was whole. Like most of the practice swords it was nicked, and polished at the hilt end with sweat. It was of white oak, as was his. He rested it against the fence, point to the earth. "What happened?" he asked.

Vargo flexed his elbow. He wasn't wearing a helmet either. "I was clumsy," said the second grumpily. "It's all right. My arm's numb." He nudged the sword with a boot toe. "Damned unhandy things. Give me my axe."

"A man with any skill at all could split you with a sword before you got close enough to use that axe," said Ryke.

"Then I have never fought a man with skill," said Vargo, grinning. He swung his elbow in a circle, and swore.

"Maybe not," said Ryke.

He worked apart from the others for a while, practicing strikes; slices and lunges and sweeps to take off a head or gut a belly through leather; pushing his muscles till they ached and creaked. Under the bright cold afternoon sky the sweat ran down his sides, soaking his clothing. The powdery ground, part sand, part snow, clutched at his feet.

When he had had enough of solitary practice, he returned to the equipment shed and dragged out a leather shield. Fastening it to his arm, he went to find a partner. He prowled the edge of the Yard. Ephrem and Kinnard hacked at each other in the shadow of the fence. Ephrem looked fresh, but Kinnard was clearly tiring. Ryke shouted to stop them. Kinnard breathed like a runner. "Rest," Ryke told him. He lifted his sword. Ephrem smiled, without malice. He wore no shield.

"Ryke, do you want my helmet?" Kinnard called.

"No," Ryke called back. He circled, trying to put the sun in Ephrem's face. Ephrem swung at him two-handed. Ryke parried the blow, sword on sword, feeling the shock of it shiver up his arm. Ephrem was strong, heavy-chested, as was Col. Under the round helm his face grew serious. He hacked out again. Ryke took the blow on his shield and swung at Ephrem's unprotected side. The southerner leaped back to let it slice harmlessly past him, and stepped in again with his great two-handed swing. Ryke wondered where he'd learned it. He parried it, and then another one, measuring the shorter man's timing. His hands stung. He let Ephrem back him up. Ephrem swung another time, and Ryke ducked. The wood whistled over him. He lunged at Ephrem, holding the sword in both hands, and heard the southerner gasp as the tip of it thudded into his breastplate. He staggered, chopped, and sat. Ryke leaned on his sword. His wrists hurt from having held it steady. Ephrem's chest heaved. "Are you all right?" Ryke asked.

"I can't get my breath." Ephrem sat on the ground and huffed. Finally he got to his feet. He pulled the breastplate off and undid the laces of his shirt. There were purple lines on his brown chest where Ryke's blow had driven the edges of the leather plate into the skin.

"Put your shirt back on; you're sweating," said Ryke. "Better let the surgeon check to see if you cracked a rib."

"It's all right," said Ephrem. He swung his sword arm and grimaced.

"See the surgeon anyway," Ryke said. Ephrem trudged away.

Kinnard looked apprehensive. He bit the end of his mustache. "You want a second bout?" he said, bravely lifting his sword.

"No," said Ryke. His sword arm ached. He took the shield and wooden blade back to the shed, feeling moderately pleased with himself.

This night's dinner in the hall was simple and subdued compared to the previous evening's festivities. As if repenting for the eels and wine, the cook had made everything with onion. Ryke ate sparingly, having no wish to spend the night shuffling between his bed, the guard posts, and the toilets. The messengers sent word that they preferred to eat alone this night. Col told the servants to feed them in their chambers. He did not call for Errel. There were no fights.

At the close of the meal, he turned to his commanders. "Meet me in the apartments when you have seen to your men." The commanders looked at one another, surprised. Held scowled, and went to make rounds. Gam stumped to the stables. Onran went to flirt with the kitchen maids and steal a slice of goose. Ryke stayed at table. The servants cleared around him. He did not understand why the messengers had not come to table. It disturbed him. Anything that might catch Col's attention disturbed him. The kitchenboys snuffed out the torches with their long-handled snuffers. The huge room darkened. The dogs gnawed at the stew bones. He felt warm breath and a cold nose on his leg. It was the black wolfhound. He stroked and scratched her, steeling himself to do the thing he did not want to do, which was to meet with Col Istor in the room that had been Athor's.

The dog trailed him across the court, but it would not follow into the apartments. It was only a hop from the hall to the north stairway. There was a page outside the door. Ryke hesitated. He did not want to enter the room. "Are they all there?" he said. The page shook his head. The heavy door was open a crack. The brass plating shone on its iron hinges. Ryke rubbed the smooth metal lightly. Generations of pages, he among them, had measured their height by the ornate brass, and polished it with their breath. He unloosed the lacing of his shirt and went in.

Col was standing at the fire. He looked irritated. Onran sat on a chest beneath a window hung with blue velvet. Held leaned on a wall. Gam was absent.

Ryke sat on a stool. The colors in the room had changed. Col had moved the big wardrobe with the carved doors, and had brought in a huge blackwood table. It was littered with sheets and scrolls of paper, the stuff of record keeping. Athor had preferred to leave the record keeping to Jaret the steward, who had died in the fighting. Col had no steward. Over the mantel hung a thing Ryke had never seen: a diamond-shaped shield, big enough to cover a man from neck to crotch, worked with gold, silver, and bronze to show a serpent eating its own tail. It was a symbol he had seen before on things of Anhard making, but never done so well. Beneath the plating, the shield itself was iron. He imagined a man in battle lugging it up a hill or dragging it in retreat. It looked unscored by blows, and he guessed it had been given to the Keep in earnest of some truce (long forged and long abandoned) by a ceremony-minded Anhard lord.

Gam strolled in. He smelled of the stable.

"Can we begin now?" Col said. He put his thumbs into his belt. "I want you to know that I am accepting Berent's truce offer and will keep truce until the spring."

Onran said, "Does that mean we can't continue raiding?"

"That is what it means," said Col. "Officially speaking."

"Then how will we know Berent's strength?" objected the youngest commander.

Col smiled. "I'm no seer. But I think the territory around Cloud Keep will shortly suffer a plague of outlaws."

"Trappers might be better," said Gam.

"Outlaws carry weapons," said Col.

Onran and Held started to argue whether the outlaws should make day or night raids. Ryke let his attention wander. The room smelled of beeswax and dried jasmine. When Athor slept in it, it smelled of dog. The door to the sleeping room was open two handspans. A candle passed across the opening. A woman looked at the men. Her hair fell down her shoulders and her back in an amber curtain. It was Becke. Their eyes met. Unhastily, she drew back.

Col looked suddenly bored. He thumped the table to silence the argument. "That will do. Good night, commanders. We join at table tomorrow to feast our guests." Ryke stood up. "Ryke, stay." Surprised, Ryke tensed. He saw Held look from the doorway with a suspicious, jealous stare. Col motioned him away. The page closed the door.

"Come here," Col said. Ryke approached the table. His heart hammered. He could not read Col's face. The messengers betrayed us, he thought. Slowly as he dared he let his right hand drop toward the short dagger in his belt.

"Can you read?" asked Col pleasantly.

The words were so unlike the ones he had expected that he had to repeat them to himself as if he had gone witless. "I can read runes," he answered. He marveled that his voice did not shake. "Athor bade me learn when he made me watch second. I cannot read the southern script."

"Can you read these?" Col pushed a scroll across the table. Ryke spread it, holding it open with both hands. The dark lines wavered down the page. Some were so faded he could not make them out. The roll was dusty. Ryke squinted. The first letter of some lines was larger than the others.

"*In the seventh year*—something—*reign*, I think—*of Kerwin, Lord of Tornor*—something about Anhard—" The runes for K, L, and T had been filled in with gold ink.

"Who was Kerwin?"

"Athor's grandfather? Great-grandfather, maybe."

Col hooked a stool with his ankle and sat on it. "You know where I found these? In the watchtower. Mouse turds all over them."

"I didn't know they existed," Ryke said. "What are they?"

"Histories! Records. Great houses keep them. The Med family in

Kendra-on-the Delta has a room filled with them, and a woman whose work is to keep them clean.''

"You lived in Kendra-on-the-Delta?"

"I served the Med family for five years," Col said. "I led troops against the Asech." Ryke nodded. He knew who they were: a strange people that lived south of the Galbareth in houses made of skin. "I rode with Ewain Med and with Raven Batto."

"Is that the man who was outlawed?" Ryke asked, remembering the story dimly.

"So the news even reached this place? Yes, that's the one. He killed a cousin of the Med family, which was stupid, because the Med family rules in Kendra-on-the-Delta. But that was ten years ago." He walked to the window and opened a pane. "Do you know any music?" he said.

Startled, Ryke said, "No."

"That's too bad. In the south we sing a lot." Softly, as if to the night, he said, *"The hills and stars are my companions, and all I do, I do alone.* Do you know that one?" Ryke shook his head. Col dropped the curtain. "The weather's still clear," he said. "Will it hold?"

"Probably not. There's a wetness in the wind."

"And that means more snow, I suppose. I wish spring would come. Winter's no time to learn to love a land. *For I am a stranger in an outland country,"* he said. "That's the song." He sat on the stool and laid one hand on the topmost scroll. "I want you to read these to me," he said.

For a witless moment, Ryke almost answered, *"But I'm leaving.* He caught his breath. Heat rose in his face, and he cursed to himself. "I suppose I could," he said, making the acquiescence grudging.

"If you won't, say so. I'll find someone else."

"I'll do it," Ryke said. Col's dark eyes stared into his face. He wished the chief would look away. A log fell into the fire. He glanced down to the scroll beneath his elbow.

Col said, "Does that surprise you, Ryke? That I want to love this land?"

"Yes."

"If I don't, it will destroy me." Ryke said nothing. "I suppose you would like that."

Embarrassed, Ryke shrugged. Col's hand lay before him, palm down. He had huge tendons; they stood up like roots out of shallow ground. Ryke heard a whisper of cloth and a clink of metal from within the sleeping room. He did not turn. The candlelight flickered on the Anhard shield. The serpent seemed to writhe. He tried to remember what Athor had hung over the mantel, and could not. They were Col's rooms now; there was nothing of Athor left in them. The knowledge made him angry and oddly desolate. "Is that all you want from me?" he said.

Col looked at him. "Thank you. Yes." Ryke released the scroll. The thick paper curled, ends toward middle.

"Good night," he said. He turned his back on the chief. As he passed the sleeping room door he glanced through it, but all he saw was the steady flame of the candle and the shadows of the hangings round the curtained bed.

five

That night Ryke could not rest. He made his rounds assiduously. The weather held. Ill weather would both aid and hinder their escape; fine weather would aid pursuit. He did not know whether to curse it or bless it. At the main gatehouse the guards were discussing the ghyas' (presumed) sexual habits. The barracks smelled most foully of onion. He walked the walls. From the turrets of the outer wall he looked down toward the village and the surrounding farms and fields. The wolfhound found him pacing the parapet and came to stalk beside him. He wondered whom she would find for company and comfort after he was gone.

On one round, on the pretext of checking the doors, he took a lantern with him. He walked through the apartments, swinging the feeble yellow light from side to side, till he came to the middle stair. He saw his own footprints in the gathered dust. He scuffed them over. At the bottom of the stair, he unbolted, went through, and then carefully bolted from the outside the telltale middle door.

By morning his eyes felt filled with sand. After change of watch he went into the hall. The serving window was up. Leaning near it, he drank three cups of thick mint tea. His mouth dried and his slack senses tautened.

He went over his preparations in his head. Errel had one travel pack. His own Ryke had hidden in a hole made by two crossed beams in the roof of the west postern gate. To it he had tied a child's-weight bow that he had found in the empty apartments. He had not been able to find arrows to fit it. In his right boot, as always, he carried the Anhard skinning-knife. He wished there were a way for him to take his sword.

"More?" said the serving girl. She leaned through the window to smile at him.

He handed back the cup. "That's enough." The hall doors swung inward. Col, Held, Onran, Gam and the messengers entered. The girl skipped inside the kitchen to warn the cooks. The ghyas (it was easier to think of them as that than to remember that one of them was a woman) wore travel furs. Ryke walked to join them. The messengers did not look at him. Col sat. The servers arranged the platters in front of him.

Held was restless. Twice he rose to listen. "What's the matter with you?" asked Col.

"Something feels odd."

Ryke sweated. Held was the least imaginative of men. If he went into the kitchen he would see Errel.

"You're nervous as a woman," said Gam. He was grumpy because Col had insisted he eat in the hall, not at the stable. He reached across Ryke to spear a bacon strip.

"I'll look around," Ryke offered. Onran glanced up, astonished. It was Onran's watch. Ryke left the table quickly before Col could order him back. He stepped into the kitchen. Errel was not there. He went to the barracks and the stable. The ghyas' horses—tough barrel-ribbed steppe horses with tails like brooms—stood waiting. A light east wind blew. Ryke crossed the inner ward to the main gate. The men at their posts at the gatehouse looked bored.

He returned to the hall. The maid was serving eggs and roe. "All's well," he reported. He sat in his place while a server filled his plate. Col frowned, intuition roused. Ryke swallowed. He could scarcely taste the food. He wondered if Col could see the sheen of sweat he knew was on him.

Held said something soft to Onran. The young commander flared. He slapped the table. "There's naught amiss on my watch, damn you. Keep your tongue civil."

"Don't give me orders, stripling," said Held.

Onran stood, sputtering. "You—!"

"Shut up," said Col. His eyes flicked obsidian at his commanders. Held shut his lips tight. Onran's shoulders hunched and relaxed. The messengers ate. "Onran, sit." Onran, scowling at Held, flung a leg over the bench. "Ryke." Ryke jumped. "Was there anything amiss on your watch last night?"

"Naught save an excess of onion."

Col's lip twitched. "I shall have to speak to the cook." He leaned both elbows on the table. The messengers pushed their plates aside. Ryke could not look at them. "You are no doubt anxious to complete your business," he said.

Norres said, "It's a three-day ride to Cloud Keep."

"I wouldn't want Berent One-Eye to think I did not give his offer thought. My answer to him is, I accept his offer of a winter truce, and will treat his son as if he were my own. I will return the boy with proper escort after the second thaw. At that time the truce will end." He spoke as if he had been making truce and breaking truce all his life.

"We bear witness," said Norres. That was all there was to it. Ryke gazed at the tapestries opposite. The masons in the picture, at their eternal labor, did not look impressed.

Norres said, "Thank you for your hospitality."

Col grinned across the breakfast dishes. "I would not be found less generous than Berent." He gestured to a kitchen-boy. "Go see that the messengers' horses are ready."

Now, thought Ryke. His knees felt weak. Col stood. So did his commanders and guests. Norres and Sorren drew on their gloves. "See that the main gate is open," Col said to Onran. As the young commander strode away, Col said to Held, "Don't ride him." They strolled from the table. The kitchenboys rushed to collect the platters before the dogs got at them.

At the hall's tall entryway, Ryke said, "Excuse me." Col nodded. Ryke crossed the courtyard. It took all of his will to keep himself from breaking into a run. The wind was rising; Col's banners snapped. He went through the inner wall to the outer postern gate. The guards were telling stories in the gatehouse. He reached up into the crossbeams for the travel pack. "Open the gate," he said.

"What's that?" asked one of the men as he put his shoulder to the bar. The door opened inward. He backed up.

"It's for the messengers. Col's order." His wet palms skidded on the leather straps. "Close up," he said to the guards. He stepped into the light. Obediently they closed the door. He heard the bar thud. The watchtower's shadow streamed toward the road like a finger pointing to freedom. He walked into it and nearly fell over Errel. The prince crouched against the stone. He wore travel furs and over them the pack. There was a scrape on his cheek. The bandage on his hand was filthy.

Ryke dragged his furs from his pack, heart racing. "How did you get outside the wall?" he whispered.

"Climbed," said Errel. He stood up. "Did you bring me a bow?"

Ryke twisted to stare at the rough-faced stone. "I didn't know you had that skill." The outer wall was four times the height of a man. He pushed his arms through the slits in the cloak.

"Need teaches," said Errel dryly. "I have it now."

Ryke took the bow from the pack. "I found this."

Errel turned it in his glove hands. "It might be the one I learned on," he said. "Did you bring arrows?"

"I couldn't find them." He heard the sound of hooves in snow. Clumsy in his haste, he strapped his limp pack to his back. In a moment, he thought, the guards will open the gate to see where I have gone . . . He looked at Errel. The prince was turned away from him, bow in his left fist. The hoofbeats sounded nearer. The messengers rounded the corner, riding without haste along the curve of the road.

Ryke squinted. The snow was so bright it seemed polished. He shaded his eyes. The first messenger saw them. Ryke could not see which of them it was. He decided it was Sorren. She lifted a hand. "Hola!" she called. It was Sorren. Errel ran down the shadow of the watchtower to meet her as if it were a street. Ryke trembled, fearing to hear at any moment a shout from the wall.

No one shouted. No one was watching. Sorren aimed the horse at Errel. He ran three steps beside her, and then leaped. The horse bolted out of the shadow into the light. Norres entered the shadow. Ryke saw the arm outstretched for him. He grabbed it. He was hauled to the horse's back. "Go!" he pleaded.

"Hold my belt," grunted Norres.

Ryke tucked his fingers into the tough leather. Norres leaned forward. They clattered over a bridge. The Rurian lay in sculpted ripples under it. The horse was moving easily under the double burden. Ryke risked a look behind. The Keep rose silently behind them. The road was empty. No one was following them. He wanted to shout with relief, until it came to him that he might never see the castle again.

Snow dropped on his neck from a swinging branch. The road went through a stand of evergreens. Ryke pulled a hand free and yanked his hood over his head. "How long will it take us to get to Cloud Keep?" he asked.

"Three days with two. Four with the four of us," said Norres.

Sorren slowed. "Don't stop," said Norres.

"There's no pursuit," said Sorren. Errel turned around. Ryke grinned at him over Norres' shoulder.

"Even so. We'll stop when we get to the fog."

Sorren nodded and urged her horse forward. Ryke kept on listening. There were men among Col's troops who knew this country better than he did. But there was no noise behind them. At last the scrubby trees thinned out. The road wound steeply up and seemed to end in a thick grey mist. They dismounted. "Watch your step," Norres warned. They went slowly forward. The clouds closed in at their backs.

Errel took the lead. Norres dropped back to listen for pursuers. The clouds drifted thickly over them. Fog dripped down the rocks. Errel led them smoothly. Ryke remembered that before the war the prince had been accustomed to hunt this country. He knew it at least as well as Col's raiders. In a few places the trail was so steep it was more like climbing than walking. Sorren walked between Ryke and Errel. It seemed like hours before they stopped. "Let's eat," Errel said. They waited for Norres to come up with them. Ryke's legs ached. He had gotten soft. His back burned with weariness and tension.

They ate in a hollow off the trail. Col had supplied the messengers with food for the horses and for themselves. Ryke had packed both his and Errel's pack with strips of dried meat and cheese. Nevertheless, there was not enough food to keep four people going for four days. Errel said, "We shall have to hunt." The little bow lay across his knees. He put it down and unwrapped the bandage on his hand. The bruise had subsided. He tried to move the middle finger, grimaced, and wrapped the hand again. He wore the ring of the lords of Tornor on his left hand.

Sorren stood up. "Let's go if we're going," she said. She pulled her hood over her hair. Ryke clenched his teeth and rose. His thighs felt like lead. Errrel went ahead. Sorren followed. Water droplets clung to the grey fur of her hood and glittered like the stone.

They went on. It grew colder; the wind cut at them like knives. Ryke's hands slipped on the rocks. He wondered if someone had made this path, or if it was natural, made by wind and water. His chest hurt. He caught himself panting. They stopped to rest to windward of some scrubby spruce. Errel hunkered down on his heels. Ryke leaned to see what he was doing. He was cutting at the low boughs of the tough little trees with his knife. "Arrows," he said.

"What will you fletch them with?" Ryke asked.

"I'll find something." He chopped at the stick, working awk-wardly with his left hand.

They went on. Ryke wondered what had happened to the sun. He had lost all sense of direction save telling down from up. He got a fit of the shudders. "Here." Sorren passed him a flask. Ryke took a long swallow. The drink burned his throat and warmed his stomach. He took some more. His shivering stopped. Respectfully he corked the flask and handed it back to Sorren. Life moved in him. He stamped his feet to make the blood go. Sorren's legs went up and down, up and down. They rested again. Ryke leaned back against the rock, hearing the fall of water somewhere, dreaming of summer, a hot sun, a blue sky, warm rain.

They stopped when the grey turned to darkness.

Ryke said, "Shouldn't we set a watch?"

"What for?" said Norres, coming up behind him.

"Pursuit."

The ghya laughed. "They won't chase us in the dark."

At the messenger's direction, Ryke and Errel took off their boots, washed their feet with snow, and rubbed them briskly until they were dry. "What for?" Ryke said.

"It keeps the feet from freezing," Errel said. "It would be better if we had a fire," he said sadly. "I don't suppose, in your travels, you learned the secret of burning snow, or rock."

Sorren looked up from cutting jerky into strips. "Alas, no."

They slept in a tiny cave, no more than a scoop in the rock. There was just enough room for the four of them. Norres and Sorren slept wrapped in one cloak, their arms about each other. Outside the shelter, the wind moaned.

In the middle of the night, Ryke roused. Errel was shivering. Ryke felt the shudders against his own backbone. He rolled over onto his other side. Putting an arm around the prince, he fit his chest to Errel's back and hugged him close, sharing his warmth. The shivers stopped. Errel's breathing evened. Ryke lay wakeful, listening to the wind. Finally the cold numbed him, and he drowsed into uneasy dreams.

In the morning he had to shake his left arm vigorously to bring feeling back into it.

The second day was just like the first day, except they went down more than they went up.

Ryke's chest ceased to hurt. They rode part of the day. They came out of the fog onto a stony plain, dotted with scrubby trees, covered with ice-scummed snow. The clouds hovered over them like a giant's hand. The shaggy-coated horses moved stolidly across the steppe. They camped the second night in a stub-filled hollow. Norres lit a fire. The tree stubs hissed and smoked. The horses munched their feed. Men and beasts crowded close to the scanty heat. The clouds covered the stars. Norres passed the flask around. Ryke took a mouthful of the potent liquor, and rolled up in his cloak while his belly was still warm.

Errel sat up, bow and the two arrows he had made across his knees. He had fletched the arrows with a lock of Ryke's hair, stiffened by evergreen sap. The sap served as glue. Ryke rolled over at the bow's twang. "Did you get something?" he said. His mouth was muzzy with sleep.

"Missed." In the last small flare of the fire, Errel's face looked cut out of stone. Ryke fell back to sleep.

In the morning there were chunks of meat searing on a fire. "What was it?"

"A yearling fox," said Errel.

"I'm surprised it came near enough to be taken," said Norres.

"It knew traps and trappers. Not hunters," said Sorren. Her hair fell over her eyes. She brushed it back. For a moment Ryke saw the woman in the shape of her face, the lift of her cheekbones, he clear and beardless skin. Then it was gone. She was neuter, unknown, a ghya.

They rode the third day across the steppe. The mountains marched on their right. Toward evening the wind lifted and the cloud cover broke. The sun stained the sky red and purple. Errel and Sorren talked in low tones. Ryke could not hear what they said. As night came, they heard the lifted voices of wolves prowling south. The horses shifted nervously at the sounds, huddling side by side as the wind snapped and sang. Toward morning it rained. Ryke, Errel, and the ghyas rolled together to lie beneath the smelly shelter of their cloaks. They did not sleep. The rain pounded at them, runneling under their backs, soaking them from beneath. It ended with the dawn, and they rose wet and cursing. The sky was blue as a heron's wing. The clouds sped toward the dark humps of the western mountains. Norres pointed. "There's Cloud Keep."

It was a toy castle tucked between two hills. As they rode toward it, Ryke imagined the steppe in summer, a great open meadow covered with thigh-high grass, fragrant and warm as milk. The bleak space disturbed his mind. Smoke from housefires marked where a village lay to the south. He looked for birds, but saw none. The horses plodded. Up to the very gate of Cloud Keep, theirs were the only shadows.

They stopped just before Cloud Keep to give the horses rest. Ryke took his knife from its bootsheath and examined it for rust. The blade was clear and calm as water. He wrapped it again and stuck it in the sheath. Errel ran a finger along his bowstring. He had kept it dry by taking it from the bow and fastening it around his waist. "I've been thinking," he said.

"Yes," said Ryke.

"Berent will not necessarily be pleased by our arrival. It's within his right not to take us in."

"But where else can we go?" Ryke said. He swept a hand in a circle to the steppe. "He must."

"We will see what he does," Errel said. He did not sound worried or angry, only thoughtful and a little curious.

Unlike Tornor, Cloud Keep had no tower. Its stones were smooth, unveined, and grey. At the gate of the Keep stood guards holding pikes. They wore Berent One-Eye's badge, the head of the mountain cat in gold silhouette on scarlet. They crossed their pikes as the horses walked up to them. Norres said, "We are the messengers returned from Tornor Keep. Let us pass. You know us."

The men eyed Errel and Ryke. "We know you," said one. "We do not know these men."

Errel leaned down from his place behind Sorren. He held out his left hand with the ring on it. "Look here," he said. "Do you know this crest?" The gatemen conferred. Then they signaled to the guards within, and the gate opened. The travelers rode into Cloud Keep. They dismounted. It was wonderful to be out of the wind. All the dogs in the Keep were barking. They looked toward the inner gatehouse. The sun blazed down at them without warmth.

Four men walked through the inner gate. The foremost of them wore a muslin patch over his left eye and a red wool gown. The others wore linen, mail, and leather. Their boots kicked up dust. Ryke felt uneasy. Berent was lean and grey, a dusty withered old man. His one eye turned to Errel.

"My lord of Tornor," he said. "Welcome."

six

"Your eye is good, my lord," said Errel. He sounded amused.

Berent said, "You look like Athor."

"Do I?" They embraced lightly. Errel's boots squelched. Berent's robe was grease-stained. The jingling of the horses' bridles was the loudest sound in the castle. The silence hurt Ryke's ears. Errel stepped back from Berent and turned to wave at Ryke. "This is Ryke. To keep me alive he became Col Istor's watch commander, but he remained loyal to me these four months, while Col Istor held me captive."

Berent looked at Ryke, cocking his head on one side like a bird. Ryke bowed. "My commanders," said the old man, pointing to the three men. They bowed to Errel as Berent said their names. Two of them looked like him. Ryke judged them to be his sons. Perhaps the third one was, too. And there was yet another son who was to be sent to Col as hostage. Odd that such a dried-up stick of a man should have so many sons, when Athor, lusty and strong as he had been, had had just the one.

Berent One-Eye must have been strong once. But no longer, Ryke decided. He walked at Errel's heels, through the guard's door into the inner ward. The Keep had an incomplete, sleazy feel to it. One of the commanders said, with an air of doubt in his voice, "We heard that you were dead, my lord." It gave Ryke a wrench to hear Errel being called that.

Errel said, "As you see, I am not." They walked past the Yard and the barracks. There were no men circling in the Yard. Belatedly, a page came running from the stable to take their horses. Berent led the way to the great hall himself; not, Ryke thought, a task that the lord of a Keep should do. He saw few men, and most were servants, and those were old. They went into the hall. It was smaller than Tornor's hall, and smokier. The smoke rose to the ceiling and out a skylight. A fire burned in the massive square firepit. The room smelled of peat. As at Tornor, the walls were covered with cloth, some with pictures, most without. At one bare spot in the wall, iron hooks upheld a giant club with spikes thrusting wickedly out of it. It had the look of Anhard on it. Ryke tried to imagine the man whose weapon it had been. It looked too heavy for one man to lift.

He was sweating beneath his furs. A servant girl shuffled in with wine. Ryke sipped some. It made his stomach churn. He wanted bread and meat.

Norres gave Berent One-Eye Col Istor's message. "A winter truce," said the old man. "That is good, though less than we had hoped."

The oldest-seeming of the commanders said, "No more than we could expect from a southerner and a thief." Memory made Ryke grin. Once he had called Col that to his face.

Berent plucked at the sleeves of his robe. "This strife comes at an ill time," he said peevishly. "Would that Athor of Tornor had not fallen!"

Errel said, "I wish that, very much." He turned the light brass goblet in his fingers. "I thank you for your welcome, my lord. But I must ask you plainly, how firmly do you offer it? Col Istor is now your ally.''

"Say, rather," said Berent, "that there is truce between us which I am loth to break."

"If he asks for me, as he well may, you will be obliged to give me up to him, or break that truce."

"Were you pursued?" said one of the commanders.

"No," said Ryke.

"But we may yet be," said Errel. "My lord, please speak plainly. Will you shelter us or no?"

The commanders looked at their hands. Berent said, "Lung fever plagues my men. We are at half strength, and those that are left are trembling on their feet. Athor was my friend, my ally, but since you put it to the question I must answer you, I cannot grant you shelter for more than three days. Forgive the cruelty of my caution. I will give you horses, food, and weapons of your choice, but I cannot put my Keep in jeopardy for one man's sake."

"I had to ask, my lord," said Errel. Ryke put his hands flat on the board. Three days was the shelter a Keep granted to any man, even an outlaw, in winter. Errel had tried to warn him that this would happen. Errel had guessed, or known, or seen it coming in the pattern of the Cards . . . We shall have to go on, he thought. His whole body ached at the idea of more riding. We shall have to go on to Pel Keep.

If Berent were Athor—but Athor was dead. Anger rose in his heart, not for himself—who was he, a soldier, no one—but for Errel. He cleared his throat.

But Berent said, "My lord, the page will show you to your room." They stood. The moment passed. They left the hall and went into the courtyard, through a door, and up a stair. The anger left him. He yawned till he could hardly see. He did not care what Berent did to him as long as he was going to be allowed to stop walking and sleep.

*   *   *

Food revived him. They were brought to a room smaller than the rooms at Tornor. It had a fireplace and a scuttle filled with peat. Tubs of warm water and a tall pile of linen towels awaited them. In the luxury of safety, they pulled off boots, shirts, tunics, every stitch, and sat naked as babes in the warmth. There was a fresh layer of reeds on the wooden floor and a feather quilt on the huge bed. Errel wrapped himself in the billowing quilt.

He combed his hair with a wooden comb that he found in a chest. Ryke scrubbed himself with a brush. The water turned scummy with grease. He sat beside the tiled hearth and fed peat bricks to the flames until they roared. Errel was humming. Berent's words seemed not to have troubled him. Ryke looked for the resemblance to Athor that Berent had spoken of, but could not see it. A servant scratched at the door. He lugged in a tray with food. Errel ate steadily through it. Ryke stuffed himself with fresh-baked bread. The rich smell made him dizzy. He lay back on the bed, wondering where the ghyas were. Norres and Sorren. He reached a hand to the wall to steady himself. Under the painted hanging cloth, the wall was cold.

"No watch to stand tonight," said Errel.

"No somersaults to turn," said Ryke.

Errel stretched. "*For I am a stranger in an outland country,*" he sang. He had a clear tuneful voice.

"Don't sing that," Ryke said, startled into protest. It was the song Col Istor liked. He hauled himself off the soft pillow-strewn bed and walked around the room. There was only one tapestry in the chamber—the one by the bed. It showed a hunting scene, a wolf at bay. The room was dark. Its two windows were mere arrow slits facing north, and they were both shuttered.

"What troubles you?" said Errel quietly.

"This—" Ryke flung a hand out. "Why did we come here?"

Errel answered, "We came because this is where Norres and Sorren had to come." He smiled. "It's not perfect. But I find myself with no inclination to return to Tornor."

"No," said Ryke. "Not without an army." He knew what was niggling his peace. "I thought Berent would have some use for us.

For me," he amended. "Against Col. I want to fight him." He walked
to the fire screen. The clothes which hung on it were dry. He pulled
them off and sorted them apart.

"Why?" said Errel.

Ryke held out the clothes to him. The prince made no move to
take them. His blue gaze was suddenly compelling. Ryke shifted under it. He had thought the question rhetorical.

"Why?" said Errel again.

"He killed Athor."

Errel bowed his head. "A good reason," he said after a moment.
With his right hand, he turned the ruby ring around and around on
his finger. His ribs were patterned with scars. Ryke wondered if any
of them were of Col Istor's making. He thought, I would kill him
anyway, my prince, for what he did to you. He could not say that.
He remembered Col's words. *I wish to learn to love this land.* It will
destroy you anyway, thief, he thought. It does not love you. The
pleasure of fighting burned through him, and his right arm tensed as
if he held a sword. He saw himself armed and armored, riding in the
vanguard of Sironen's army.

He laid Errel's clothes on the bed. He pulled his tunic on over
his head. "Do you think Sironen will take us in?" he asked.

Errel said, "I can't see why he wouldn't." He picked up his shirt.

"I would hate to be Berent's watch commander."

"You think him coward?" said Errel.

"He doesn't want to fight. What hope has his Keep, with a lord
who thinks like that?"

Errel's head popped out of his shirt. "You heard him say it yourself," he said. "His men are dying of the lung sickness, and probably
not only here but on the farms and in the village, too. The lord of a
Keep has other things to consider besides war and its making."

The crisp tone stung. Ryke said, "The business of a Keep is war."

Errel did not answer him at once. The silence grew uncomfortable. Ryke wished for something to break it. He pulled his breeches
on, and his boots. The leather felt brittle from the heat, and he looked

in the chest for oil to grease it with. Finally he said, "I'm sorry, prince. I spoke out of turn."

Errel smiled oddly. "No. You didn't. But tell me, Ryke, do you know why Tornor Keep was founded?"

Ryke let the chest lid fall. There was no oil within. "Every farm-boy knows the answer to that question, my prince," he said. "The Keeps defend against Anhard."

"Of course," said Errel. He leaned back into the down softness of the pillows. "But men built the Keeps. They didn't grow like the mountains. The architects and masons and carpenters who built the Keep came out of the south, and so did the gold and the cloth and the grain with which they were paid. The first Lord of Tornor was a southerner, a rebel out of a southern town, who was given the choice between death and exile to the mountains. He chose exile and the cold; he chose to raise his sons to love the mountains, and call the northland home, and despise the green soft hills of the south. Your father's father's father, two hundred years back, was a mason in Kendra-on-the-Delta. And mine—" Errel smiled—"was a rebellious younger son."

"Does it say that in the scrolls?"

"The scrolls?"

"The records in the tower. Col showed them to me."

"Were there records in the tower?" Errel fell silent. "I wish I had known," he said sadly. "Jaret would have loved to see them. He knew all this history; he was a scholar."

Ryke swallowed. His mouth felt dry as his boots. Rising, he searched for something to drink. "A mason?"

Errel flapped one hand. "That was a guess. I don't know. He could have been anything, a carpenter, a soldier."

"A smith's son," said Ryke. He found a ewer. He looked at his arms, at the fine gold hairs that crisscrossed them. Southerners were dark. He was not a southerner. Yet not all southerners were dark, nor were all northerners blond. Redheaded Vargo's skin was fair as his own. "I could be cousin to Col Istor."

"You could."

Ryke shook his head. Tornor was his home. He wished Errel had not told him how the Keep had come to be. It was just a story, he told himself; he didn't have to think about it. He lifted the pitcher to his lips. "Cousin, I will kill you," he mumbled against the smooth mouth of the jug. The water was cool and sweet. The promise made him feel better. He glanced at Errel, but the prince had not heard the soft words. He sat with his elbows resting on his knees, staring into the leaping fire.

They were left solitary till the afternoon. Ryke catnapped, lying fully clothed on the woolen cover of the vast bed. It was lovely to wake and sleep and wake again out of the reach of the wind. A page came to get them. He had spiky light hair and pale blue eyes, pale as marshfire, and a thin clever face. "What's your name?" Ryke said to him.

"Ler, commander." He brought Errel his cloak, and Ryke his, and held the door for them, leaning all his slight weight on it to keep it open. He took them to Berent's apartments. Berent was there with two of his three commanders. The room was hotter than the great hall; Ryke took his cloak off. The boy Ler lifted it from his arms and hung it on an iron hook. He had to stand on his toes to reach it.

"Get us wine," said Berent. The boy slipped from the chamber and returned with wine and cups. He served Berent, then Errel, then the commanders. Berent watched as the child moved round the room from chair to chair. The lad was quick and graceful. The old man's face kindled with affection and pride. Ler came to stand beside his knee. Ryke wiped his face. The apartments were hung with cloth, and the air was thick and sultry. The chairs and stools were all of dark wood. They say old bones need heat, Ryke thought. He sipped the wine. It was warm.

Berent touched the boy on the shoulder. "That's sufficient," he said. "Go thou. If I need thee, I will call."

As the boy left the room Errel murmured, "You are well-attended, my lord."

"Ler is my son," said Berent. Ryke was startled. The boy looked to be no more than ten, and he knew that Berent's lady had died young. Some Keep's woman had borne the boy. "My lord, and commander, I know well that this truce Cloud Keep makes with Col Istor will last only as long as the southerner wishes it to last. Can you tell us aught which might strengthen our defense against him when he comes?"

Errel signed to Ryke.

"He has three hundred men at Tornor," Ryke said, "and one hundred fifty more at Ziliz Keep. His men are expert in reconnaissance. He moves fast. His men hate the cold but they fight well, cold or no. It will be hard for them to keep a supply line open over the pass, especially in thaw when the streams rise."

The door opened swiftly. The third commander strode in with a muttered apology. Ler scampered in to serve him.

"How long before he comes?" asked Berent.

"Two or three months," Ryke said.

Ler's eyes moved from face to face. The boy was missing nothing of the talk. Berent saw it and said sharply, "Go outside." The child left.

"He is your pledge to Col," said Errel gently.

"Aye," said Berent. He folded his hands in his lap. Ten years back would have been in the middle of the Anhard war, Ryke thought. Berent would have had both his eyes.

Tav, the oldest son, said, "How does he think?"

Ryke frowned. He was better at answering questions about supplies.

Errel said, "He is ruthless and careful. His greatest flaw is that he tends to overlook the obvious." He smiled with a corner of his mouth. "He should never, for example, have kept either Ryke or me alive."

"Let's be glad he did," said Tav. Errel bowed slightly in response.

"What are his horses like?" asked the second son.

Ryke answered. "Well-kept and strong, but they're not mountain-bred. He'll have trouble with them on the plains. They'll tire."

"Have you bowmen?" asked Errel.

"We have some," said Tav. "Not enough."

"If you put them in the cleft when he comes you might be able to hold him off for quite a while."

"We might," said the second son doubtfully.

Berent tapped the arm of his chair. It was carved at the base with the snarling visage of a mountain lion. "In two months the wagons will come from the south. We will have grain and meat enough to withstand any siege."

"Col does not like to siege," Ryke said. "He storms."

Berent thrust his maimed face forward like an angered bird. "Cloud Keep's wall has never been breached."

Errel said, "Nor, until he did it, had Tornor's."

Ryke squirmed surreptitiously on the hard wooden seat. He was sore from four days of riding and rock-climbing; he longed for a cushion.

Berent called, "Ler." The boy came in. "Bring the commander a pillow."

Ryke flushed. Errel said, "Bring me one too, child." Calmly he took it and pushed it behind his back.

Tav said, "I would send to Sironen."

Berent said, "I fight my own battles."

"Sironen has men to spare."

"Perhaps, perhaps not," said his father. "*I* have not the supplies to feed an extra watch."

"In the spring—"

"Who knows what will happen? Col Istor may attack Pel Keep first, choosing to fight Sironen when he himself is strongest." Ler held out the cushion. Ryke took it. He smiled at the boy. Ler reminded him of someone, he could not think whom.

Tav said, "Surely if Tornor—I beg your pardon." He hesitated, and continued, "If Col Istor had planned to attack Pel Keep before

Cloud Keep, he would have mentioned it to his commanders." He looked at Ryke.

Ryke said cautiously, "Col likes to keep his plans a secret, even from his commanders." Ler sat cross-legged by a chair, clearly hoping his father would not notice him. Ryke realized whom the boy reminded him of; it was himself at thirteen. The boy wore a thick leather belt, a copy of his elders'. It had a round metal buckle and a sheath, but no knife. Ryke thought, If he is old enough to act as page for the lord of the Keep he should wear a knife.

Later, under the heavy warmth of the feather-quilt, watching the fire dance in the grate, Ryke said into the darkness, "Did you mean what you said about Berent, my prince?" He rubbed his nose to warm it.

Beside him, Errel said, "What was it?" He sounded sleepy.

"That he would make a good dogsboy."

"No," said Errel. "Why should I tell Col Istor the truth about the capabilities of a man he will have to fight?"

Ryke tugged the quilt higher on his chest. "I was wrong about him, I think," he said. "I thought him fearful and weak."

"You no longer think him a coward? I'm sure he would be pleased with your change of heart." The words fell crisply through the chill. Then Errel said, "Forgive my ill temper, Ryke. I'm sick of war talk."

Fighting is easier than talking about fighting, Ryke thought. He turned on his side and put his cheek in the pillow, trying to get his face warm. "Berent will lose," he said.

"Yes."

"Why does he give his son into Col Istor's hands?"

Errel said, "Because he knows he will lose. I don't think he'll surrender; he has too much pride for that. When it comes time to fight, where is it safest for the boy to be? In Tornor."

"You said he had the soul of a wolf," Ryke said. "What if Col threatened to kill the boy unless Cloud Keep surrendered? I would not want to be Berent then.''

"I named Col *wolf* to tickle his vanity," said Errel. "He is a man, no different than you or I." He rolled over in the bed. His voice grew more distant. "Unless Berent breaks truce, Col will not hurt the boy."

"He is ruthless, you said that, too—"

"Even wolves forbear to kill their rivals' cubs."

The next day Ryke went to the stables to choose horses. They stood tall, shaggy-maned in their winter coats. They snorted at him. He fed them fistsful of hay as he felt them over. A cat leaped disdainfully out of the hay pile. Stableboys trotted in and out, trying to look busy so that he would not ask them to do anything. He had nothing for them to do. He picked out a sturdy grey gelding for himself and a chestnut stallion for Errel. Errel had taken the small bow into the Yard to shoot. Some of Berent's men had joined him; Ryke heard his clear voice calling instructions.

Tav came into the stable. "I was looking for you," he said. Ryke straightened. "Ah, did you pick the big one?" he said, running a hand down the grey's long jaw. The horse nudged him in the chest.

"Yes."

"He'll serve you well. I broke him myself," said Tav.

"I'm sorry—"

"No. You'll need him more than I. I'm pleased to see him go." He had a pleasant voice. He put an arm through Ryke's; his shoulder was thick with muscle beneath his woolen cloak. "Last night you said that Col Istor plans to disguise his men as outlaws. Come and tell me more." Ryke cast back to the conversation in the watchtower. He had not really been a part of it.

At dinner, in the hall, the talk was not of new wars but of old ones, of the war with Anhard-over-mountain, tales studded with the names of men now dead. Tav and Ashe, Berent's second son, fought over the battle in which Athor had killed the Anhard king. Ryke remembered waiting for the signal which brought the Keep's men into battle: the lifted battle staff. He remembered the heat . . . Just before the signal was given, he had watched a bee foraging for honey in the cup of a blue daisy, its legs fat with pollen. He wondered if it had ever gotten back to the hive. "Do you remember?" Ashe said to Errel.

"Not well," said Errel quietly. "I was fourteen. I was on the wall with the archers. I remember being very thirsty." The old man nodded and said nothing. Ler stood at Berent's elbow, eyes flickering with excitement at the war talk.

Errel was eating with his left hand; he kept his right hidden in his lap. "Did you injure the hand again?" Ryke said across the board.

"No," said Errel. "It hurts."

"It's only been six days since it broke."

"I know when it broke," said Errel. He wrestled with a capon leg. "If I don't use it, it will stiffen."

"Quite right," said Ashe.

"You could give it a bit more healing time," Ryke said.

Errel held it out and flexed the fingers. The middle finger would not bend. "It's *my* hand," said the prince with unusual irritation. "I can barely draw that damned child's bow."

"Enough to try anyone's temper," said Tav. Ryke grunted. Norres and Sorren had not come to the meal; he wondered why not. Perhaps they had left. Their task was done.

"Are the messengers gone?" he said.

"They requested that we excuse them," said Tav. "They are being served in their chambers."

Uncharitably Ryke thought, They were wiser than we, who sit here roasting to death. But he recalled that they had done the same at Tornor. One of the watch seconds began to tell the story of the man who had been nailed to the front door of his own house. Ryke found himself disbelieving it, though he had believed it before. Probably the ghyas had simply killed the man.

The moon, a gleaming crescent, floated on the peak of the western mountains. Errel and Ryke crossed the inner court to the apartments.

The stars stood out against the winter black. Ryke shivered. The walls and shapes of the Keep were not those he knew. Even the ring of his boots on the courtyard's stones seemed subtly changed from the sound of the stones of Tornor. He felt lonely, even though he was safe, unwatched, among friends. "What is it?" said Errel softly.

He didn't know how to say it. "Nothing, my prince."

They had scarcely lit the candles in the sconces when someone rapped on the door. Ryke opened it. Norres and Sorren stood in the doorway. "We want to talk," said Norres. Ryke backed away to let them in. He sent a page for wine. When it came, Ryke sent the page away and poured it himself.

Errel lifted his cup to the ghyas. "Neither Ryke nor I have had a chance to thank you properly," he said.

Norres said, "We have been long indebted to you."

"You are no longer," Errel said.

Sorren said, "We came to find out what you intend to do, now that you are homeless." She leaned back in her chair, one arm across her lap, the other braced upon it, chin resting on the back of the lifted hand. Ryke found himself leaning forward to see her better. Her pale blue eyes were depthless as the sky. The man's tunic and breeches did not disguise her anymore. Her mouth was wide. He wondered what it would taste like . . . Norres was looking at him, grey glance like the touch of a sword. If they were lovers, he thought, what did they do? He flushed. He was thinking such things because he had not been with a woman in a long time. Fumbling for the wooden wine cup, he lifted it to his lips and drank deeply. The wine was warm and cinnamon-scented, and very strong. The word she had said so calmly, *homeless*, reverberated in his head.

He put the cup down. "We ride to Pel Keep," he said, not caring that he was speaking out of turn. He wiped his mouth with his hand.

Sorren looked at Errel. The prince said, "Where are *you* going now?"

"South," said Norres.

"How do you decide where to travel?" Errel asked.

Sorren said, "We listen to the rumors in the villages and on the roads. We follow war, like the crows."

"A convenient occupation," Ryke said.

"What do you mean?" said Sorren.

"There will always be war."

"Maybe. Maybe not," she said. Ryke drank more wine. He realized he had not been even slightly drunk in five months.

"Always," he said. He loosened his shirt. "Always."

"What war do you ride to now?" Errel said.

"No war," said Norres. "We're tired. We're going home."

"Where is home?" said the prince.

Answering syllables pattered like rain. "Vanima."

Ryke laughed. The others looked at him. "There's no such place," he said. His tongue was thick with wine. "It's a children's tale." *Vanima*—it meant Van's Valley. It was a place in the western mountains, mythical and inaccessible, a place of always summer. He had loved such tales as a child. "It isn't real."

"It's real," said Norres. "We've been there."

"Truly?" said Errel. "There is such a place? And is Van a real person?"

"Real as you are," said Norres.

"Can you go back?" asked the prince. Ryke reflected, you never could, in the stories. Norres nodded. Ryke drank again, wondering about what was happening beyond the Keep, wondering what Col Istor was doing. The back of the wooden chair hurt his head. He wobbled up, senses swimming, and walked to the bed. "How long does it take to get there?" Errel said.

"Eight days' ride from here," said Norres.

"Ah," said Errel. Ryke looked up. His heart thudded without reason.

"Come with us," said Sorren.

Errel clasped his hands on his knee. "I have a war to fight."

"That war will not be fought for another three months, and what will you do in the meantime? Beat your head against Pel Keep's walls? Come with us." Her voice was music. On the wall, the trapped wolf snarled at the hunters. Ryke lay back on the bed.

"Eight days' ride?" Errel said.

"Yes."

"Are strangers welcome in the valley?"

Norres said, "They are when they arrive with friends."

Errel stooped over the bed. "Ryke."

"Uh."

"Shall we visit Vanima?"

Ryke grinned. It was pleasantly ridiculous to agree to step into a fiction. "I'll go anywhere," he said recklessly. "West, south, anywhere." The pillow was cool; he tucked his turning head under it. None of this was real. Behind, above, around him, voices murmured: summer, the land of summer, Vanima.

s e v e n

They left Cloud Keep at mid-morning the next day.

Berent and his commanders said farewell to them at the Keep's main entrance. Berent thanked the ghyas for their help in obtaining the truce with Col Istor. He thanked Ryke for all the information he had revealed about the war chief's plans. Ryke bowed. Tav stepped up to clasp his hand and stroke the grey horse. "Good fortune on your travels," he said.

"Thank you," Ryke said. " 'Ware outlaws."

"We shall," promised Tav. The red horse, excited, spun in a circle, and Errel reined it in. Berent spoke softly to the prince. The old man had given them food, clothing, and weapons. Ryke touched the hilt of the dagger at his belt. The sheath bore Berent's crest: a mountain cat. Errel had a dagger and the little bow and a quiverful of goose-feather-fledged arrows. He supposed that Norres and Sorren had the weapons they had come with. They sat silently on their horses, enigmatic and unapproachable, cloaked in their difference. The outer gate opened. Errel pulled the chestnut into line. They rode from the Keep. The guards on the battlements lifted their bannered lances in salute.

The steppe stretched grimly out before them. Due south rose the smoke of a village's fires: they rode toward it. Ryke brought his horse next to Errel's. The stallion nipped at the grey.

"Berent didn't ask where we were going."

"Safer for him," Errel said. "If Col Istor should have occasion to ask him if he saw us, he can truthfully say he harbored us for two nights, as is the custom, and then saw us gone, and that he doesn't know where we went."

"And then he can hope that Col believes him," said Ryke.

They rode through a village. There were few people in the streets, and the windows of the houses were shuttered. Three women leaned on the wall of the well, talking. They looked at the riders incuriously. A pig ran out of an alley, pursued by a gaggle of children. The animal squealed at the horses in fury. The children shouted and flung themselves on it. Errel's horse bucked its hind legs in irritation, and he held it down one-handed, swearing at it. "Why did you pick me the one with the temper?" he said.

"I'm sorry, my prince," said Ryke. He started to offer to exchange his grey for the chestnut, but thought better of it.

"Sorren says I will have to get used to being called just 'Errel.' There are no princes in the valley. Do you think you could try to do that?"

"No," said Ryke.

Errel grinned. "You don't believe in Vanima," he said.

"No, prince."

A chicken marched across the road. Errel's horse snorted. Errel called it names. Its ears pricked back. "Child of a mongrel donkey." It tossed its head. "My father would have loved this horse," said the prince. "He loved things he could subdue."

"He was a good man," said Ryke.

"He was a good lord," Errel said. "As a man, he was no better than any of us.'' Ryke frowned. Errel had said just such a thing of Col. It irked him to think of Col Istor and Athor of Tornor ranked together. ''Don't scowl at me. I loved him and admired him. But he was not a gentle man.''

''I don't know what you mean,'' Ryke said.

''Never mind.''

They passed a bog. The houses of the village curved in a circle around it. Women in cloaks and boots chopped at the dark earth with spades. To Ryke's eye, the ground looked as cold and unyielding as the stone. They came out of the village. Before them lay the steppe, decorated with dirty white clusters of sheep and an occasional green pine thicket. Dogs barked rings around their charges. Ryke remembered watching the sheep as a boy, before he was old enough to go to Tornor. He had suffered through it, impatient to be older. He did not recall it with pleasure. He looked west. At the horizon lay a line of orange-gold hills, tipped with white, fading into distance. West was a road that went directly from Cloud Keep to Pel Keep: they were not on it. ''How close will we come to the Galbareth?'' he said, remembering the trip south with his father.

''I don't know.''

''Close enough to see it?''

''I don't think so,'' Errel said gently. ''No.''

They passed by another village. The steppe was so grazed down that they did not need to follow the road. The backs of the village houses looked like humpbacked men sitting in a row.

When he looked back, Cloud Keep had shrunk till it was almost indistinguishable from the rocks at its back. The sky had turned a bright portentous blue. Birds wheeled over them. Errel's chestnut scampered like a colt. Ryke's big grey plodded. Errel kicked the chestnut into a run and brought it back. ''He'll do.''

The first two nights they slept under trees, on pine needles. The trees dripped moisture. They lay quietly, unmolested by wolves, but Ryke woke and slept and woke again. The sound of the water disturbed him; it was nothing like the drip of fog over rock.

The following day the land turned a sly new green. The trees

were tipped with red growth. Banks of snowdrops lay in the hollows
of hills like the last remnants of winter. Ryke found himself twisting
and turning on his horse's back, trying to see it all. They now rode
due west, but still the line of mountains (orange in the morning, blue
in the evening) grew no larger. "Wait," said Sorren.

The road they followed was nothing more than a cart track. The
day they saw the snowdrops they passed through two villages. The
doors of the houses were open, and the aroma of baked bread steamed
from the doorways. The lush scent made Ryke's stomach growl. In
the meadows around the town the men and women were planting.
They stooped over the turned fields, shoots in their hands, singing.
They waved to the travelers.

That night they sheltered in a woodcutter's lean-to. Sorren went
looking for a stream. She brought back two skins full of water and
then disappeared again. Ryke walked downstream and came upon her
scrubbing at something in the cold creek water. The sunset light was
fast fading. He could not see what she was washing. There seemed
to be a lot of them, all the same shape. She looked briefly at him.
"Blood rags," she said, seeing where his gaze went. "Was there
something you wanted from me?"

"No," he said. He went farther down stream and urinated against
a bush. He went back along the stream, but she had finished and had
gone on ahead of him.

There was a blackened ring of stone outside the lean-to. Norres
built a fire in it. Errel went up the forested hillside. Ryke leaned
against a fallen log. The firelight fingered the tree trunks. He heard
the twang of the little bow. Errel came back with a hare. Ryke skinned
and spitted it. Fat dripping from the carcass made the fire hiss and
sputter. In three days of traveling the plain had turned to hills and
the hills to meadow and forest so smoothly that he had not noticed it
happening. "I don't understand where we are," he said fretfully.

"Southwest of Tornor," Sorren said. She sat beside Norres, her
arm resting on Norres' lap: an intimate gesture.

"We're riding to the valley between the Great Mountains and
Galbareth," said Norres.

"Can we see it from here?"

"Galbareth? No. We're too far from it," said Sorren. She leaned forward, out of the circle of Norres' arm. Smoothing a place in the dust, she picked up a twig. "Here's Tornor." She made an X in the dust. "Here's the Rurian, flowing south from the mountains. Here's Kendra-on-the-Delta." She drew a line and an X at its other end. "Here's Galbareth. Tezera City is here. Here's Lake Aruna, and here the line of the Great Mountains. We're here." Another X. "Vanima lies five days south of where we are." She drew another line at the bottom of the picture. "That's the ocean."

Errel grunted. "Have you been there?" he asked.

"Yes," said Norres.

Ryke tried to see it as a bird might see it, small as this but alive, teeming with beasts to hunt and be hunted by.

"We traveled down Rurian when we left Tornor," said Sorren, touching the map. "We went into Galbareth. The farm folk were friendly. We worked in the fields. After harvest we went back to the River Road. We went all the way to Mahita."

"Was it hard?" said Errel.

"Sometimes." Sorren smiled at Norres. "But we were never sorry."

"Where is the Asech country?" Ryke asked.

Sorren made a smudge with her thumb between Galbareth and Kendra-on-the-Delta. "We never went there. The Asech tribes are not friendly to strangers."

"Why did you ask that?" said Errel.

"Col learned war in the Asech country, chasing the tribes."

"How do you know?"

"He told me."

"Ah."

Norres reached over Sorren's shoulder and rubbed the map out with a firm hand. "Let's sleep." Sorren smiled, and rose. They stood side by side, shoulders touching, seeming twins, as they had that first time Ryke had seen them in the watchtower . . . There was no difference in the shape of their bodies. Norres had taken off the fur-lined overshirt.

"But you are—" he bit his words silent. Linking hands, the two women walked into the woods. Ryke slid into his cloak. He felt tricked, and knew that was stupid. Norres' sex had always been there for him to see. He wondered what had kept him from seeing it before. The women returned. He heard the sounds of bodies touching and shifting. He looked up, seeking sky. The tree tops joined like black lace overhead, trapping the crescent moon in their design.

"Good night," said Errel.

"Good night," Ryke said.

"Good night," said a voice from the other side of the fire.

Then there was silence.

At dawn, Errel read the Cards.

Crows sailed above them as he laid out the pattern on top of his cloak. The painted colors glittered. The crows swooped close, hoping that the Cards were something to eat. "These are the Cards of the past," Errel said, touching them one by one with his left hand. His broken finger stuck out, away from the others. "The Demon is a portent of violence and domination." Dressed in white with green flames around his head, the Demon grinned. "The Sun, reversed. The Lord, reversed. The Messenger." He looked at Sorren. "That's you."

Sorren nodded.

"These are the Cards of the present. The Wheel of Chance. The Death card. That means transformation, a new way of thinking. The Wolf. The Stargazer, reversed. These are the Cards of the future. The Scholar, reversed. Unorthodox ideas. The Phoenix. One of us is going to be tested. The Weaver. A person of power. The Mirror, reversed. One of us is a pessimist. That's Ryke."

"I don't feel pessimistic."

"But you don't believe in the Cards," said Errel. Still using his left hand he swept them into a pile.

"Change, unorthodox ideas, a test," repeated Sorren. "Is that good?"

Errel shrugged.

"I can learn," Ryke said. "I'm willing to learn." He glanced at Norres. But she was scuffing her heel into the ashes of the fire and did not look at him.

He mounted the grey, angry. He told himself he had no reason to be angry, but the words did not stop the tightening in his chest. Errel could have told him what the ghyas were. Ryke wondered why he had not. Sorren sat her horse holding the rein of Norres' bay. "When will we reach this magical valley of yours?" he asked.

"Five days more," she said.

"Is it really summer there?"

"You'll see."

Errel said, "After a winter in Tornor, it feels like summer here." He stretched contentedly. "Spring comes early in the south."

Sorren said, "Southerners say it comes late in the north." Norres took the rein from her. "We'll stop tomorrow at a village. A friend of ours lives there." She leaned low over her horse's neck to avoid the sweeping branches. They wove through the trees. The scent of early flowers rose around them. A butterfly fluttered over Ryke's head. Its wings were yellow with black markings. They went down a slope and up again and came out of the trees onto a grassy hillside. Their shadows pointed in front of them, toward the white-capped mountains.

All morning they rode west, keeping to the crest of the hills. Sheep grazed on the hillsides, tended by children and fuzzy dogs. In the valleys, the young shoots lay in the rich earth, soaking up the new sunlight. Blackbirds wheeled over the fields. The sun shimmered off their iridescent wings. Brightly colored pieces of cloth waved like banners from poles set at intervals in the fields. "What are those?" Errel asked.

"They keep the birds away," said Sorren.

"That's a good idea," Errel said.

They stopped for a midday meal beside a stream. Norres cut a willow switch and used a piece of thread from her shirt to tie a thorn to its end. She dug in the soft loam near the stream till she caught a worm. She dangled the baited thorn in the stream. Almost at once there was a flurry in the water, and the switch dipped. Drawing it toward her, she reached into the water. She brought out a fish by the tail. She did it four times, while Sorren build a fire. The fish were not much longer than Ryke's hand, with yellow skins that shimmered in the light like the blackbirds' wings.

They ate everything of the fish except the fins and bones and eyes. "What are these fish called?" Errel asked.

"Yellowlings," said Norres.

"Ah. I like this country," said the prince.

Ryke looked west. He was astonished to see how big the mountains had grown. He looked south. Green hills spread with the shadows of the clouds fanned at his feet. He looked south, seeking a glimpse of Tornor's mountains, but could see only the hills through which they had been traveling. He had long since taken off his travel furs. "How far is the village we're going to?"

"Has it a name?" asked Errel.

"It's called Gerde's Spinney," said Norres. "One day's ride."

Gerde's Spinney was a cluster of wooden houses lying in a valley. The hills above it were heavily forested. The land in the valley was cleared and plowed, and the villagers were planting. A herd of long-haired goats browsed in a meadow, watched by the inevitable dirty-faced child with a switch. As they rode toward the houses the child came bounding from the meadow, goats at her heels. Errel's chestnut shied. He pulled it back. The girl-child wore her hair in two long braids. She called a question to them, in speech so swift and thickly accented that Ryke could not understand it. Sorren answered. "We come to visit Chaya; we are her friends." The child grinned, white teeth in a dark brown face, and scrambled back up the slope, goats all around her. She was no older than Ryke's youngest sister. Wearing breeches and a ragged shirt, she climbed as agilely as her whiskered charges. Ryke wondered how his family was faring.

The village was small, three streets one way, four another. An old man with a straw shade over his face slept in the marketplace beside the well. The houses were of wood, not stone. Their walls had been washed with some kind of red paint to keep them safe from water-rot. They were lower than the tall houses of the north, with steep eaves.

They stopped at a house apart from the others. Dye smells hung thick about it. The harsh steam raked Ryke's throat. He coughed. The door of the cottage opened, and a child came into the road. He was fair-skinned, comely, except that his right leg was withered. He leaned on a stick. He reached for the horses' reins. Ryke hesitated to relinquish the grey. "I can hold him," said the boy. Without a hint of mischief, the chestnut stallion followed him. Ryke let his own reins slide.

"Welcome," said a woman's voice. Ryke turned to see her striding around the side of the house. "I saw you coming down the slope." Her voice was deep and quick. "Ai, Sorren, Norres!" She opened her arms. The three women hugged in a circle. The stranger wore a hat of straw, and her clothes were scattered with spots of color, red and blue and purple and saffron. She was very tall, nearly as tall as Ryke.

Sorren said, "This is Chayatha. Chaya to her friends." She indicated Errel and Ryke, saying their names. The woman nodded to them. She was dark as Col Istor. She took off her hat for a moment. She wore her hair in a braid coiled on the top of her head.

"What brings you on this road?" she said to Sorren.

Sorren grinned at her. "We go to the valley."

"Oh? And what of them?" Chayatha pointed her chin at the two men.

"They go with us," said Sorren. "They are exiles. Van will take them in."

Ryke wondered what right this woman had to know who they were or where they went.

"Maybe. Go in the house." She pushed Sorren's arm. "Emmlith will give you food. I have cloth in the pots and cannot leave it." She loped round the side of the house again. Ryke scowled. He did not think it a friendly welcome.

The house was low and smokefilled. It smelled of sheepskin, wool, and dye. Its dimensions were deceptive; it was larger than it had seemed from outside. It had a brick hearth with a spit. Through an unshuttered window Ryke looked on the back of the house. He saw the steep roof of a chicken coop, and a pot the size of a bathing tub raised on stilts, with a fire burning under it. It was clay, Ryke thought, or tile, some substance that would not burn.

Emmlith served them goat cheese and ale. He swung easily about the room, using his cane as if it were an extra limb replacing the crippled one. Errel said, "What happened to your leg?"

"I was born so," said the boy, uninterested. "Where did you come from?"

"North," said Errel, "from the mountains."

Chayatha came in. "Emmlith, go watch the fires." The boy limped out. Chayatha poured herself a mug of ale. The mug was painted with the figure of a dancer, black on red. "It's been a long time," she said. "Too long. Three years. Last time we spoke, you were going south. I heard you joined the green clan."

Sorren stroked the green braid on her shirt front. "It was true, as you see. We have been messengers for two years."

"How did you get the green clan to accept you?"

Sorren grinned. "They think us ghyas. That was Van's idea for us, and it worked."

"And has it been what you desired?" said the dyer. Eyes bright, she looked from Norres to Sorren. "No, I think not. Ai, my poor friends, each loving what the other does not want. The road makes a weary compromise. How is it that you ride from the north in winter, traveling with two northerners?"

"We were south. But the green clan follows war," said Norres. "There is war in the north."

Chayatha grimaced. "When is there not war in the north?"

Ryke said, before he could stop himself, "This war was made by southerners."

"Ryke," said Errel, "we are guests." But the dyer laughed.

"So speaks an exile, seeking someone to blame for misfortune. I know, I was one. Have some more ale." She refilled Ryke's mug. "You've caught me at a busy time. The sheep were sheared, and the wool pressed and carded ten days ago. Since then, I have not stopped tending the fires." She stretched and yawned, a gusty sigh.

"Then we will not stay long," said Sorren. Ryke approved. He did not like the cottage. Chayatha puzzled him. Her speech was quick, too quick for a slow-thinking countrywoman. Perhaps she was from Mahita, where Sorren and Norres had met her. But if she was from Mahita, what was she doing here? She was farther from her home than he was.

Norres said, "What news from the south?"

"Nothing," said Chayatha. Drawing the cheese in front of her, she cut herself a piece, pushing the knife outward with her thumb like a man. "It's too early for the traders. They'll be here in a month or so. They come across Galbareth crushing the grain with their laden wagons as if they were on the Great South Road itself." She put the cheese knife on the table.

Norres said, "I wonder that the land allows it. Galbareth doesn't like strangers."

"What do you get from them?" asked Errel.

"Silks," said Chayatha, "spices, oil, brass and copper." She touched the copper-handled knife. "They buy our wool, cloth and thread. Especially now, they like the blue cloth."

Sorren chuckled. "I can tell you why that is. The traders tie bits of blue to their wagons and call themselves the blue clan. Truth!" she said at Chayatha's disbelieving look. "In Tezera they gather in a big hall and call themselves a guild, and make laws for each other. If one breaks the law, he is fined. They wear blue capes and hoods."

"Such nonsense!" said the dyer. "The green clan I know, the black clan I know, but what is this?" She scowled. Ryke remembered

Jaret, who had taught him the runes and had worn a black hood sometimes. Errel had said that Jaret was a scholar.

"Times change," said Errel.

"And not always for the better," said the dyer darkly. But she glanced at Errel and then at Ryke, and her face lightened. "Ah, a mystery. Two travelers, fair-haired, with clothes out of the north, one with a ruby ring on his hand, keeping company with messengers. Who are you, strangers?"

Errel dropped his left hand to his lap. "My name is Errel."

"Chaya—" began Sorren.

"Nay, let him answer. He has a tongue. Errel. That is a good northern name. Why so shy? I am only a woman, and you are a soldier. Do you fear I shall hurt you? I shall trade secrets with you. I come from Kendra-on-the-Delta. I have lived in Vanima; I am Van's sister. There. Now, show me your ring."

"My prince," said Ryke, and stopped, furious and ashamed of himself for having betrayed Errel's rank. He glared at Chayatha with mistrust, and then watched astonished as Errel reached his ringed hand across the table. Chayatha touched the sign of Tornor with one finger. The backs of her hands were stained and spotted.

"Ah," she said. The sound hung in the air. Her dark, wide eyes seemed to lose their light. Ryke's skin prickled. Norres' fingers sank into his arm. When he looked at her, she laid a finger to his lips.

"I see a place," said Chayatha tonelessly. "I see a castle on a hill." Her face twitched. "There is snow on the earth around the castle. The walls are built of black stone. I see a man in a tower. He is walking back and forth in front of a fire. I cannot see his face. I see a younger man on watch beneath the stairway. I see a woman in a red dress walking up to the man on watch. She has fair hair, where all the other folk I see are dark. I see—the tower fades. I see it from the doorway of a hut. An old woman stands in the doorway, leaning on the shoulder of a little girl. In the hut are herbs and spices and roots and drugs, a healer's stock. The hut fades. I see a castle; a tall old man with scars on his face talking to a young one who looks like him. That is—that is all." She drew a deep sluggish breath.

Errel said, "Sironen has a scarred face." Ryke thought, The man in the watchtower is Col. The woman in the red dress is Becke. He pictured her running up the stairs to Col Istor's bed.

"The healer's hut," said Norres. "I have not thought of it in years. I wonder if old Otha still lives." Putting her arm around the dyer's shoulder, she poured ale into a mug. "Drink."

Chaya groped for the mug. Her eyes looked odd. Ryke wondered if she knew what Col was doing, planning. He didn't understand what she had done. "What does your seeing mean?"

She shrugged. "I don't know. I see. *You* know. I saw what you wanted me to."

"Does that mean it isn't real? Is it a dream?"

"It's real enough. Don't ask me questions, I don't know the answers." Ryke wanted to shake her. Perhaps Col had attacked Sironen. Why had Chayatha seen naught of Cloud Keep or of Berent? He did not dare to ask her. The stink of the cottage was making his nose itch. He stood.

"I'm going out," he said.

Looming on the western horizon, the wall of mountains closed the vista. He still felt shut in. He paced in the narrow street. A horse complained. He went around the house to the shed and slid in among them, stroking them. Memories of Tornor writhed in his mind: of Tornor cold in winter, stark against a star-studded sky, grey rock in the green of spring, firm against the sudden unreliable warmth of summer, solid in the autumn rainstorms. The softness of this southern country disturbed him. He remembered how, on the visit to the grainfields long ago, he had wakened to hear the *slush-slush* of the wind in the grain. It was terrible at night, like a hundred dead men walking, and he had crawled to his father and thrust himself into the sleeping man's arms. He rested his cheek against the grey gelding's smooth flank, despising himself for the child's voice in his mind that whispered, *I want to go home.*

He left the shack. Errel hunkered down against the side of the house, under the slanting eaves. Ryke sat beside him. The prince was turning the ring around and around on his middle finger.

"What did that woman do?" Ryke said.

"She—saw Tornor." Errel sighed. We look like two beggars in the dust, Ryke thought. "I have heard of people like that."

"Is it like the Cards?"

"No. The Cards are only an instrument, like the star-patterns or the stones and sticks that other folk use to make visible the harmonies and balance of the world. The information lies in them. We read it there, like weather-lore. Even a fool knows the signs for rain or frost. Anyone can use the Cards."

"Not I," said Ryke.

"You will not, but you could learn. All it takes is the will to do so and knowledge of the shape of the tool; no different than learning to swing a sword. But Chaya's seeing is a gift you are born with, like sharp eyes or a long reach or a withered leg."

"A southern thing."

"You forget," said Errel gently, "we were all southerners once."

I was never a southerner, Ryke thought; I am of the north, and I want to go back to it. "Why did she see Sironen?"

"I don't know," said Errel.

A dog trotted out from between two houses, smelled the seated strangers, and began to bark. Errel groped left-handed for a stone. He threw it; the dog yelped as it struck, and slunk into the alley. Sorren and Norres came from the house. Sorren carried a pack; Norres a wineskin. "Chaya is tired from the far-seeing," said Sorren. "She asks us to leave. She gave us some cheese and some ale. The prentice has gone to get the horses."

Errel said, "I am afraid our presence upset her."

"It was not you," said Norres. "Chaya sees what people bring her, in their heads and in their hearts." She looked pointedly at Sorren. "Whether they know it or not."

Sorren's chin went up. "That's not true," she said. "I know what is in my heart. I have always known it." Ryke looked to Errel for enlightenment. But the prince only shrugged. Emmlith brought the horses from the shed. The chestnut looked contented, his wildness gone. They rode. At the foot of the village Ryke looked back.

Silent on her hill, the goatgirl was watching them.

eight

The coldness between Norres and Sorren lasted till evening. Their distance made Ryke uncomfortable. But in the morning he opened his eyes and saw them sleeping as they always did, arms about each other, wrapped in one cloak. It was his turn to see to the horses. He took his time, leaving Errel's chestnut for the last. The stallion danced in a circle, tossing its head away from the bit. Norres came to his aid. "Be still," she said to the horse. Magically it grew mild in her hands, standing without fighting as Ryke saddled and bridled it. Ryke brought the horses into the clearing. Errel came from the stream, waterbags over his shoulders. He turned to thank Norres, but she had turned her back, busy, inaccessible.

"Four more days to ride," said Errel.

"We turn south now," said Sorren. She stamped on the fire ashes.

The country changed yet again. The shape of the hills hardened. The green diminished. They rode past upthrust granite and clefts of many-colored banded rock. The western mountains loomed on the right, their peaks touched with snow.

"There are high places where the snow never melts," said Sorren, guiding her brown mare next to Ryke. She wore a gold-trimmed shirt that brightened the pale color of her hair and matched the smooth gold of her skin. She offered Ryke the winebag. He drank the sour ale. The air was thin, dry, and warm. Ryke wished he had a map in his head, as she did. He wanted to know where they were, where Tornor was, where the valley was. He handed back the wineskin.

Sorren said, "What do you think of the ride so far?"

Ryke shrugged. "I would rather not have had to make it." That sounded churlish even to him. "It's not bad."

Sorren said gently, "I remember how it was to leave Tornor."

"But you wanted to leave."

"I wanted to stay, too. I hated it and loved it. And I was frightened; I was only fifteen and had never traveled farther than the village."

She sat the horse as if she had been born on it. Ryke wondered if she liked living a nomad's life, homeless as any street beggar in a southern city, following war. It was a lonely life for a man to lead; it seemed to Ryke an unnatural one for a woman. "When did you leave?" he asked.

"Eight years ago."

"How is it that I don't remember you?"

"Why should you remember one girl among so many? I remember you. You were in Stane's watch. You stood day guard outside the stable all one summer. Norres and I used to meet there. Your hair was lighter then."

Stane—he remembered him; a big man with fair hair and ruddy face—he had been four years in Stane's watch. In summer a post at the stable was like standing guard over a midden. "Why did you leave?"

"I had to," Sorren said. "There was no one in Tornor who would let me do what I wanted to do. They wanted me to be Keep's woman, as my mother had been, and have children, and I wanted to live with

Norres, and ride horses and fight. I would have stayed at Tornor if they had let me do that. I love the mountains. It makes me restless to be away from them.'' They both looked west, toward the heights.

"Women don't fight."

"That was what they told me," said Sorren. "So I ran away. They brought me back and I cried, and my mother yelled at me. She told me I was a fool, that if I did as I was told I might even marry well, because my father was lord of the Keep."

"You're Athor's daughter?" The gelding stumbled. Automatically Ryke pulled its head up. Sorren nodded. "Does Errel know it?"

"Oh, yes. He knew before I did. He was first to tell me. We played together, he and I. He showed me the things he learned in the Yard. It made him so angry when I could do everything he could do." She chuckled. "But that was when we were much younger. When I became a woman he was the only person in the Keep I talked to. I told him about Norres."

Ryke bit his lip, afraid to speak and break the flow of speech. A bird called sharply from a bush.

"She was born in the Keep, too. But she was some soldier's child, and they sent her to be fostered in the village. They prenticed her to the healer. She hated healing: staying indoors and tending the pots. She ran away to the Keep and hid in the stable. She liked being with the animals. I always loved her. I planned ways for us to leave and not be found—but they were all flawed." She sighed. "I suppose that was because I did not want to go. Norres was so patient. She never cried, even when Otha beat her to make her say where she had been hiding. She could have run but she refused to go until we could leave together. Errel found a way." She brushed her hair back from her face. "He brought us boys' clothes and took us out hunting on horses from Tornor stable, under the very noses of the guards." She smiled at the memory. The eastern light glinted off her cheekbone. He wondered who had told the young prince that Athor had a daughter, and why he, Ryke, had never heard it. Sorren's hands were firm and sure on her horse's reins. Athor might have married her to one of Berent's sons.

"Would it have been so bad to marry and have children?" A picture came into his mind, at first he thought it was the Lady off the Cards, and then it turned into his sister Becke, going up the watch-tower stairs in a red dress.

She did not answer him at once. Dropping the rein, she arched her spine and pushed her hair back with both hands. When she spoke her voice had flattened. "Is your mother alive?"

"Yes," he answered.

"Mine is not. She was sixteen when she bore me. She died in childbirth the year I was eleven."

Even in the north there were teas women took which could halt the making of the child in the womb. He supposed it had been too late for such. He was a man; he knew little about those things. He said, "All women do it."

"What has that to do with me?" Sorren said fiercely. Touching her heels to the brown horse's flanks, she rode ahead, leaving Ryke alone, annoyed, and puzzled as to why she had spoken to him at all. The gelding stumbled again. Ryke halted it. There was a stone wedged into its left forefoot. He dug the stone out with his knife. When he remounted, he saw Norres and Sorren far ahead and Errel lagging, waiting for him. He urged the grey to a canter. He had not meant to anger her. He had spoken truth as he saw it.

When next they stopped to rest, he offered her some cheese from his pack.

"Thank you," she said. "Have some ale." She passed him the wineskin. He drank, and passed the skin to Errel. The sun was strong. There was a tinge of brown on the green tough grassy hills. A hunting hawk sailed the wind over their heads. The whole landscape seemed to tilt toward the mountains. The great peaks seemed, from where they sat now, to curve in, eastward, so that if they continued to ride due south they would halt at the mountains' feet. If they rode farther south they would end in the sand of the Asech lands . . .

"Ryke."

"Uh." Ryke sat up. He could not remember lying down. Errel grinned at him. He held the rein of the grey.

"Come on. You don't want to sleep here."

"I wasn't sleeping."

"What were you doing?"

"Dreaming," Ryke said. He rubbed his eyes and took the grey's rein. The answer made perfect sense to him; it took some time before he worked out why it had made Errel laugh.

Sunset of the eighth day they came to Vanima.

They turned west for the last time. They rode right at the mountains and the huge brown slabs seemed to slide apart for them, like the wooden puzzles that Ryke remembered playing with as a child ... You pushed the leaves of the puzzles to one side or another, looking for the heart of the toy, and when you found the center it was always empty. The sun shimmered on the brown rock. He was last in line. Errel was ahead of him. Norres and Sorren had disappeared around some corner or down some slope. Errel turned and waved. Ryke squinted. The stallion's head dipped; his hind-quarters bunched. Ryke kneed the grey. He came to the end of the path and looked down. The path widened. He was looking into a long green valley. He saw dark brown fields and the square corners of buildings. He eased his grip on the reins and let the horse pick its own way down the hillside.

Eyes dazzled with heat-shimmer, he realized that the snow-capped mountains had not moved. Vanima lay in a deep cleft of the foothills. The larger peaks floated against the western sky, no nearer, no farther away.

He looked for guards, and saw none. The mountains guard this place, he thought. That was fantasy. He looked for men with weapons, and saw men with hoes. He had never lived in a place without soldiers.

Errel, Norres, and Sorren stopped to wait for him. He hastened to join them. The men, working shirtless in the fields, waved. They went to the stables. The horses pushed eagerly for the water trough. A girl came out of the back and caught at the leads, talking to the thirsty animals with authority. She wore men's clothing, a shirt and cotton breeches. "We can leave our packs here," said Sorren. She said to the girl, "Where's Van?"

The girl gestured with her thumb. "At the Yard."

They walked from the stable. Errel took a deep breath. "Even the colors of the mountains are different," he said.

Ryke said, "Can anyone come here?"

Norres said, "You have to know where it is to find it."

Ryke counted twenty-odd houses fanning out from the center of the village, the well. They were made of some reddish wood. The Yard was big, too big for a small village, and it had no fence about it, only a low wooden railing over which a child could step. The ground was very dusty. Even this late in the day the place was bare, hot, and utterly shadeless. Men and women stood in a semicircle, watching one man throw a second man headfirst at the ground. At the last minute the thrown man's body made a wheel; he rolled and came up on his feet. A woman in the semicircle reached to steady him. The thrower said something to them all, and then came striding toward the newcomers.

"Well," he said to Norres and Sorren, "you've come back."

He was Ryke's size, swarthy as Col Istor, a true southerner, and he moved like a cat, all lope and stretch and ripple under the skin. He had black eyes, very wide set. Like the girl in the stable, he wore cotton breeches, but his brown chest was bare. Dust caked his arms and shoulders. He was beardless. His hair was tricolored, black and red and blond, and he tied it off his forehead with a red length of cloth. Hands on his hips, he looked at Errel and Ryke. "What have you brought me?"

"This is Errel," said Sorren. "This is Ryke. This is Van."

"What can you do?" Van said to Errel.

"I can shoot a bow. I can sing. I can tumble, a little. I can read the Cards of Fortune. I can climb."

Van nodded. "And you?" he said to Ryke.

"I lose wars," said Ryke. "I can arm wrestle. I'm a good liar." He saw Norres frown. He didn't care.

"Welcome to the valley," Van said. "Can you work a field?"

Errel said, "We can learn."

"Good. Take them to Maranth," he said to Sorren. "She'll find places for them to sleep and work for you all to do. It's warmer here than where you've been, by the look of you. We're in the middle of a heat wave. You'll have to find other clothes. Come to the Yard when you're ready to fight." He turned back to the circle waiting for him.

Norres said to Ryke, "Do you usually insult your host?" Ryke shrugged. He waited for Errel to say something. The prince was not even looking at him. He was watching Van. The look on his face was disturbing.

"I'm not answerable to you," said Ryke. "I told the truth."

Norres snorted. "What you do reflects on us," she said.

Van threw a second man. He, too, turned his body into a wheel and landed upright. Ryke could not see what any of it had to do with fighting. He turned his back on the spectacle. "He reminds me of Col Istor," he said.

The fields spread out from the village in a fan shape. Mannikins on stakes waved cloth arms in the breeze to keep the birds from the furrows. In the field nearest them the earth was dark from the blade of the plow, ready to be sown. Horses grazed in the fallow. One at least was a mare, heavy with foal. "What's that?" said the prince, pointing to a field which looked uncleared. Ryke shaded his eyes. The stalks did not have the look of weeds. They were planted in regular rows and grew thigh high.

Sorren said, "The winter planting."

"It looks like wheat," said Errel.

"It is wheat. The ground is not so hard here, nor the winter so severe. Wheat planted in fall is harvested in summer," said Sorren. "Oats are sowed in spring and harvested before the autumn rains, as in Tornor."

"Two plantings, two harvests," murmured Errel.

"This is how the planting is done in Galbareth," said Norres.

They walked down a street, the only street. The well stood in its center. The village looked deserted. No children hung about the buildings. There were no women with their spinning wheels sitting in the sun, exchanging stories—a familiar sight in Tornor village. Chickens cackled from a pen. Ryke glimpsed a stockade and smelled pig. A cat lazed on a roof, licking a paw, stopping now and then to stare with wide eyes into the street. They walked into a cottage. A woman sat at a table. A square window opened at her back. The room smelled of dust and ink and light.

There were chalk slates on the table, and parchment rolls. The woman looked up and leaped to her feet. She wore a blue and scarlet tunic, fringed with gold, and her hair was black as tar and springing loose from her head like a bush. She flung both arms around first Norres and then Sorren. "You've come back!" she said. Her voice was husky, reminding Ryke of Chayatha. On her wrists she wore circles of silver set with blue gems.

Sorren laughed. "Of course."

"Who are your friends?"

"Ryke and Errel. This is Maranth." The woman smiled at them. Errel smiled back; Ryke saw that he had taken off the ring. Ryke tried to smile. He was suddenly exhausted. He wanted a meal, a bed, silence, no strangers to confront, the company of one face, no more. The cat oozed in the window, black fur shining like coal. Maranth petted it and it rubbed against her hand, eyes slitting with pleasure.

"Where have you been?" she asked.

"South. North."

"East and west. I know. Who rules the city now?"

"The Med family," said Norres.

Maranth merely nodded, as if the question and its answer were not important. But she did not immediately speak again. Ryke wondered why who ruled in Kendra-on-the-Delta mattered in Vanima. "Ai, wait until you see Amaranth; she's grown. She's already taller than I. I think she may rival Chayatha." Her voice was quick as rain on hard ground.

"Is she well? Are you well?" said Sorren.

"We are all well. You come at a good time. It rained four days ago, and in another four it will be full moon." Going to the other side of the table, she picked up a slate. Ryke saw that what he had thought were skirts were in fact trousers, slit and bloused. "Let me find you an empty house. The cottage with the blue shutters lies empty, will you take it?"

"Surely," said Sorren. Maranth wrote on the slate. The letters curved and twisted; they looked all the same to Ryke.

"There's plenty of work to do so near to the planting. The fields grow boulders sooner than barley. Do you mind hauling rocks? I need another person to help build a water-break." She looked at Ryke. He nodded, not sure if he was being asked or told.

Norres said. "You can put me with the goats."

"I was going to," said Maranth. "Once they find out you are in the valley they will balk for anyone but you. Sorren, will you plow?" Sorren nodded. The cat walked across the slate. It sniffed at Norres. Maranth seized the animal around the middle and tossed it at the windowsill. "Out, beast!" she said. "How did you hurt your hand?" she asked Errel.

He smiled. "Wrestling."

"A one-handed man cannot hunt or cook or plow . . ." She pushed her fingers through her hair. She seemed at least as old as Ryke, but she moved with the liquid grace of a woman half her age. The bracelets jingled. Beyond the table with the slates he glimpsed the frame of a feather-quilted bed. A man's tunic hung on a hook in the wall. He wondered whose it was. It galled him to be taking orders from a woman.

It did not seem to bother Errel. "I can pull weeds," he suggested.

Maranth grinned. "A good idea. We always need weed-pullers. I hope you can tell a weed from a wheat-stalk." Wind riffled the parchments and the small woman held them down with both hands. "And the fee, if you have it," she said.

Sorren took a pouch from her pocket. Untying the strings that held it closed, she counted coins into her hands. Some of them bore the fish-sign of Tezera, some the grain-sheath symbol of Shanan, and some were marked with symbols Ryke had never seen. They were mostly silver, a few copper. She handed them to Maranth. Taking them, Maranth put them into a wooden chest with metal bindings that sat behind the desk on a stool. She took an unmarked parchment. With practiced movements, she poured water from a brass jug onto an ink-stick in a dish. She rubbed the stick with the brush until the brush tip filled, and wrote on the parchment in the black ink. Over her head on the wall behind her hung a scroll in a wooden frame, with lines of writing on it. Ryke wondered what they said, and if she had made them.

"That is well. Later at dinner you must tell me all about your travels."

"And you shall tell us all the gossip of the valley," said Sorren.

"I never gossip," said Maranth, with mock dignity. "Ai, go away. Let me work."

They went to the street. The sky had darkened; the sun was nearly gone. The face of the mountains was dark brown. "Night comes early in the valley," Errel said. From a pen behind a cottage Ryke heard the snoring grunt of pigs.

"Prince, are we to be farmers?" he said.

"My name is Errel," said Errel, "and yes, we will be farmers here, and goatherds, and whatever is needed." Ryke bowed his head, accepting it. He did not like it. He was a soldier. He felt penned in this village of strangers. The whole place seemed less than a quarter the size of his birth village outside Tornor. "Who is Maranth?" Errel said.

Sorren picked up a piece of straw from the ground. She plaited it in her fingers as they walked. "She's Van's lady. But if she hears you call her that she'll swear at you. She says: *I belong to myself, no one else.* She is the scribe and the steward of Vanima. She keeps the accounts. When the traders come to Gerde's Spinney she goes to bargain with them for the goods we need. Van calls her the Whip. He swears we would starve without her."

"Is that what the fee is for?" Errel said. "To pay the traders?" Sorren nodded. "You paid it for the four of us, didn't you. When I can, I will pay you back."

Everything was red about them: the mountains were red, the earth was red, the wood of the houses was red. Even the house roofs were red slate. They found the house with the blue shutters. It reminded Ryke of his mother's cottage. It had two rooms below separated by a wooden hinged screen, and stairs to a loft. Sorren and Norres went upstairs. The walls were bare. The grain of the wood made patterns like the current of a river. The house smelled of cedar. The bed in the sleeping chamber was soft and prickly with feathers. Pulling off his boots, Errel sank into it with a sigh of pleasure.

Ryke found tallow candles on the mantel, a chamberpot near the bed, a water jug stoppered with cork. There was a chest in the front room. He opened it. It held woolen blankets, a bolt of cloth, thread, a needle, an empty tinderbox, a belt with an iron buckle in the shape of a hand, a dagger hilt without a blade attached. Someone pounded on the door. Ryke opened it. The girl from the stable stood outside holding all their packs. He brought them in. Sorren ran downstairs. She had changed clothes. She wore a light blue tunic and soft brown cotton breeches. "Good," she said seeing the packs.

Errel said, "Where can we get clothes like that?" She pointed to the chest. Ryke returned to it. He found several pairs of breeches and three shirts folded in the blankets. He stripped off his own leather and wool and put on the cotton. The fabric felt weightless on his skin, like a woman's touch.

He had to lay his belt aside. The cotton pants belted with a simple drawstring. The shirt was decorated with embroidery: the image of the sun. He traced its rays with his finger. Norres came downstairs. Ryke saw that she and Sorren wore boots of soft skin that came only to the top of the ankle. He went to the chest again and found three pairs of soft boots and one single leather boot without a mate. One set fit him, but none was long enough for Errel. The prince pulled on his big leather riding boots. "You can have others made," said Sorren.

There was one chair in the front room. Ryke sat. This was journey's end . . . His muscles twitched with fatigue. He had never been so far from the country of his birth before. He felt displaced.

Errel laid a hand on his shoulder. "Come."

Ryke made himself stand. "Where are we going?"

"To the refectory," said Sorren. "Aren't you hungry?"

Ryke's stomach danced at the thought of food. They left the cottage. The light boots made him feel that he was walking off the earth.

For days they had eaten little but cheese and dried meat. The wind blowing down the street at them carried the smells of meat fresh-cooked, and baking bread. They passed the well. Light glistened from the windows of a building; soft light, not the hard bright light of torches. A spark winked in front of Ryke's face. He brushed at it. It winked again. "What the hell?" he said. He squinted into the blue dusk. It blinked in front of him, and he reached for it. It turned into an ash and skittered away.

Sorren laughed. "Firefly," she said.

"What's that?"

"It's a flying thing that makes a fire in its tail and carries it around like a lantern."

Errel said, amused, "Better not try to catch it."

"I want to see it."

"Wait," said Norres. She halted. They all stood still. The firefly circled around their heads, blinking. Norres extended one hand. Ryke held his breath as the fly hesitated, and then dropped to land on her knuckles. Its light pulsed and died, pulsed and died. "The fire's cold," Norres said. She shook her fingers. The fire insect spread its wings and soared off.

"You can tame anything," said Sorren softly.

The refectory's roof was steeply angled from the ridgepole. Inside, the beams were webbed with shadow. They were the same red wood as the houses. There were no weapons and no tapestries on the walls. A peat fire burned in a brick hearth. The soft light came from dishes of oil set out on the tables. Reeds textured the planks of the floor. The tables were long, with backless benches as at Tornor. At one end of the building there was a serving window. Everybody wore cotton and soft boots. Some had woolen cloaks over their arms. "Where do we sit?" said Errel.

"Anywhere," said Sorren. She pointed to a bench. "Sit there.

There's room for four. Norres and I will bring the food.'' Ryke glanced around for a head table. There did not seem to be one. The table Sorren indicated was half empty. They sat down. A man near them looked up and smiled. Sorren and Norres came to the table, each with a platter. The platters held meat (pork and hare) and cheese and a tureen of whey-colored soup with herbs in it. Ryke sipped the soup. It was surprisingly tasty. There were mugs on the table and full pitchers of wine. He poured himself a mug and drank. It was not wine, but water. He drank anyway.

Errel had asked Sorren a question. He listened to the answer. ''Everybody eats here. Everything we grow, we eat, or feed to the horses and chickens and pigs. And everybody takes a turn in the kitchen, doing some kind of work, cooking, cleaning, baking, slaughtering. We hunt, we fish. There are no servants in Vanima. Everyone works and learns the same.''

''What do you learn?'' said Errel.

Sorren said, ''How to fight.''

Farther down the bench from the man who had smiled, Ryke saw a woman with a baby at suck. She wore her hair in two long braids. He looked around. He saw the girl from the stable. He thought he saw one of the men from the Yard. The place confused him. People ate, or talked in low tones. There seemed to be no commanders, no distinctions of rank. One of the people at the serving window came around it and sat at a table, eating with the others. No one carried weapons. It was all wrong, and yet the feel of it was familiar, like a new shoe that has been made exactly to the pattern of an old one. It felt like a Keep.

He drank more water, wishing there was wine. Errel and Sorren talked. Three people walked through the door; a man, two women. The shorter woman was Maranth; he knew her by her hair. Someone waved to her, and she strode in that direction. The other woman and the man went to the serving window. Carrying platters, they came to the half empty bench. The man was Van. He sat without ceremony. The woman sat beside him and Ryke realized that she was just a girl. She had a great bush of hair like Maranth, held at the nape by a clip of leather, and a slim passionate face, vivid in the light from the oil dish. Like Van's, her hair was tricolored. He looked from one to the other. "Ryke," said Van, pointing at him. "Errel. My daughter Amaranth."

There was bread on the table, too. Van tore a slice. He dipped the bread into the meat sauce. His motions were quick and neat, without waste. "Where are you sleeping?" he said.

"The cottage with the blue shutters," said Sorren.

"Ah." He drank. The others were silent, waiting for him to move or speak. His presence imposed a silence. The prince sat quietly, right hand cradled in his left, watching him. Ryke's nerves itched.

Rudely he thumped his elbows on the table, breaking the quiet. They all looked at him. He said to Van, "What is this place?"

Van stopped sopping his bread. His eyes were a brilliant black, like jet or the kind of veinless black marble that quarriers sometimes brought out of the mountains, or like the depths of night between the stars . . . Ryke looked away. The back of his neck was cold. "Vanima," said Van. "The land of summer."

"Where are you from?" said the girl across the table. Her eyes, too, were black, but they did not have Van's terrible springing power. Ryke glanced at Errel. The prince smiled at the girl.

"From the north," he said.

"What happened there?" pressed the girl.

"A war."

"Did you lose it?" Errel nodded. "Who won it?"

"A southern thief," Ryke said. He didn't want the prince to say more than that. He didn't want him to talk about Col Istor.

"Not all things out of the south are ill," said Van. He leaned back a little, putting his face in shadow. It made him easier to look at. "You know the southern word *chea*?"

"No," said Ryke.

"Yes," said Errel. "It means—balance."

"Balance. Chea. Yes. Out of it comes the word cheari. You know that word?" Errel smiled. "It has been corrupted. It means juggler, fool. Once it meant something much more powerful."

"The dancer," said Errel.

Van's eyebrows lifted. "You're a northerner," he said. "How do you know that?"

"From the Cards of Fortune," said Errel. "The first card, which has no number, is the Dancer. He is sometimes called the Fool. He stands at the center of all things."

"I didn't know that," said Van. "I have heard of the Cards of Fortune, but I have never seen them. The southern scholars say that dance is sacred, because the dancer represents the chea, the balance of the world." He put the tips of his fingers together, making a circle. "The symbol for that balance is the sphere, the whole." He was talking directly to Errel, leaning toward the prince. At his elbow, the girl looked bored. "All things balance: night and day, the seasons, the patterns of the stars; all move in their circles, as do we, moving from birth to youth to age to death, whether we desire it or not. But just as the word cheari has corrupted to mean trickster, so do human beings corrupt the chea, destroy the circle and the balance."

"How?" said Errel.

"By killing. By making war. You asked me what this place is. This place restores the balance." He grinned. "At least, that is my hope. I teach a way of fighting that does not break the balance because it does not kill."

Errel was nodding as if this speech made perfect sense to him. Ryke said, "What good is fighting if you can't win?"

"Who said you couldn't win?" said Van. "Skill lies in winning without killing." His eyes glowed. "There's no skill in causing death."

The big shadowy room had stilled. At other tables men and women were nodding their heads. Ryke grew annoyed. There was no way to make war without killing. Van's talk of balance was all words. He imagined going to Col Istor and saying, *Go home, you have broken the chea!* The expression on Errel's face disturbed him. He looked seduced.

"I was a cheari for a little while," the prince said softly. "I'd like to see what your chearis do."

Van nodded. "We'll show you," he said, and rose.

He went toward the door, the girl in his wake. On the way to it he stopped several times, leaning to talk with one or another person. Ryke fought back his dislike for the man. Sorren and Norres left the table to bring the empty platters back to the serving window. Ryke edged closer to Errel. "Are you really thinking of staying here?" he said.

"For a little while," said the prince. "You don't want to."

"I think I'm too old to learn new tricks," Ryke said. "I was taught: When you fight, you kill."

Errel said, "I would not want you to do something against your nature. If you don't wish to stay here, go."

The soft permission was like a blow. "I swore an oath," Ryke said.

"I'm curious," said Errel. He leaned his chin on his clasped hands. The bandaged finger stuck out. "Aren't you?" Something burned at the edge of Ryke's field of vision. He couldn't tell if it were a shooting star or a firefly framed in the window. He gripped the table.

"No."

nine

The meal was over. Norres and Sorren returned from the serving window. Errel rose. They went out the door. A cold wind blew down the tunnel of the street, cutting through the thin cotton of Ryke's clothing. He rubbed his arms, wishing he had brought a cloak. A lithe figure leaped by them: the girl Amaranth, wild-eyed and light-footed as a colt. They went to the blue-shuttered house. Errel lit the candles. Ryke found wood and laid a fire in the hearth. The room filled with the smell of pine. The two women went upstairs to the loft. Sorren called down, "Good night."

Ryke and Errel went to bed. Errel slept immediately. Ryke could not sleep. His muscles twitched. In the grate the sticks assumed the shapes of buildings. Twigs made a tower. Ryke wondered if the shape was an omen of Tornor. Lulled by the heat and Errel's steady breathing, he watched them fall into the fire.

At last he slept. He woke once in the night; the room had chilled. The fire was out. He fell asleep again. He dreamed. He was in a room. As is often true in dreams, he knew the room without being able to say where it was. He thought it might have been a room in Tornor. The room was hot. He went to the window to open the shutters. They stuck. He had to force the latch. At last one opened. There was a wolf's head in the window, glaring at him, teeth bared, dark eyes glittering. It began to climb in the window. He backed from it, feet moving terribly slowly, looking for a knife, an axe, his sword ... He could not find them. The wolf grew bigger. In the dream he yelled for help. He woke up, gasping. The blanket was over his face. No wonder he had had a bad dream. He pulled the wool out of his mouth and nose. It was morning. Sunlight striped the red wood of the walls. He lay quiescent while the sweat dried on his chest and hips. Errel slept beside him. The warm red room was like the heart of summer.

The house creaked. Norres and Sorren were awake; he could hear them walking above him. Someone ran down the stairs. He heard a door open. He heard the sound of water. His mouth was dry. He rolled from the bed carefully, so as not to wake the prince. His shirt and pants were on the floor. He dressed. There was a water jug and basin on the bedside table. He poured water from the jug into the basin and washed his face. The design on the stone was the same as the one embroidered on his shirt: the image of the rayed sun. He rinsed his mouth and spat. Errel rolled over. "Uh."

"Good morning," Ryke said. Errel sat up. His hair was spikey. Ryke carried the basin full of dirty water to the door. A soft breeze trickled into the room when he opened it. He threw the water into the street. It glittered in the air like the eyes of his dream-wolf. Ryke brought the basin to the bed and refilled it with clean water. He wondered if the dream meant something.

Errel said, "Ryke, you do not have to do things for me. I am not a prince here, remember, and you are not, in any case, my servant."

"I don't mind," Ryke said. If the dream meant something, Errel ought to know of it ... If the room were Tornor, then the wolf was Col Istor. Ryke decided he did not need to bother Errel to tell him that.

"Did you sleep well?" said Errel. He dunked his face in the basin.

"Yes," Ryke said. Remembering there were no servants here, he shook the blankets out and hung them in the windows to air. Sorren waved to him from a rise behind the house. She was emptying the chamberpot.

The sky was gemlike: hard, clear, pure. Errel dressed. In the daylight his tall boots looked incongruous. Norres came downstairs. She was smiling. Her shirt was open at the throat. The soft material molded to her. She looked happy, younger, and untroubled. Ryke felt a stab of envy toward her joy. She lifted a hand in greeting and went outside. "Are you ready?" said Errel. "Let's go out."

The red slate roofs of the houses gleamed in the morning light. Already the fields had people in them. On one hill, spotted with stands of fir and cedar, Ryke saw the scattered sleek bodies of the piebald goats. They pushed among the trees, snatching at the low branches. "That's where I go," said Norres, following his gaze. She kissed Sorren lightly on the lips. "Later, love." Sorren led the two men toward the fields. A woman shouted to a horse. The planted fields were edged with marigolds to keep the insects off.

"How old is this place?" said Errel.

Sorren's brow lined for an instant. "Ten years," she said. "I remember hearing Maranth say that she and Van came to the valley when Amaranth was four."

"It must have been lonely for a child," said Errel.

"No lonelier than a Keep," said Sorren. "But they were not alone for long, and there are other children here now."

It bothered Ryke that there were no guards posted to watch the trails along the mountainside. Anyone could come here. But he remembered what Norres had said; you would have to know the way. On the western horizon, an eagle skirted a precipice, sailing on a down-draft. Once more Ryke had the feeling that the mountains themselves were the valley's guard.

A sound penetrated his thoughts. *Whap. Whap.* He glanced around for the source of the noise. "Do you hear—?" he slapped his thigh with a cupped palm to imitate it.

"Yes—" Errel looked at Sorren. She grinned, and pointed to a red hill. Ryke squinted into the sunshine. He could not see what she was pointing at. Then he saw it: a building like a tower with a wheel on its turret. The wheel revolved. Its spokes were vanes. *Whap*, they said as they circled.

"It's a windmill," said Sorren. "Vanima is short of streams, so the mill runs on the wind. If you ride into Galbareth you see them standing in rows on the horizon, like giants waving at each other. We need the mill to grind the grain."

"Wouldn't it break if the wind got too strong?" asked Errel.

"Yes. I don't know how to do it but there's a way to stop it from turning."

"Does it freeze in the rains?"

"No."

"Huh." Errel watched the turning blades, hand shielding his eyes. "I'd like to see that."

They went into the field. The earth steamed. Errel worked his fingers. He had left the bandage off his hand. The broken finger was crooked. "Weeds for me," he said cheerfully, and strode into the wheat field. The pale green stalks brushed his boots. He looked, Ryke thought, like any village fieldhand.

Sorren pointed up the slope. "I see Simmela with a pitch-fork," she said. Ryke squinted into the sunlight. He saw two people digging. About five rows behind them a man guided two horses hitched to a wheeled blade.

The man behind the horses was named Dorian. He greeted Sorren as if she were an old friend. Ryke walked with him to where the people dug. Simmela, with the pitch-fork, was a woman. The man, Lamath, held a pointy-headed spade.

As the sun moved up the sky they walked ahead of the plow, digging out stones and boulders, piling them to the left, building neat cairns between the furrows. Lamath explained that the stones were left in the field to catch the water runoff when it rained. Insects scuttled over their feet. The sunlight thickened like water, till it seemed to Ryke they waded through the musty heat. Lamath and Simmela flipped the stones expertly from the earth. Dorian caught them and laid them ready for Ryke to pile. Below them Sorren talked to the horses. Ryke's back muscles burned as he bent, turned, lifted. His palms blistered. He started to fall behind the others. He forced himself to keep up with their pace.

Finally Lamath signaled for a rest. Simmela strolled back to the plow and returned with a laden waterskin. She offered it to Ryke. "You look as if you need it." The water tasted faintly of leather. It was wonderful. While the bag passed round, Ryke tried to find the place where they had started. He was amazed at how far they'd come; across nearly a quarter of the field.

"Your nose is red," said Lamath. Ryke rubbed his face. The skin was dry, hot, and tight. "Put some dirt on it," the southerner advised.

At the next stop they drew straws to see who should go to the refectory and bring the lunch. Dorian lost. He loped toward the village. "Though really you can say he won," said Simmela. "He gets to wash his face and drink as much as he wants."

Dorian returned with a basket. From it he produced a full water-bag, bread dripping honey, cheese, meats, dried fruit, and a sack filled with small hard sweet blueberries. They sat cross-legged in a circle on the hot earth with the basket in the middle, and ate. Simmela poured water on her head, slicking her hair to her face like an otter. "Aah." The skin around her eyes crinkled with pleasure. Her eyes were dark blue, like the berries.

At noon, when the sun's heat was dizzying, they all stopped. Sorren unhooked the traces and brought the horses into shade. Sweat gleamed on their flanks. Lamath shouldered the spade. They walked out of the furrowed fields. In the fallow the grazing horses stood like stones, tails alone twitching. A hawk sailed in the hot sky. The wind-mill's blades turned in lazy rhythm. *Whap. Whap.* Ryke's back felt like wood. His hands stung. His face and arms were fiery. The crown of his head was too hot to touch.

Sorren came to walk beside him. She was as red as he. "Riding is ill preparation for plowing," she said grimly. "You use none of the same muscles."

"Will there be more to do later?" Ryke's attempt to keep exhaustion from his voice did not quite succeed. Simmela heard.

She chuckled. "No. If we worked longer we would be too tired for the Yard. We did a lot today. Three days and the field will be ready for sowing, right on time."

"In time for what?"

She turned to look at him. "On time for the full moon." Her tone was matter-of-fact. "We sow the field in its light." Ryke remembered stories he had heard of dead men walking out of the earth. Once he had heard Jaret speak of them. *Fables*, the old steward declared. *Tales to frighten children*. Perhaps they were. "The moonlight quickens and strengthens the seed," said Simmela. "This is the custom all through Galbareth. They don't do this in the north?"

"No," said Ryke.

"How strange," she said.

Sorren said, "You don't know the north. It's not a country made for farming."

They halted at the well, and drank, and soaked their faces in the bucket. The cool liquid soothed Ryke's skin. He gulped water till his belly swelled. He wondered if Errel was still in the wheat field. Dorian said, "In Galbareth, the women weave hats of straw which the folk working in the fields wear on their heads. The sun is not so fierce here but perhaps there is a woman here whose fingers recall the skill and who would be willing to make one or two. A day in the sun counts nothing to me"—he extended a dark, ropy arm—"but fair skin burns more easily than brown." He glanced from Sorren to Ryke.

"I can manage," Ryke said.

Sorren sighed. "It's a good idea. Seven years ago, I wore such a hat to reap my first harvest in Galbareth." She put her palm lightly to the top of her head. "By autumn harvest, my poor hair will be burned near white."

Ryke returned the dipper to its peg. "Is there only water to drink in the valley?" he said.

Lamath grinned. "Hard to get used to, isn't it? Van says fermented drink dulls the reflexes. After eight years without, I don't miss it.''

Sorren said, "I didn't realize you have been here eight years." She glanced at Ryke. "That's as much as Norres and I were gone from the north."

Lamath nodded proudly. "Saying it makes it seem long," he said. "It hasn't been—but in the early years, there were days when I thought I could kill for a taste of wine."

From the well they walked to the blue-shuttered house. Lamath and Simmela strolled in front of them, heads together, arm in arm. The air within the house was close and unmoving. Errel sat in the chair. He had poured water into the stone basin, and was soaking his feet in it. His face was red, and his long hair tangled with wheat straw. He caught Ryke's eyes and laughed softly. "The southern sun is naught like the one we are used to, is it? Sorren, I think you might have warned us."

"How, warned you?" she said. "It has been three years since I worked a field. Truthfully, I forgot what it would be like."

"In Galbareth they live in the sun," said Errel. He moved his feet in the basin and winced. "And we think farmers soft."

Sorren lay down on the floor. "I think I will stay here till dinner," she said. "It will be hot as a fire in that loft."

Ryke took a pillow from the bed and brought it to her. "Thanks." She stuck it under her head. This close to her he could see the fine smooth grain of her skin, delicate despite the flush of red that overlay it, and the tiny squint lines at the corner of her eyes, now creased with dirt. She smiled at him. "It's not Tornor, but it's not so bad, is it?" she said.

He shrugged. It made his shoulders hurt.

When Norres came in, she halted in the doorway with her hands on hips. Ryke lay on the bed; Errel was in the chair; Sorren lay supine on the floor. "What's the matter with you?" she said. She wore a wide-brimmed black felt hat.

Sorren lifted her head. "You stink of goat," she said.

"Of course I do. This room looks like a battlefield. Are you all sick?"

Errel said, "Only a little sore."

Norres regarded them. Her lips twitched. "You do look red," she said. "Wait here." She went out the door again.

Sorren said, "I have no intention of moving."

Norres returned holding a clay pot. She knelt beside Sorren. Dipping her fingers in the pot, she spread white salve over Sorren's face and hands. "What is it?" asked Sorren, sitting up. The salve gave her face a masklike look.

"Burdock tea and beeswax," said Norres. She brought the pot to Ryke. The goat smell hung on her hands and clothes. He took a dollop on his finger. The salve was cool and aromatic. "Good for burns and blisters."

Errel striped his face with white. "Where did you get it?"

"Van keeps a cupboard filled with such stuff. I took it." She frowned at Errel's bare feet. "Tomorrow before you go to the fields put hemlock powder in your boots."

"I would as lief go barefoot to the fields," said Errel.

"Do that, then, and poultice your feet with hemlock tonight. Van has some." She took the pot back. "I'm going to bathe," she said, and went out.

Slowly the salve drew the heat from Ryke's face. The sun was falling toward the mountains and the shadows were long in the room. Errel said, "So Van knows healing as well as fighting. He knows the old tongues, and their history . . . What was his name before it was Van?"

Sorren looked at her hands. "I don't know," she said.

Ryke thought, That's not true. She does know.

"Does he ever leave the valley?" Sorren shook her head. "Chayatha said she came from Kendra-on-the-Delta, and she is his sister. He could be a scholar of that city."

"Does it matter?" asked Sorren.

"No," said Errel. "I simply wondered."

At dinner Maranth drew Norres and Sorren off. "Now you shall

tell me all about your travels,'' she said. Simmela and Lamath stopped
to greet Ryke. As the people from the kitchen came to clear the tables,
the girl Amaranth appeared at Errel's elbow. She wore a red cape
with slits for sleeves.

"Come to the Yard," she said.

"Why?" asked Ryke.

She turned a dark stare on him. "My father wants you to see a
chearas." She vanished into the shadows.

"What's a—what she said?"

"I'm not sure," said Errel. "Save that it has something to do
with chearis. Let's go." He rose. Ryke grabbed a final handful of
berries from the basket on the table and followed him to the street.
The wind was as chilly as it had been the night before, and he was
glad that he had remembered to bring his travel cloak. The gibbous
moon bulged in the sky, bright as silver plate. Against the black
silhouettes of the mountains, the village looked tiny. Ryke wondered
how many people lived in it. He asked Errel, not expecting a response.
"About a hundred," said the prince. "But people come and go."
Sorren told him, Ryke thought. They went to the Yard. It was lighted
by a ring of torches set on long stakes. The wind snapped the flames
into sparks. People made a half circle in the dust. The torchlight
falling on their faces made them all look alike. A woman in red silk
waved to them. It was Maranth. They went to her. The silk made a
sound as she moved. It reminded Ryke of the wind in the grain.

"Sit here," she said, leading them to the front of the crescent.
Five people stood in the patterned circle cast by the torchlight. Van
was one. He too, wore red. We are audience, Ryke thought, for what?
He sat. Maranth joined the five in the ring, making six.

Van stamped. The sound drew silence. He stamped again, in
rhythm. Within the audience people began to clap, softly, picking up
the beat. The six people made a circle, hands clasped, facing inward.
They moved in it, all stepping alike. Ryke glimpsed Maranth smiling,
Van intent, two men, two women. They spun, leaning backward,
slow, fast, faster, and their joined hands opened. They whirled from
each other. They made two chains and wove around each other, break-

ing and rejoining. They paired and moved around each other, feet beating out a design. They circled and turned and leaped, hair tossing in the torchlights. Sweat gleamed on their foreheads. Their boots made patterns and their hands made patterns and the hands clapped them into a circle and out again, till they seemed to give off sparks like the flames. They joined hands and whirled, fast, faster, and then stopped, stamping one, two! Ryke hadn't thought that it was possible to stop so completely in the midst of motion. One of the women bowed her head. Her arms trembled. Ryke realized that he was sweating into his fur, as hot as if he had been moving with the dancers. The circle broke. Everybody cheered.

Van loomed over them. Sweat dripped from his hair. "That is half of what we do," he said, He stepped past them. Maranth took his arm. The other dancers were surrounded by people laughing and praising them and talking about the dance.

Sorren and Norres appeared at Errel's elbow. "What did you think?" said Sorren: She sounded exhilarated.

"It was beautiful," said Errel.

It was, Ryke thought grudgingly. His eyes hurt. He rubbed the sweat from his face. He wondered what it had to do with fighting. It was beautiful but empty, empty as the words Van had spoken at last evening's dinner. The balance at Tornor had been broken, yes, and the way to restore it was to kill Col Istor and make Errel lord of the Keep.

"Ryke looks sour," said Norres. "He didn't like it."

"It isn't that," said Sorren. She thrust her arm through Norres'. "Ryke doesn't understand what it's for."

Shadows moved from pole to pole, sniffing out the torches. People moved, still talking, out of the starlit Yard. They talked about dancing and about the plowing. They all wore the same clothes. Ryke glimpsed the girl Amaranth beneath a torch. Sorren was right, he thought. He didn't understand the place.

*   *   *

The next day it was just as hot.

Norres disappeared before they went to sleep, and brought back hemlock leaves and a metal pot in which to steep them. She made a thick tea and soaked a pair of linen hose in it. Then she cut the hose at midcalf and had Errel put them on. In the morning there were only a few tender spots on the soles of his feet. He thanked her gravely. They went out into the sun. At noon, as before, they broke off work and gathered at the well. Even Simmela grumbled about the heat. A few clouds floated out of the north. She lifted her face and shaded her eyes to watch them. "Good," she said.

"What do they mean?" Ryke asked.

"They mean this heat will cool. Too much sun and the seed will bake in the soil. Now we must hope it does not cool enough to rain. If it rains the seed will rot."

"Too bad there's no weatherworker in Vanima," he said.

She nodded. "It is too bad." He hadn't expected her to take the comment seriously. In the village, folk jested of one another, *Ah, you must be a weatherworker*, but he had never heard of anyone who could truly move weather at will. Weather was fickle. It seemed as if it would be a tricky talent. He was a lot less tired than he had been the day before. He took a third dipperful of water, drank half, and splashed the rest on his face.

Sorren jogged his elbow. "Let's go to the Yard." Ryke could think of no reason not to. They passed three people, two men and a woman up on a roof, eating blueberries, surrounded by piles of red slate. They waved. Sorren waved back.

"Are there many women in the valley?" Ryke asked.

"Why?" said Sorren.

"I was just wondering." The black cat lolled on Maranth's doorstep. It swiveled its head to watch them pass.

"No," said Sorren, "not unless things have changed, and from what I can see, they haven't. There are a few. Women do not learn about the valley, and even when they do, it's hard for them to come here. Most don't want to." Ryke pursed his lips. That made sense to him. He couldn't see why any woman would want to learn to fight when she didn't have to. But he wasn't going to say this to Sorren.

There were thirty people in the Yard. Dust puffed in the hot, barren space. Some held wooden swords. No one wore armor. Paired, they circled; feinting, parrying, thrusting. From what Ryke could see of them, they were quick and good. More had short sticks, carved and weighted like knives. Ryke sucked his belly in reflexively. He hated knife fights, for all that his long arms made him practically invulnerable. Van strode from pair to pair. In one part of the Yard, away from the others, a group of six, two women, four men, were dancing. The steps were less mysterious seen in daylight, but they looked just as strenuous. The circling fighters wore boots. The dancers were barefoot. Sorren's body twitched. "I can't stand it," she said. She stepped over the railing. Weaving through the moving bodies, she went to Van. He grinned and nodded.

Ryke watched her find a wooden knife and a hank of rag to tie her hair with. One member of a circling pair agreed to take a rest. She edged in sinuous as a snake, light on her feet as a milkweed pod. She was fighting with a man who was taller and heavier than she. But she was quicker. She tapped him when he least expected it. When he lunged she was not there. Once or twice her movements seemed slowed and uncertain, but that was because she was out of practice. Ryke was suddenly very glad that he had never had the urge to challenge the ghyas. Alone he might win, but if Norres fought like Sorren, together they would have killed him. Without knives, of course, it would be very different. Without a weapon to make close quarters dangerous, the bigger, stronger, or fresher man would win.

As if she had overheard his thought, Sorren said something to her partner. She left him for a moment. When she came back she was not carrying the wooden knife. Ryke craned his neck to see more clearly, but there were too many other people in his way. They circled. The man's knife hand moved in little thrusts, feints. Sorren turned with his motions, keeping one side and then the other facing him, swiveling her hips in a parody of the dancers to present him with a smaller target. Suddenly he thrust upward toward her belly.

She wasn't there. She had turned away. For a moment it looked as if she were turning her back to him. Ryke couldn't follow what happened next, but suddenly she had the knife and the man was face down in the dirt. Laughing, she nudged him gently with her foot. He stood. The left side of his face was streaked with dust.

That was a trick, Ryke thought. He rubbed his nose and realized that Errel was standing beside him. "Did you see that?" he said.

"Sorren? Yes."

"How did she do it?"

"I don't know," said Errel.

"It was a trick. In a real fight she would have been spitted."

"No," said Van. The big man had come up catlike on Ryke's left. He was bare-chested; there was a small dense patch of reddish hair on his chest. He stank, and his breeches were stiff with dirt and sweat. "It was no trick." His size and his speech still reminded Ryke of Col. But his manner—there was something about him of Athor.

He said, "I don't believe it."

"Want to try?" Van reached a long arm out to one circling couple. They stopped at once. He gestured toward a knife and held it out, hilt first, to Ryke. "Here." Ryke glanced at Errel, but the prince's face told him nothing. He stepped over the rail. His heart began to pump. He would have to make this very fast. He crouched a little. Van's dark eyes gleamed. They circled. Ryke chopped at Van's belly and chest, pushing the southerner around to face the sun. I know a few tricks myself, he thought. Suddenly he laughed distractingly and in the midst of the laughter, struck, angling the point of the wooden blade up for the rising thrust.

Van was not there. Hands gripped his shoulders and he was thrown back onto the ground. He landed jarringly on his spine. His head rang. The knife skittered from his fingers and went in among the feet of the watchers. Someone picked it up. He rose, puzzled and furious. He reached to grapple and Van evaded his arms and slapped him lightly across the face. The blow was enraging. He punched and felt his fist hit muscle hard as board. Van grunted, and hooked his neck with one arm. He thumped down on his back again. He got up and was thrown. Got up. Was thrown. He got his elbows into the ground. They stuck there. His vision was blurred. He couldn't breathe. People made a circle around him, whispering. They seemed very dark and tall against the sunlight.

Errel stooped close to him. "Come on." He caught Ryke's hand and pulled up. Ryke stood, wavering, and leaned on him. His left ankle hurt sharply, not enough to be broken. His head buzzed. He let Errel lead him from the Yard.

He recognized the color and smell of the blue-shuttered house. He sat in the chair. Cool hands felt him. "Wiggle your left foot," said Sorren's voice. He hadn't seen her. He wiggled his left foot. She probed his ribs. "Does this hurt anywhere?"

"No."

"Good, then nothing's broken." There was a metallic taste in his mouth. She touched his head. He hissed. His neck burned. There was a whispered conference. "You want some water?"

"Yes."

Errel brought him water. He slurped it awkwardly, not wanting to lift his head. A door opened and closed. Errel took the mug away. Ryke gasped as different fingers hurt his head. "Damn it—"

"Shut up," said a deep voice. The fingers probed his neck. "Let me have your head." Ryke tried to relax his neck muscles. Very gently, the hands rolled his head around on his neck, first one way, then another. Suddenly they whipped his head all the way to the left, very fast. He yelled. His eyes watered with pain. He heard a crack. The pain subsided. The hands let go. Van came round to look at him. "Would you like to learn how to fall?" he inquired.

"Fuck you," Ryke said.

"All right." He blurred noiselessly away.

Ryke gathered breath and called to him. "Wait." He came back. There were red hairs on his arms. His wrists were outsized for his hands; they were thick with muscle, big as fence posts. "I'd like to learn how to fall," Ryke said.

Van smiled. "Good. Don't go to the field tomorrow. You can begin to train in the Yard." He sounded much like a commander assigning a post. "You're going to feel when you wake as if a horse jumped on you. Show up anyway. Eat first, lightly. If you aren't there by noon, I'll come get you."

"Fuck you," Ryke said again.

Van's voice was genial. "You don't say that to me outside this room." He left. Ryke closed his eyes. He heard the sound of flints being struck, and looked. Sorren was kneeling by the hearth, a pile of rags beside her.

"What are you doing?" he said.

She answered without turning. "Making a fire to heat water for cloths for your neck."

Ryke rotated his head slowly. It still ached, but not the way it had. Sorren moved from the fire. The flames were almost invisible. They licked upward at a pot. Sorren stood in a patch of sunlight. This is your fault, he wanted to tell her. Angrily he said, "Where I come from, you fall when you're dead."

Her mouth twitched. "I come from where you come from, remember?"

"Armies don't fight like that."

"What good are armies?" she asked.

The question made no sense. He shook his head, and yelped at the pain. "I don't understand it," he said, meaning her, meaning Van. She bent over the kettle. After a while she brought a cloth and draped it over the back of his neck. Water dripped down inside his shirt. The heat was soothing. "Thank you," he said.

"You are welcome."

His back was sore where he had fallen on it. He could still feel Van's grip on his neck. He wondered what would have happened if he'd had a sword. He guessed it would have ended the same. Sorren took the cloth away and brought it to the fire. Ryke watched her move. She was light as the girl Amaranth. "I'm too old to learn new tricks," he grumbled.

She thought this was funny; she laughed at him. "How old are you?"

"Twenty-seven."

Dryly she said, "You'll learn." She dipped the cloth in the hot water and wrung it out.

"Why are you doing this for me?" he said.

"Why not?" She moved behind him. With gentle movements she laid the hot cloth across the back of his neck.

t e n

In the morning Ryke was indeed as sore as if he had been ridden.

The pigeons talked in the eaves. It was very pleasant just to lie in bed. Errel lay beside him, still asleep, head turned away from Ryke. Between the runneled scars, his back was pale and smooth as the bark of a silver beech. Ryke's elbow brushed the prince's spine; Errel made a slumbrous sound but did not wake.

Footsteps sounded overhead. Sorren and Norres came downstairs. Errel turned and stretched. He sat up, shaking the hair from his face. "How do you feel?" he said to Ryke.

"I'm all right." Errel stood to use the chamber pot. Ryke pushed the coverlet back. His muscles creaked. His left ankle hurt. He forced himself to stand on it. Sorren looked round the edge of the wooden screen that hid the bed, grinned, and popped her head back out of sight.

"Tell me when you're dressed," she called. Ryke felt for his clothes. The shirt and breeches that he had worn the day before were stiff with dirt.

"Wait," said Errel. Wearing only breeches, he went round the screen. Ryke heard him unbolt and open the lid of the chest. He grabbed for the coverlet as Sorren pushed the screen aside.

"What are you doing?" She reached for the shirt with the embroidered sun on its back and for his filthy breeches. "Those are mine."

She put her hands on her hips. "Someone has to wash them. I'll go to the tubs while you're at the Yard." She skipped from the chamber. Errel laid a clean pair of pants and a shirt on the bed.

Ryke scowled after Sorren. "You look like a Keep washerwoman!" he shouted. She was out of sight, but he heard her chuckle. He let go of the coverlet. He did not need to be reminded that he was bound to go to the Yard. He dressed. Errel had borrowed from somewhere a pair of soft boots. Sitting in the chair, he worked his feet into them. Ryke shook the blankets free of dirt and hung them out the window. The skin on the prince's face and arms had browned. Except for hair, Ryke thought, he looked like a southerner.

Sorren trundled out the doorway, arms full of laundry, calling good-byes over her shoulder. Ryke looked out the window at the brown and green landscape. The air was dry, and the colors rich and clear as if they had been painted on the hills. It looked nothing like the north. Ryke closed his eyes. He willed away the mountains. But when he opened his eyes, they were still there, drenched with sun. He ached for the delicate gleam of green leaves on the grey stone that meant spring in Tornor.

Turning from the window, he told himself not to be a fool. Errel finished lacing the boot ties. He stamped and stood. "That's better." Pulling his hair free of his collar, he lifted a hand in farewell to Ryke. Ryke watched him go, thinking of the wolf-dream. Maybe I should tell him, he thought. He swept the two downstairs chambers with the straw broom that sat beside the hearth. Recalling Van's command, he ate sparingly. The sun made red patches on the rough-grained floor. He went to the Yard. As he was searching for Van, Maranth came up to him. Her hair was tied severely in one thick braid. She had taken her bracelets off. She had to tip her head back to talk to him. "I'm going to teach you how to fall," she said. "Watch."

She fell backward, curled her body into a wheel, and came upright in one fluid motion.

"Did you see that?" she said.

"No."

She showed him again. "You have to tuck one leg and sit," she said. He balanced on one leg. "Use your arms. Lean on this shoulder." He sat, and could not get his legs over his head. "Kick harder." He kicked, went over suddenly, and landed on his crossed legs in the dirt. "Better," said Maranth. He tried again. "It's no more complicated than learning to walk, and any babe learns that." He tried yet again. She showed him how to tilt his head to one side so that he did not hit it. At last he did it awkwardly but without mistake. She clapped her hands. "Good. That was right." Patiently she drilled him. When he could fall backward and come up from kneeling or from standing, she showed him how to fall forward and rise unscathed. The dust packed into his beard. His face itched; he understood why most of the men in Vanima went clean-shaven. "Again," she said. His mind went back to boyhood. He had learned to thrust, recover, parry, thrust with an old wooden sword in just this way, over and over, until his lungs hurt and his head ached from being clouted for mistakes. This was not much different.

Van walked over to watch him. Ryke clenched his teeth as he rolled in the dust and waited for the man to say anything. One word of disparagement, he thought, and I swear I'll kick his eyes out of his head. Somehow.

"Here," said Van. He had held out his arm, curving it like a bow's crescent, elbow rotating outward, thumb pointing at the ground. "Try turning your arm like this. You may find it aids stability." He did not stay to see if Ryke obeyed him, but walked to another part of the Yard where two men fought with wooden knives. Ryke tried curving his arm. It did help. Maranth appeared with a wooden knife in her fist.

"Now we shall have some fun," she said.

She gave him the knife. The hilt was warm and polished with use and sweat. She faced him and told him to attack her. He did, thrusting lightly at her breasts. "Not like that," she said with disgust. "A real attack." He shrugged, feinted a few times, and lunged. Her hand closed on his wrist, and he felt her foot sweep his legs from under him as she jerked him forward. He flailed and fell on his face. Chagrined, he rose slowly. At least he had kept his grip on the knife. "Why didn't you roll forward?" she said. "Do it again." He attacked her again, prepared to fall, and her hand came up and hit him in the face. He yelped and fell backward and returned gracelessly but competently to his feet. His head throbbed, and his nose stung. "That was better," she said austerely. Her manner reminded Ryke of Jaret. "Do it again."

He attacked. She knocked him down. She worked him until he staggered. He forgot that she was a woman, weaker than he, smaller than he: she was a voice, a fist striking in the sunlight. When the sun was high and the Yard nearly shadowless, she told him he could go. At the other side of the Yard six dancers spun in a linked circle. In the house with the blue shutters he shucked his clothes and fell across the bed. He woke once, and felt the warmth of wool over his bare back. Someone had thrown a blanket over him.

He woke a second time to find Errel gently shaking him. "Uh." The prince's hair was damp; he had bathed. The sunset light stretched lean and red across the floor.

"Don't you want dinner?"

Ryke struggled up. His muscles were stiff. At the foot of the bed lay the clothes with the sun emblem, clean and smelling of ash soap. He put them on.

In the refectory, he passed the woman with the braids. She carried her baby on her back in a cloth sling. The child was plump as a capon; his arms and legs bobbed. "Hello," she said. Ryke brought a tray of food from the serving window. He and Errel were nearly finished with the meal when Van left the table at which he had been sitting with Maranth and came to join them. He wore black and scarlet, and his hair was tied back with a silver clip in the shape of a running horse.

Ryke's shoulders tensed. The southerner laid one palm flat on the table. "Sore?" he said. The light from the oil lamp touched his face with gold like a mask. He smiled at Ryke.

"Some."

"Will you come to the Yard tomorrow?"

Ryke glanced at Errel. But the prince was simply listening, hands clasped on the table. The middle finger of his right hand stood away from the others. "Why should I?" said Ryke.

Van said, "Maranth taught you how to fall. I can teach you how to fight."

There was challenge in the words. Ryke scowled. He stared at Van. It was hard not to turn away from the gaze of those lucent, powerful eyes. "I'll come."

"Good." He shifted his look to Errel. "You wanted to see what chearis do," he said.

"Yes," said Errel.

"And now you have seen."

"Yes," said Errel. "I have." If it was a struggle for him to look at Van, he was not showing it. "My curiosity is satisfied."

"Come to me when you want to learn more," Van said. He lifted a hand and returned to his seat, moving with his graceful feline stride.

Ryke wondered what it was Van expected Errel to want to learn. "What does that mean?" he said.

Errel said, "It means Van hopes I will do what most of the folk who come to this valley do—give up my old life and learn to be a cheari."

"Does he think I'll do that?" Ryke demanded.

Errel laughed. "I doubt it," he said, amused. "He's not blind."

Ryke nodded. He can see the northern blood in me, he thought. He must know that northerners don't renounce their trusts. He wondered how much Van did know of him and of the prince. Sorren or

Norres might have told him who they were, and that they were in exile.

Across the room, someone began to sing in a clear tenor. *"For I am a stranger in an outland country, I am an exile wherever I go; The hills and stars are my companions, And all I do, I do alone."* Music filled the shadowy hall. The words tore at Ryke's heart. He turned to Errel.

"My prince—" He hesitated. Errel was not looking at him. He sat on the bench, head bowed as if he had suddenly been turned to stone.

The singers ended the song and started another. Ryke said, "My prince, let's leave."

They returned to the cottage. The moon had risen above the mountains; it was a hairsbreadth from being full. Errel drew his clothes off. His face was taut with thought; Ryke wondered if he was thinking about Tornor.

He said, "Ryke, have you said aught to anyone here of who we are and where we come from? Have you spoken my name, or my rank?"

"No," Ryke said. No one had asked him save the girl Amaranth, at table the first night.

"That's good," said Errel. He pushed both hands through his hair. A shutter banged.

Ryke walked to the window to tighten the shutter latch. "Everyone can see we are northerners," he said.

"That—yes." Errel got into bed. "That's not important here, haven't you noticed? The people who live here seem to have given that name up." The candle by the bedside flickered frantically and he shielded it with a cupped palm. His hand glowed. "As they must have given up family, friends, home, for a vision, a dream not of their making—" he stopped. "Are you going to stand by the window all night?"

Ryke rested uneasily. He wished that Errel had not spoken of dreams; he was afraid that he might dream of the wolf. He dozed, and jerked awake to see the moonlight questing across the floor like a tongue. At last he fell asleep, warmed by Errel's warmth against his side.

He woke into sunlight to find himself alone. Errel had risen, dressed, and left, moving so quietly in the red room that Ryke had not even felt him go.

He dawdled. He took the pitcher to the well and returned with it to the house, wondering if the prince would come back. He went to the refectory. Errel was not there, of course. He was probably in the wheat field. Amaranth was swinging on a post. He thought of asking her if she'd seen the prince—she roamed the slopes like the wind, watching everyone, and he suspected she knew where everyone was— but she slid suddenly out the door. He heard her calling. "Diktaaa!" He went to the Yard. Maranth was not in the great dusty space. Ryke found a corner to himself. He practiced the rolls she'd taught him, watching other people out of the corner of his eye to make sure he was holding his arm right. He began to feel less awkward. Nearby, two small boys, wordless as puppies, tumbled in the dust in imitation of the adults. Ryke went forward and backward till his head spun. Rising from a forward roll, he found Van in front of him. The big man held a wooden knife.

He tossed it, caught it out of the air, and turned the point at Ryke. "Yai!"

The sound was a blow. Weaponless, Ryke crouched, weaving, turning himself into a small, moving target. He was outmatched; he knew it. Suddenly he was fifteen, back in Tornor's Yard, hearing in his mind the older men say, *You can tell where the hands will go from the feet, you can tell where the mind is from the eyes.* He tried to remember what Van had done with him when he had held the knife. He had no idea what it was. Van struck at him, a slow blow, and he stepped to one side and parried with his forearm, striking down. Van moved behind him, quick as light. He turned; the knife changed hands and leaped for his throat; he jumped back, his hands lifted, crossed to catch. It was a feint; too late he saw the hand drop.

The knife point like a tooth raked his side. He was dead. If the knife had been steel he would have died.

Van said, "Hadril, come here." The man so named had just stepped across the low barrier to the Yard. Immediately he came. Van gave him the knife. "Attack me," he said. The boy (he looked no more than seventeen) obeyed, moving with light dancing steps. He feinted once and thrust in. Van stepped to the knife-hand side, put his right hand on the thrusting wrist and his left hand on Hadril's neck, and with a turning backward step, flung the other man down. Hadril rolled and came upright gripping the knife. "You see?"

"Not exactly," said Ryke.

"Slower," said Van, and Hadril repeated the thrust slowly, as if he were sleepwalking. Van counted as he moved to show Ryke the steps. Then he motioned Hadril to attack Ryke. Hadril grinned. At the end of the lunge Van had him stop as if he had been turned to stone, and told Ryke to move around him, counting. *One:* glide to the side; *two:* sweep the knife hand down; *three:* clasp the collar or the hair; *four:* bring the two hands down together and turn. When Ryke could do the steps from memory, Van told Hadril to attack him, slowly. He moved. Hadril fell, and the knife flew out of his hand. He came out of the fall and rose rubbing his neck. One of the playing boys scampered after the knife. "Not so hard," said Van. "If he hadn't known how to fall, you might have snapped his neck."

"Sorry," said Ryke.

"Do that until you don't have to think about it," Van instructed. Hadril, smiling, took the knife from the waiting boy's hand. Van walked to another part of the Yard.

They did the steps over and over until the sun beat at their heads and made them stop. When Ryke forgot the steps, Hadril counted for him, voice deepening in unconscious imitation of Van. Van returned. He took the knife from Hadril and attacked Ryke, slowly, and let Ryke throw him. "Good," he said, and gave Hadril the knife. "Go rest." Ryke went to the well to wash. Sorren was there.

She smiled at him. "You've been training." She carried a brown sack over one arm. It smelled of barley seed.

"Did you finish the washing?"

She punched his arm lightly. "Yes. Do you think I am so slothful as to take two whole days at it? I'm going mushrooming." She waved the empty sack. "Up on the ridge. Want to come?"

He hesitated. He wanted to find Errel. That was stupid, senseless. If the prince needed him he would be told. He would not run after Errel like a child needing reassurance. "All right."

"Let's get another sack." They went to the storeroom. The big white chambers were packed with supplies: wood, skins, furs, cloth. In one room sat the last of the winter food stores: flour, aged beans, potatoes dry as sticks. Ryke wondered what winter was like in the valley. He lifted the lid of a bin. It was empty, stinking of salt fish. He asked. "Easier than at Tornor," Sorren said. "It snows less. The woods are always thick with game."

They climbed the valley's sloping side past the fields to the forest. The trees were mostly evergreen with some alders and white birches. They grew in rows, as if they had been planted like the wheat. They were covered with green cones like tiny sour apples. The ground was springy with layers upon layers of fallen needles. Sorren pointed at a cluster of mushrooms, their caps rose and white, thriving against the dark bole of a tree. "These are good," she said. "Don't pick any that are green or pure white. They're poison." Ryke twisted the soft stems from the bark, somewhat nervously. The trees grew straight as swords. From one great fir a garrison of squirrels watched him, tails fluffed. Sorren moved to another patch. Her fingers danced on the tree trunk. She was faster than he.

He found himself watching her surreptitiously. Sunlight touched her cheek, so angled that beneath the pine dust he saw the gold hairs glinting. The scar under her left eye was paler than the tanned skin around it. She looked like Errel. He had never seen it; he saw it now. She turned her head in his direction and he quickly felt for a mushroom. A derisive squirrel chattered in the tree crotch.

It was as if there was a man inside her. Perhaps there was; that might be the thing that made her seem unlike all the women he knew. He wondered if there was a man hidden inside all women. He thought of Norres, of Maranth, of Becke. He thought of his mother. If there was a man inside women, was there also a woman inside men?

"Ryke!" He turned. Sorren was grinning at him. She led up her sack; it was a quarter filled. "Lazy!" The squirrel spoke again. Her smile was light and as impersonal as flowing water. He reached for another mushroom.

At evening meal Errel was preoccupied and grim. Ryke tried to watch him without seeming to. But every once in a while he would look up to find the prince's gaze resting on him: a look oddly without warmth or anger, as if Ryke were a table or a tree. It made his skin prickle worse than the moonlight. The cold eyes lidded. In a moment they opened again, looking this time at Sorren.

"My prince, is something wrong?" Ryke asked.

"No," said Errel, "I'm thinking."

They walked to the cottage. The valley dreamed in the blue dusk, its red-roofed houses and planted fields neat and formal as a tapestry. Within the cottage, Errel closed the shutters. Ryke knelt, tinderbox in hand, to make a fire. The door opened. "They are here!" said Sorren. She came into the room. "We saw you come in; why did you leave the refectory?"

Errel said, "Why should we have stayed?"

Sorren pushed a shutter open. Light streamed in, catching on the brass of the fireplace tongs, turning them silver. "The moon's up. It's time to make the sowing."

Ryke stilled his fingers on the flints. He did not want to go. His head danced with tales of ghosts. He looked at Errel. The prince's face was set, as if he knew already whose ghost was waiting for him.

"Take those off," said Norres. Ryke jumped. She stood behind Sorren. He had not heard her step across the threshold.

"What?"

"Take your boots off."

Errel said, "This is a southern custom—is it needful that we be there?"

"Yes," said Sorren. "Everyone in Vanima comes to the sowing."

Ryke saw the prince reach to his boots. He laid the flints down and fumbled with his own boot ties. His hands were stiff and clumsy. At last the boots came off.

Barefoot, he followed Sorren into the street. Errel walked behind him. The dust was cold. The full moon blazed above the toothy mountains. The valley was alive with light, and restless as a pregnant woman. A crowd had gathered at the big building abutting the refectory: the village storerooms. As Ryke reached the crowd someone stuffed a sack into his hands. It was filled with barley seed. He slung it onto his left shoulder. Simmela gestured to Van beneath the light of a hand-held torch. Nobody spoke, save once a child's voice cried shrilly and was swiftly hushed.

Ryke wanted to ask what to do, but the thick silence weighted his lips shut. Someone took his left hand; a second hand seized his right. He was caught. Linked, he climbed to the waiting field, part of a line. The earth pressed upward between his toes. The night birds called. When the villagers reached the field they freed each others' hands. Their shadows fell northward as they weaved through the furrows. They stitched the earth with life. The peaks of the western mountain glittered like bone; snow hit by the moonlight. Van walked at the head of the line, holding the torch.

When all the seed was pressed into the soil, they joined hands a second time. Simmela shouted. The high wordless yell echoed like a falcon's scream from the nearer rocks. The hair on Ryke's arms lifted. His skin prickled. The wind went *slush* in the wheat. He trembled. He told himself not to be a fool, it was the wind, the wind only and he was cold . . . Van lifted the torch in both hands, and brought it swinging down against the earth. Now there was no light at all but the light of stars and moon.

Ryke gathered his senses and made himself stop shaking. The line weaved down to the valley floor again. Once Ryke looked back. He caught his breath. Dark, misshapen figures loomed in the fields, ragged, skeletal guardians . . . He remembered the cloth and straw mannequins. Laughter broke in his throat. He was afraid to laugh aloud. He coughed. The others had come in ahead of him. Errel sat in the chair, water basin at his feet. Sorren was lighting a candle at the hearth.

Errel said, without lifting his head. "Ryke, would you latch the door? One visitation is enough for any night." Ryke pushed the iron pin through the bolt. Sorren took the candle to the stairs. As she mounted, the candle wick spurted fatly. The light flared off Errel's cheek. The prince lifted his head, frowning slightly. Ryke shivered. He had never seen Errel look so like to Athor.

eleven

A changeling strangeness hovered around the house the next few days.

The day after the sowing, Ryke walked in to find Errel sitting tailor-fashion on the floor, dealing out the pattern of the Cards. He glanced round. "Go away," he said. Ryke retreated. He had glimpsed two of the Cards: the Illusionist and the Demon. He did not want to see any more.

By the morning of the third day he was jumping at the fall of a shadow. He could not believe he was the only one to feel the change. Errel was silent; his face closed and harsh. Ryke hung the blankets out the window and swept the floor—his morning rituals. There was sand in his beard from the training in the Yard. His skin felt itchy and sore. He decided to shave. He searched through the chest till he found a razor with a bone handle and a silver-plated mirror. The mirror's frame was a woman's head: her face the handle, her streaming hair the sides. He stropped the blade on a piece of leather and mixed a bowl of soapsuds. He pulled at his face, peering into the glass.

He could hear Errel and Sorren talking outside. The ceiling creaked. Norres was upstairs. He gripped the razor and sliced. The cool blade scraped his skin. He swished the razor in the basin. Errel and Sorren came in. Sorren cackled. "Look at Ryke. He's turning himself into a southerner!" She grinned as she went up the stairs, chamber pot in hand.

A curl of soapsuds soured Ryke's tongue. He spat. "Oh, shut up." Where his beard had been his skin was chalk white. It made him feel conspicuous. He wiped his face and tossed the soapy water out the window.

"Are you going to the Yard this morning?" Errel said.

Ryke turned. "Yes," he said.

Some of the pinched look was gone from Errel's face, and his voice was gentle. "I would like to walk with you."

Sorren and Norres came down the stairs. Sorren brushed Ryke's arm in passing. "How are you getting along with Van?" she said.

"All right," Ryke said.

"He'll work you till your feet fall off. If you want a change, come and fight with me today." She grinned at him. Her hair was tied back with a red rag. A pulse lifted and fell in the suntanned hollow of her throat. Her shirt bore the brown embroidered figure of a running horse.

"I'd like to do that," he said truthfully.

They went to the Yard. Sorren went to get a knife from the rack. Ryke watched as Van leaned over the barrier to talk to Errel. He waited for the cheari to call Maranth. But Van listened to whatever Errel said, and then beckoned him across the barrier to the dancers' side of the Yard.

A hand grasped his wrist and his feet were swept out from under him. He gasped as he landed on his side in the dust.

Sorren loomed over him, arms akimbo, knife in her fist. She kicked his leg lightly. "Pay attention."

The next three days, Ryke trained with Sorren, and Errel worked among the dancers, learning their steps. "He takes to it well," Sorren said once. Ryke was surprised. He had not noticed her watching the prince. She added, without any change in her tone, "I suppose that's because he's had practice in tumbling."

In the afternoons, Ryke, Sorren and Errel went to the wheat fields. The work no longer wore Ryke to tatters. Errel's hair was white from the sun. They made a rhythmic unit of motion in the furrows.

On the day of the quarter moon, it rained. They stayed in. They sat in the front room. The rain dripped from the eaves in a pewter curtain. Norres went out once, grumbling, to milk her goats. Sorren mended shirts. Ryke patched boots, using rawhide thread and a leathermaker's awl. His boots were worn over both big toes.

Errel rummaged in the chest. He brought from it the quiver and arrows that Berent One-Eye had given him.

Sorron said, "What are you going to do with those?"

Errel said, "Watch and learn." Laying the arrows out in a circle, head toward him, he took the leather sheath off his axehead. The steel blade shone blue in the sunlight. With sharp measured strokes, he beheaded the arrows, severing the broadheads cleanly from the shafts. The axe blade made a straight clean line in the red floor planks.

"You'll leave splinters in the floor," said Sorren.

"I'll rub wax into the wood," Errel said.

Ryke's shoulders ached from sitting. He shook them loose. Errel set the arrowheads, one by one, to the side. The truncated arrow shafts looked deformed without their heads. The sight made Ryke's stomach queasy.

Errel slipped the sheath onto his axehead. He said to Ryke, "Is it all right with you if I use the razor?" He brought it from the mantel. Taking the arrows one by one into his lap, he stripped the quills from the shafts.

Sorren said, "I suppose you *will* get around to telling us what you're doing."

Errel said, "I heard Maranth complaining about the dearth of brush sticks. I thought I'd give her these to use."

Ryke's fingers slipped on the awl. He held it still. "Don't you think you're going to need arrows?" he said.

Errel's lips thinned. He was frowning over the razor. He stroked downward along the shaft in one smooth line. Lightly he picked the vane from the tiny attachment of the quill. "If I need more, I can make them." He turned the shaft. "There are plenty of birch trees in the hills."

The rain brought the fringed barley stalks lifting practically overnight from the sodden ground. It brightened the wheat to gold—and strengthened the roots of the weeds. The people of the valley swore.

"It's not fair," said Simmela, swinging her hoe as if it were a scythe. "There are always more weeds than people."

The second day after the rain Ryke went late to the fields. He was at the very summit of the wheat field, chopping at the tenacious weeds with his hoe, when he heard the jingle of riders on the path. He straightened to welcome them, to call to them.

They came slowly down the slope, six of them, single file. The westering sun spilled light like water down the sides of a mountain peak; the eastern sky was a dark, placid blue. The horses looked weary. The foremost rider said, "Is this Van's Valley?" It was an odd question. It was more than an odd question. Ryke moved up the slope to them, tightening his grip on the hoe.

The foremost rider was a woman. He reached for her horse's bridle, and she swung a leg over and slid from its back. Her teeth gleamed like shell in her dark face. Her skin was so brown that it was almost black. She was narrow-cheeked, tall, and lean; she wore riding leathers and a broad-brimmed grey hat. Under the brim her hair curled round her head like tendrils. "My name's Domio," she said. "This is Vanima, isn't it?"

At her back, one of the still mounted riders said, "It must be. It's where Osin said it would be."

"Be quiet," she said. "Get off your horses. We look like the vanguard of an army up here on the slope." They obeyed at once.

Ryke wondered at her authority. The way she held herself reminded him of Sorren. Her horse snatched for the wheat. Imperturbably she held it back. "Osin sent us," she said. "He is Yardmaster at Mahita. He trained us and told us how to get here. We carry greetings and messages from him to"—she closed her eyes and then opened them—"Maranth, Simmela, Chaya, and to Van—" she shaded her face with her hand. "May we enter?" The restless horses stamped.

He could not hold them on the hill staring into the sunset. "What are you?" he said.

"We are a chearas."

He showed her where to go along the ridge to find the path to the village. "Thank you," she said, mounting. He did not wait to see how well she followed his directions. Hoe in hand, he hastened down the slope.

He caught Van just as the dancer was leaving the Yard. "Strangers coming," he said. He pointed. "They say someone named Osin sent them from Mahita, and they have never been here before. Their leader is a woman named Domio. They call themselves a chearas."

Everyone in the Yard had gathered to listen. "Osin!" said someone. "I saw him in Mahita before I left it."

"If they have never been here how did they know the way?"

"How many of them did you say there were?" said Sorren.

"Six," Ryke said.

Van silenced the talk. "Enough. Let us meet them." He brushed the sand from his forearms. "Hadril, go get me a shirt, and tell Maranth to come, if she's in the house." Hadril raced off. Surrounded by his dancers, Van strolled toward the well. "Ryke, you can put that hoe down." He sounded neither worried nor surprised. Ryke grinned. He laid the hoe against the front wall of a house. He had been gripping it as if it were a pike.

The riders came into the street. The horses surged toward the smell of water. Ryke picked a splinter from his palm. Van took the shirt Hadril gave him. "Maranth?" he said. The boy shrugged. The sun brightened the faces of the riders to gold. Crickets screeched in the wheat. There were more people at the well than had been at the Yard, many more. Ryke's heart began to thump.

The riders dismounted. Their horses tugged them forward, wild to get to the water troughs. Uncertainly the riders held them back. "Let them drink," Van said. Maranth came from the refectory. The strangers' cloaks were dusty. One other of them was a woman; the rest were men. They wore hats of stiff felt, and pieces of red cloth on their arms like a badge. Their horses were of southern stock, sleeker and taller than steppe horses. They nosed at the troughs, tails switching. The riders pulled them back before they could drink too much.

Domio said, "Osin sent us from Mahita. We are a chearas." Her black eyes flicked from face to face.

Van said, "Welcome to Vanima."

She caught her breath audibly. "You are Van?" The big man nodded. She swept the palms of her hands together in front of her chest, fingertips pointing outward, and bowed to him, a gesture Ryke had never seen. *"Skayin,"* she said. Her eyes glowed. "Osin sends you greetings, and hopes that you will accept us as a gift and a token of his respect. He is Yardmaster in Mahita now."

The people listening murmured. Sorren said softly in Ryke's ear, "When we were in Mahita there was no Yardmaster." Maranth ducked under Ryke's arm and came to stand beside Van. Her silver bracelets glittered. Van said her name, and Domio greeted her from Osin. Maranth smiled broadly. Ryke glimpsed Errel standing apart from the others on the opposite side of the well.

"From Osin? Ai, welcome! You must be hungry; come and eat. Dikta, Amaranth, take their horses. Is Osin well? You must tell us everything. Why are you all standing about in the street like cows?" Effortlessly she drove them ahead of her to the hall.

The newcomers distributed themselves among the tables. The one at Ryke's table was named Lyrith: he was chunky and young and a little confused at being the center of so much attention. He turned from side to side to answer questions as he packed in food. He had the appetite of a young bull. "We rode upriver to Tezera, and across Galbareth. We left Mahita just after the full moon."

"Did the Asech bother you?"

"They sniffed at us outside the city gates, but when they saw we had no carts they left us alone."

"Who rules in the city?" asked Simmela.

"The Med family." He dipped eager fingers into the stewpot. The back of his hand was blotched with freckles.

"Where did you sleep?" asked Orilys.

He grinned. "We slept in barns when we could. But mostly we slept on the road."

Sorren said softly, "While you were in Tezera, did you hear any news of the north, of the Keeps?"

Ryke leaned forward to hear the answer.

Lyrith groped for the water pitcher. "None I recall." A hand fell on Ryke's shoulder. He looked up, to see Errel. He pushed against Sorren to give the prince table room. As they crushed together, Lyrith explained how Osin had come to be named Yardmaster in Mahita. "He challenged anybody in town to best him, and no one could do it. When he beat the head of the city guard they offered him the job and he wouldn't take it. They had to do something, so they made him Yardmaster."

"When was that?" asked Sorren.

Lyrith put a finger in his mouth and poked out a piece of gristle. "Two years ago."

The tide of speech rose and fell at the other tables as the same questions were asked and answered. Nearest to them, Van sat beside Domio. She had taken the grey hat off. Ryke saw his lips move. The dark woman smiled and touched the red scarf around her arm. Ryke wondered what she was telling him.

Errel's voice said in his ear, "What is this for?"

He had reached across the table to touch the cloth on Lyrith's arm. Shyly Lyrith said, "Osin said that since we were chearis, we should have an emblem, like the traders and scholars and messengers. He picked red for us to wear because, he said, Van wears a red scarf."

There was a silence. The shadows moved over suddenly thoughtful faces. Norres, on the other side of the table from Sorren, said, "Does that make us the red clan?"

Lyrith said, "I don't know."

After the meal they went to the Yard. The sky was pure as mountain water. The stars overarched the peaks in a great bridge. If it were solid, Ryke thought, a man might walk across it from one side of the world to the other. The people of Vanima staked the Yard with torches. The air was heavy with the scent of honeysuckle. Domio drew her chearas into the center of the space. They danced; they ended the dance with a stamping, spinning circle and a full-throated shout that brought half the watchers to their feet.

It reminded Ryke of a battle yell.

"The red clan." That was Sorren, at his elbow. "I like that." Murmurs of assent rippled across the dark street. The crescent moon sat athwart the peaks like a hat. We've been gone from Tornor just short of a month, Ryke thought. We left on the night of the new moon.

"I don't," said Van, somewhere behind them.

"I do," said Maranth. "Isn't that what you want the chearis to become—a clan? That's what those strips of red cloth mean. We should all wear one."

"Everyone in the valley?" said Hadril.

"No," said Maranth. "Not everyone here is a cheari."

Ryke surprised himself by saying aloud, "Maranth's right." He knew he would never be a cheari. The dance was opaque to him. His body would not learn to mesh and blend with others'. But he could fall, he thought, and he had learned how to counter a blow without meeting it head on.

The next day Maranth dragged the bolts of red cloth from the store-room. Sitting in the sun by the refectory, she, Orilys, and Sorren cut and hemmed red strips for each cheari in the valley. Maranth tried to make Amaranth help, but the girl was having none of it. She pranced toward the stable, calling loudly for her friend.

Ryke, coming from the Yard at midday, heard them talking. "Don't scold her," Sorren said.

"Why not?" said Maranth. "She won't sew, she won't scribe; she's no more help to me than one of the goats."

"Scolding sets her back up," Sorren pointed out. "Wait. She'll come around."

Maranth snorted. "What will make her do that?"

"Something, or someone. I did." Sorren smiled. "She reminds me of myself at her age. I was a wild child. Besides, consider who she is."

Maranth said. "She's my disobedient daughter."

"She's the daughter of two rebels," said Sorren. A string twitched in Ryke's mind. He lingered at the well to listen. Their voices carried easily down the street. He leaned both elbows on the wet stones.

"I was not a rebel," said Maranth.

"You followed Van into exile. Wouldn't your family have taken you back?"

Maranth laughed and turned a piece of cloth. "I didn't ask them."

Their voices dropped as Lyrith walked out the refectory door. Ryke strolled to the blue-shuttered cottage. Insects thrummed in the tall meadow grass. A bird called from a berry thicket, its song limited, clear, and precise. Errel sat in the chair.

In his left palm he was holding the ruby ring of Tornor.

When he saw Ryke, he closed his fingers loosely around it. "It is well with you, my friend?"

Ryke's neck prickled. He wanted to say . . . He wanted to ask. . . . "I was just at the well," he said instead.

"And?"

Ryke repeated what he had overheard.

Errel leaned forward, elbows on knees, tips of his fingers together, making a circle. It was Van's gesture. "What do you think it means?" he said.

Ryke scowled. He scratched his neck. "It fits something I once heard, but I can't remember what it was." He stared around the cottage, as if something there might tell him.

Errel said, "Did you ever hear the story of the outlawing of Raven Batto?"

"Yes," Ryke said. "I talked about it once, with Col—" He halted. "You think Van is Raven Batto?"

"It could be," said Errel.

"Col knew him. He told me." It seemed important; he didn't know why. The bird called again. Errel leaned back in the chair. Ryke shivered. I shouldn't have mentioned Col, he thought. The prince's eyes were bleak as blue stone.

Ryke went by himself to the field. He thought, What will you do if he decides to stay, and not to leave? It could happen. He had not wanted to see it or to admit it. He could go to the stable, take a horse, ride from the valley alone . . . no one would stop him. And then what? The wind stroked his face like a hand. He was bound to Errel, as a river is bound to its rocks. He had shirked his morning shave. He touched his chin, feeling stubble.

The chearis coming from the Yard or from the field to the evening meal all wore strips of red cloth round their heads or arms or necks. Because of that, or perhaps because of the new people, the hall was festive and noisy. The two boys—Ryke now knew they were Lamath and Simmela's sons—played Catch Me in the aisles between the tables. Hadril sang. Amaranth, to tease her mother, climbed to a rafter and perched there, legs swinging. Maranth did not scold her.

After the evening meal the valley settled into a lazy, starlit silence. Ryke and Errel walked to the cottage behind Sorren and Norres. The two women leaned together, arms about each other. The air was sweet and warm as wool. Ryke looked for the moon, but it was not yet risen. Norres hummed. Ryke knew the song. He was glad she was not singing the words; he didn't want to hear them. Errel stepped lightly beside him. The prince was smiling. Ryke wanted to ask him how much longer they would stay in Vanima. His fingers itched for a real, not a wooden, sword. Twice he cleared his throat to speak.

But he was afraid to ask. He was afraid of what Errel might choose to answer.

Norres stopped at the doorway. "Wait here," she said. She went inside. In a few moments she came out with a blanket bundled in her arms. The cicadas shrilled in the fields. Sorren and Norres spread the blanket in the street in front of the house, and they all sat on it. Ryke took his boots off. A firefly came to investigate them, flying in erratic spirals.

Two shades drifted through the street, silent as smoke. It was Van and Domio. The dark woman had changed clothes to the dress of Vanima: a cotton shirt, drawstringed breeches. The breeches were too short for her and the cuffs rode up nearly to her knees. She was saying, "I think I'm going to like it here."

"Don't fall over us," warned Sorren.

"We won't," said Van. In the darkness his voice seemed deeper than usual. Ryke squinted, trying to see his face. He wondered what Van would do if asked: *Are you Raven Batto?* He decided he didn't need to find out. "What are you doing out here?"

"Enjoying the spring," said Sorren.

"Ai, these northerners," said the dancer. He sat on a corner of the blanket.

Sorren punched his shoulder. "You've never been north. What do you know? If you want to hear about the north, ask me, or Ryke or Norres or Errel. No, don't ask Errel or Norres. They don't like it. Ask Ryke or me."

"Didn't you like it?" Van said to Norres.

She said, "I hated it. It was cold and ugly and everyone always said no."

Errel said. "That's not a fair picture . . ."

Norres laughed. "No one said no to you."

There was a small silence. Sorren reached her hand out and stroked Norres' shoulder. "That's over," she said.

Domio stretched her long legs into the dust. She leaned back on her hands. Her teeth flashed white in her dark face. "In Tezera we heard there was war in the north," she said.

Errel's head came up. Sorren turned. "But Lyrith said there was no news of the north," she said.

Domio was scornful. "Lyrith wouldn't notice a war if they fought it under his nose."

"Whose war?" said Errel.

The tall woman frowned. Her broad brow furrowed to a V. "The Keeps were fighting. I don't remember names. Is there a Keep whose lord is one-eyed, an old man?"

"Yes," said Errel. "Cloud Keep's lord is Berent One-Eye."

"Well, he's dead," said the dancer. "The other one, the one he was fighting, killed him."

Ryke swallowed. Errel bowed his head. Emboldened, the firefly settled on the white fall of his hair. Softly the prince said, "I feared so."

Ryke wondered why he felt no grief. He remembered Tav, whose horse he took, and the other brother whose name he couldn't recall. He remembered the boy Ler, who had served his father so deftly, wearing a belt with no knife. He wondered if Col had had the child killed to make up for having left Errel alive. He was no woman to weep aloud but his eyes were dry as bone.

"Col must have attacked Berent as soon as we left Cloud Keep. He probably used Berent's giving shelter to us as his excuse." Errel's voice was raw. Yes, Ryke thought, feeling for his boots. It was the sort of thing Col would do.

A hand came out of the darkness and closed over his own. It was long and cool; it said, *Be still*. He sat, holding a boot. The firefly rose from Errel's hair. Van's deep voice said, "You could tell me what you're talking about."

Errel stood. The hand tightened. "Wait here," said the prince. "I'll show you." He went into the house. Ryke heard the noise of the chest lid hitting the wall. Something fell on the floor. Errel came back to the blanket. He held something out to Van. "Look—do you know what this is?"

It was the ring. Van took it. It glimmered as he held it in the scanty moonlight. "Yes," he said. "It's the crest of Tornor Keep. How do you come by it?"

"It's mine," said Errel.

The little hairs lifted on Ryke's arms. Van said, "You're lord of Tornor? To my knowledge, Tornor's lord is a man named Athor, somewhat older than you."

"Athor's dead," said Errel. "I am his son."

Domio said, "Excuse me." Tactfully she retreated. The familiar knot of pain clenched in Ryke's chest. He tried to picture Athor as he remembered him best, huge, golden, roaring with laughter, surrounded by men and dogs. The image was faded and silent. Ryke was frightened. He had loved the old lord like a father, more than he had loved his own father—why could he not remember him?

Errel gazed at the dark hills as if he could look through them. "My home is in the hands of a man named Col Istor. He came out of the south with an army at the very beginning of winter. He killed my father. He kept me alive and made me his jester. I wore paint and made him laugh. Ryke became his commander. We escaped to Cloud Keep, Berent One-Eye's domain, when Sorren and Norres came to Tornor. They'd come as messengers to arrange truce between Berent and Col."

"And you think Col used the escape to claim that Berent broke the truce. I heard." Van shooed a gnat from his face. Heat lightning flickered in the north. A line of light limned the hills. He held the ring out on his palm. "Well, Errel of Tornor, what are you going to do?"

Errel said, "There's another Keep, Pel Keep, ruled by Sironen. He's a tough old man. He had a good army. Col will have to fight him. They may be fighting now. I should join him."

"There are horses in the stable," Van said.

Still Errel did not take the ring. Ryke thought, Why are we sitting here? He started to stand. The hand closed on his wrist. A sudden gust of wind blew dust against his face. He coughed.

Errel said, "I don't want to."

There were beads of sweat around his hairline. The night leached the color from his eyes. He looked like a ghost. Steadily he said, "Tornor was never mine. It was my father's, and then it was Col's."

Ryke opened his mouth, to speak, to plead, to rage—and Van's brilliant gaze seared him. The words stopped of their own accord. The dancer tossed the ring in his hand and caught it. "You don't want it?"

"No," said Errel.

"Then here." Van held out the ring. "Take it. Take it!" Errel took it in his fingertips, as if it were a coal. "Now throw it away. Toss it into the street or into that bush." He stabbed a finger toward the line of berry bushes beside the house. Ryke's heart thudded in his throat. Sweat rolled down his sides. He felt feverish, and deadly cold.

Errel's arm lifted. His muscles tightened. Then the breath heaved out of him in a great sigh. "I can't," he said.

"You want Col Istor to have it?"

Errel shook his head.

"Then it's yours," said Van.

Sorren lifted her hand from Ryke's wrist. It ached. He wondered if she had left a bruise. His shirt was wet. He smelled his own stink. The lightning broke again, closer. The wind skittered through the meadow. The tall grass rustled. Norres said calmly, "We should go in. It's going to storm."

Nobody moved. Van said, "I knew a man named Col once, ten years ago, in another life. He was a soldier, a smith's son, from a village near Tezera. A clever man; big shoulders, big hands, black hair and eyes."

"That's him," Ryke said.

"I wouldn't want to fight a war with him," said the dancer. "Not without knowing a trick or two."

Errel said, "I don't understand."

Van tapped the tips of his fingers together. "I have to talk to Maranth," he said. He started to say more, and the thunder growled.

He waited for it to stop. "I had a thought—would you object if, when you leave here, some of us went with you?"

Errel said, "I wouldn't object."

Ryke's left leg was numb. He rubbed his thumbs into the calf. The thunder spoke again. A hand touched his shoulder. He looked up. "Ryke," said Errel, "I'm sorry. I should have told you."

He still looked like a wraith. But the hand on Ryke's shoulder was warm, strong, and real. "Prince," he said, "you don't have to apologize to me." It was all right; he would not have to ride north alone. Errel had not repudiated his oath.

t w e l v e

Amaranth appeared on the doorstep the next morning as Errel was emptying the pot. "Would you come to our house, please?" she said in one breath, and then bounded away.

Ryke glanced at Errel. The prince brought the pot inside and set it on the floor by the bed. He sat to pull on his boots. "I suppose we must."

Most of the night the rain had held off, but it had finally arrived just before cockcrow, falling with a great rumble and rush, saturating the ground, and leaving a morsel of water on each leaf, stem, and cobweb. The valley seemed covered with a fine net of light.

They walked to Van's cottage. Van sat on a stool. Maranth stood in the middle of the floor, arms akimbo. Her bracelets jangled. Her hair stood out from her face like a squirrel's brush. As Ryke and Errel walked across the threshold, she turned to glare at them. "For ten years we have been no farther from Vanima than Gerde's Spinney, and now we are to leave and fight someone else's war in the north.''

Errel said, ''I did not ask for company, lady.'' He looked at Van and his eyebrows went up.

Maranth spoke before Van could answer. ''I am going with you.''

Ryke leaned on the wall. He had slept but he was not rested; he had dreamed about something, he did not know what. His mouth tasted ugly. Errel looked at Van as if he wanted to object. Van spread his hands. ''I thought you'd better hear it yourself.''

Errel said, ''Do you agree?''

Maranth snorted.

Van said, ''What I think doesn't matter a whit. *You* can argue if you like, but I doubt it will do you much good.''

Maranth said, ''It won't.'' Her silken trousers swirled like skirts about her thighs. Perched on her slates, the black cat licked its paw. ''Besides, you need me. Do you know what it is he wants to do?'' she said to Errel.

''No,'' said the prince, ''save that it's a trick of some sort.''

''That it is,'' said Maranth. ''I will let him tell you the details. But it needs a chearas to go to Tornor and dance for this man Col.''

''A chearas,'' said Errel.

Van put the tips of his fingers together. ''From what you said of Col Istor, he'll welcome a troupe of dancers. We'll need a true chearas, three men, three women, and you will have to be one of them. The success of the trick depends on your knowledge of Tornor.''

Errel frowned. ''Col will know me.''

The southerners looked at each other. Maranth said, ''We can disguise you so he won't.''

''Col has very sharp eyes,'' said Errel dryly.

''I know Tornor,'' Ryke said.

''Yes,'' said Van, ''but you are not a cheari.'' Ryke wondered what the scheme was. Even disguised and part of a chearas, Errel would be in danger if he entered Tornor. Maranth was walking around the prince with a measuring eye, as if he were a pig she was about to kill.

"What good can a handful of people do against an army?" he said.

"We won't be alone," said Van. He looked very pleased with himself. "You said there's an army at Pel Keep, right? We'll bring it with us."

His confidence made Ryke's spine hurt. He arched his back to relieve the spreading ache. He wanted to argue but he didn't know how. He thought, What if Sironen won't lend you his army? But he was afraid to say it; speaking it might make it happen. He thought, I am jealous of Van because he can help Errel and I cannot. He felt shamed and spiteful. The sunlight bounced off the script in the frame on the wall.

Maranth said, "Who will teach in the Yard when you are gone?"

"Reohan," said Van. Reohan was one of the best and most tireless of the chearis. "The traders will be here soon. Who'll bargain with them?"

Maranth chuckled. "Simmela can go. She can take Amaranth with her, it's time she took over some of my tasks, made life easier for her failing, aged mother." She drooped, pretending to be feeble with age, and then straightened, resilient and graceful as a young tree. "I'll take our riding leathers from the chest, *chelito*." She marched to the back of the house.

Errel thrust both hands through his hair. "Skayin," he said, "are you sure you want to do this?"

Van said, "I have reasons." The words rapped out, short as a command. For a moment Ryke saw Van as he had been when he was Raven Batto, captain of the guard in Kendra-on-the-Delta. Rising, the dancer strode into a back chamber, and returned carrying a long parchment roll. He knelt on the floor to stretch it out. It was a map. Ryke put a toe on one corner. Dust flew up from the paper; it made him want to sneeze. Errel brought an ink-dish from the desk and put it on the third corner. He put his left hand on the fourth.

Van tapped the scroll. "North. South. East. West." He laid a finger on humps that were supposed to be mountains. "We're here, as far as I have ever been able to determine." He slid the finger north, toward Ryke. "Here's Pel Keep. Four days' ride as the eagle flies, but it will probably take us five. It's hill country until you get to the steppe." He spoke with authority. Ryke wondered if he had been there. But Sorren had said Van did not know the north. Jaret had talked with the same authority about history that had happened before he was born. Perhaps, Ryke thought, that voice was part of the training of the scholar.

He bent over the scroll. It was plain. There was no gold ink. The lines were grey in spots. Around the borders there were rows of southern script.

Errel said, "Does Maranth truly mean to come with us?"

"She doesn't say what she doesn't mean," said Van.

"Who else should go?"

"We'll need six," Van said.

Ryke said, "Sorren would go." Van and Errel both looked at him in surprise. He flushed. He had not known he was going to speak— her name had just emerged from his mouth.

"Did she say so?" said the prince.

"No."

"Speak to her," said Van.

"I will," said Errel. He flexed his right hand. "It's a good idea. She knows Tornor." He rose. The scroll curled where he'd been holding it. Walking to the window, he leaned on the sill. He was wearing the ring of Tornor on the middle finger of his left hand. "How much time before we leave?" he said to Van.

The dancer frowned. "We'll need some time to practice as a chearas," he said. "Say, three or four days."

The black cat decided it wanted to go out. It leaped to the sill. Its tail batted Errel's chin. He made a grab for it but it slithered away. "Does anyone in Vanima have a hunting bow?" he asked.

Ryke stiffened.

Van said, "No. We try to keep weapons out of the valley."

Ryke licked his lips. He said, "There are old logs in the store-room, prince."

Errel glanced at him. A smile curled the corners of his mouth. "Are there?"

They walked to the Yard: Van, Maranth, Ryke, and Errel. It buzzed with talk. Van shouted. "Listen!" His deep voice dominated the other sounds. "Shut up and listen." The mutter quieted. The dancers and the folk in the fighting pairs crowded around him. He put his hands on his hips, surveying them all.

He said, "Give me a moment. This is hard to say." The silence thickened. Ryke wished there were a wall he could lean on. Van said, "I'm leaving Vanima." He held up both hands, palm out, as if to press back an outcry. No one spoke. The scent of honeysuckle drifted through the Yard, fragile as the winter's first snowflake.

"I'm going north. Maranth is going with me, and some others. We won't be gone long, two months at most." He turned his head from side to side, seeking out faces. "The valley thrives. It's spring; not an ill time to be on the road. If we leave soon, we'll be back before the harvest." His voice grew stronger. The people in the fields had stopped their work and were turning to look down at the Yard. Ryke had a sudden vision of Vanima at the center of the mountains, and the world stretching flat around it, like a stretched and flattened bowl.

Someone said, "Who will rule the Yard while you are gone?"

"Reohan," said Van. Reohan lifted a hand in protest. Van looked at him with that kindling stare, and he gulped and was still.

"Where are you going?" said Hadril.

"North. You need know no more than that."

"What if you don't return?" said Lamath. Everyone gasped. Van put his hands on his hips and cocked his head.

"Do you think I won't?" he challenged. No one dared to answer. His voice gentled. "I might not. But I came to Vanima to teach, and if I don't come back, you know enough to teach each other. The art I made will live. It spreads without me, now." He let his hands fall from his hips. "There, that's enough. Let's work. Hadril, get me a knife.'' Hadril obeyed. A dancers' circle formed. Orilys' voice rose, shakily counting. Ryke stepped across the barrier quickly before someone beckoned him. He was not a cheari; he was not part of the dream. He didn't want to be. His dream was Errel lord of Tornor, and Col Istor dead. He went toward the toolshed for a hoe.

He stayed all day in the fields. He found himself enjoying the bite of the hoe against soil, the song of the insects in the wheat, the smell of earth, the heat, the sweat stinging salt on his lips, and the dirt. At dinner he was through before he realized that Errel had not come in after him, and in fact was nowhere in the refectory. He left the hall in a hurry. A hunting owl swooped past his ear. Light shone through the cracks in the blue shutters. Pushing open the door, Ryke smelled the fragrance of a peat-brick fire. Errel sat cross-legged beside the hearth. Two candles burned on the mantel. An oil dish on a stool puddled the floor with a circle of yellow light. The planks were littered with woodshavings. Axe in hand, Errel turned and turned a stave of wood, paring it thinner. To keep his hair from falling in his eyes, he had bound it with a rawhide thong. He held the axe in his right hand. The crooked finger did not seem to hamper it. At his feet Ryke glimpsed the serpentine waxed length of a linen bowstring.

Errel held the stave still for a moment; feeling some imperfection with the ball of his thumb. Ryke saw the line of the grain delineating sapwood from heartwood: the sapwood white, the heartwood auburn. He said, "I didn't know there was yew in these forests."

Errel said, "There must be. I found two logs of it in the storeroom. The first was wind-twisted, but this one's straight. It may not be any good. If it splits—" he pointed to the corner by the bed. Standing in it were four more staves. "I'll try one of those. They're hemlock." He lifted the axe. It made a singing sound as it fell through the wood, sure as if it moved of itself.

It took one more day before the bow was done. Errel brought it to full draw; it did not split. He made a handgrip of buckskin for it, backed it in white vellum, and painted on either side of the grip the red eight-pointed star in a white field, badge of Tornor. Rubbed with boiled linseed oil, it shone and felt like silk. It stood beside the bed gleaming like a snake. Waking in the dark, Ryke imagined that he saw it move. But when he blinked he could see that it was just a staff of oiled wood.

The next day Errel brought a split of white birch from the store-room and made ten arrows. He fletched them with turkey pinions. With a stiff tapered brush, borrowed from Maranth, and an ink stick, he sat in the noonday sun and marked the cock feather on each of the arrows.

At sunset he said, "Would you go with me to the stable? I want to set up a target."

Dikta hitched a plow horse to a cart. Ryke and Errel loaded the wagon with four tied hay butts. Ryke climbed to the carter's seat. "Where do you want to go?"

"Up the path to the mill," directed Errel. Ryke clucked to the horse. The path showed the passage of other carts; it was covered with ruts. The bales bounced each time the wheels caught. Before they reached the mill Errel pointed to two tall beech trees, their copper leaves limp with the heat. Ryke backed the cart up to them and rolled the hay bales to the dirt. He propped the bales against the tree trunks.

Errel paced off his shooting length. He strung the bow, nocked an arrow, drew, and shot. The shaft spun in the air and whipped deep into the hay. He shot all ten. Ryke waited till the bow was unstrung before he stepped to the target. All the shafts had hit near the center, though none had come as close as the first. Ryke pulled them free. He had seen Errel shoot six arrows into a cluster so tight that you could not wedge a hand between the shafts.

Chayatha arrived.

Ryke and Sorren were lying in the dip of a clovered slope. The dyer rode down the narrow path on a ribby piebald mare. The horse was blotched with black and red and white as if it, too, had been spotted with paints. "The traders must be here," said Sorren. She sucked on her finger. "Damn all thorns." They had been berry-picking, and she had stabbed her finger with a thorn. In revenge, she had eaten a quarter of the berries before bringing the sack to the kitchen. Her fingertips and lips were blue.

"Is it still bleeding?"

"No. It's stopped." She lay back into the grass. "I ate so much I don't want to move."

"Now who's lazy," said Ryke. She grinned sideways at him. She had a stain of blue on one cheek. "There won't be any berries in the north."

"I know," she said. (That morning, in the back of the house, she had said, "Errel told me. We'll go with you.")

Someone was coming toward them. Ryke lifted on an elbow. It was Norres. Sorren sat up. She patted the ground beside her. "Come sit," she invited.

Norres shook her head. "I thought you might want to come with me to greet Chayatha." She looked at Ryke. Not you, said her eyes. Her grey stare made him uncomfortable. He looked away.

Sorren groaned. "I'm stuffed." Wordlessly Norres turned. Sorren leaped to her feet. "Hey." She caught up to the other woman. "That wasn't a no, love." They went down the hill, Sorren's arm around Norres' shoulders. Ryke lay back. All morning he had been thinking of Tornor, trying to see it clearly, and had found that he couldn't. He told himself not to let it trouble him. Tornor was there. But his inability to see it frightened him. It was as if the Keep and the north had grown suddenly mythical.

A grouse flew out of a thicket, squeaking fury. Someone else was climbing the hill. It was Hadril. He waved. Van, for reasons which he had not said, at least not where Ryke could hear them, had picked him to be the sixth member of the chearas. He was barefoot, shirtless, and dripping wet.

He fell into the grass with a satisfied grunt. "Uh."

Ryke couldn't help smiling. "What is it?"

"We've been dancing. And dancing. We just finished. I poured half the well on my head." He rolled on his back. His arms and chest were covered with chill bumps. "Ah, the sun feels good." He arched his hips, artless in pleasure as an animal.

Ryke felt a small knot of tension between his hips. He stared away from the boy. The clear voice said, "I don't believe I'm really going north. Ryke?" Ryke turned his head. Hadril was sitting up, knees to his chest. "I couldn't say this to anyone here," Hadrill said shyly. "But I can tell you. I know it breaks the chea and I know it's wrong, but I want to see a war."

"You will," Ryke said.

"Chayatha's here."

"Yes. I saw her."

"She's making Errel's hair red."

"What?"

"She said it would help to disguise him."

Ryke slammed a fist on the ground. "Stupid southerners." There would be nothing more conspicuous in Tornor than a redhead. "Shit." He rolled upright. The grouse bounced away from her nest again, yelling at him.

He trotted to Van and Maranth's cottage. Errel sat on a chair. He was wearing a bright red shirt. His hair had been cut short, and it stood out from his head in greasy spikes. The henna powder looked like green mud and smelled like alfalfa. Van, interested in everything, stood watching the smelly process. Ryke had forgotten how tall Chayatha was. It made it hard to fight with her. "Everyone will look at him," he said.

"Yes," said the dyer. "But they'll see his hair and his clothes, not his *face*. You see?"

Grudgingly Ryke decided that it made sense. "What if Col recognizes you?" he said to Van. "Or you?" he said to Sorren.

"He won't," said Sorren. "My hair is longer. Besides, I'll be a woman, not a ghya. Norres won't talk very much, so he won't remember her voice. I'll do all the talking."

"You do anyway," said Chayatha.

Amaranth came in. She wrinkled her nose. "It stinks in here. What are you doing?" Chayatha told her. She giggled. "What are you trying to disguise him as, a fire?"

Van, Maranth, Sorren, Norres, Hadril and Errel danced farewell to the valley that night in the Yard. The torches bled sparks into the moonless sky. Errel's copper hair changed him into something grotesque and exotic. Ryke fretted. He paced, too restless to sit with the others. The audience was as solemn as if someone had died.

"Read the Cards," he said to Errel when they entered the cottage.

He waited for the prince to object, to laugh at him, to say: *You don't believe in the Cards* . . . Errel opened the chest. He dug out the travel pack that he had carried from Tornor and took the Cards from it. They were wrapped in a length of red silk. He shuffled them. The backs were faded from handling. The picture on the back was the same on each Card: a red star on a white field. On some of the Cards the white was grey. Ryke wondered how old they were.

Errel laid out the pattern on the floor in front of the fireplace. The fire sprang in the hearth. Ryke stared at the pictures. He had never noticed before how beautiful they were. On the Messenger Card the horse seemed to move. He had no idea what he wanted the Cards to tell him. The Lord in the Card had a black wolfhound at his feet, like Athor's wolfhound bitch. It was carefully drawn, painstakingly drawn. *They take pains.* Col had said that, about Sorren and Norres. He would look for Col's face in the Cards.

"The Cards of the past," said Errel. "The Lord, reversed. That means bondage or an inheritance lost, or both. The Wheel means chance, luck, or fate. The Messenger means new understanding, or new information, or help from an outside source. The Lady reversed means poverty, inaction, and war."

Col was in all of those Cards, Ryke thought. Grimly he said, "Go on."

Errel touched the next line of Cards. "The Stargazer. That means plans, or truth. The Illusionist means misunderstanding, fantasy, and self-deceit. The Sun means achievement of desires. Some part of our plan is based on fantasy, but not enough to turn them wrong. The Archer means a challenge accepted, a decision made." He touched the final line. The Wolf leered from under his hand. There, thought Ryke, there was Col. "The Wolf. The Lovers. Appetite or passion may lead one of us to an unexpected choice. The Eagle. One of us will make a sacrifice. The Tower. The overthrow of present order.''

The picture on the Tower was of a tall tower being struck by lightning, breaking, crumbling . . . Ryke imagined it to be the watchtower at Tornor falling, carrying Col Istor with it to a certain burial. He thought, I don't want him to die that way. I want to kill him myself.

"Does that mean we'll win the war?" he asked.

Errel pushed the Cards back into a pile and trussed them with the silk. The fire glinted on the ruby ring. "It doesn't say that," he said. He glanced toward the bow in the corner. Irony tinged his tone. "The Cards are rarely so—direct. It doesn't say we'll lose." A spark leaped the fire screen and fell next to his hand. He licked his thumb and put it out.

They left the valley at dawn.

Van woke them, tapping twice on the door. Errel rolled at once out of bed. Ryke wondered if he had been lying awake, waiting for the sign. He went naked up the stairs to the loft, calling softly to Norres and Sorren. An indistinct voice answered. "Down in a moment." The pigeons spoke from the eaves in self-satisfied tones. Ryke scrubbed his face with his palms.

He pulled their travel packs and clothing from the chest. They dressed in wool and leather. The wool smelled of cedar. The clothing was stiff, scratchy, and hot. Ryke sat on the edge of the bed to wrestle with his riding boots. When he stood, the heels tilted him forward. He felt off balance. Errel wore the red shirt Maranth had given him. It was just a little too large. The red hair, cut short to his shoulders, made him seem a stranger. Ryke wondered if he would seem so to Col.

He splashed water on his face. He was sleepy. He had lain awake in the night, turning and turning the plan over in his mind, seeking the fantasy, the flaw. He couldn't bear the thought that something might go wrong. He thrust the shutter back. In the west the sky was black. Eastward, daylight flushed the peaks with gold. North one bright star shone like a beacon.

Norres and Sorren came downstairs. Sorren was smiling. Norres was silent, more remote than Ryke had ever seen her. Her eyes were steely and grim. Ryke remembered that night in Berent One-Eye's Keep when she first spoke of Vanima. She had called it *home*. He took the covers from the bed, knowing that he was doing it for the last time. Errel helped him hang them over the windowsill. Norres stood by the hearth, hands in her pockets. Sorren, frowning with impatience, watched. "You don't have to do that," she said.

They walked to the refectory. Birds sang from the eaves and the thornbushes. The doors of the other cottages stood wide. People leaned in the doorways. "Good-bye," they said softly, into the muted morning. "Good luck on your journey. Come back." No one wept outright, but Ryke could hear the tears in some voices being firmly restrained. Dorian waved long-armed from a loft window. The wooden soles of their boots bit the dust of the street, leaving little half-moon tracks in their wake. Maranth's cat prowled, ears pricked, oblivious to the soft voices calling through the dawn. It was stalking a lizard.

Norres scooped it up. It wriggled and then settled into her hands to purr. She rubbed her face against its fur. It licked her chin. She dropped it. Chayatha stood by the well. She embraced Norres and then Sorren, and murmured something to them that Ryke could not hear. Then she turned to Errel. She whispered something. The prince nodded. Lastly she faced Ryke. Her tunic was spotted and colored and it smelled faintly of dye.

She peered at him. She was not wearing her hat. Her hair, like Van's, was tricolored, black and red and blond. She tapped him on the chest. Her finger was bony and hard. "At the end of the road you will find your heart's desire," she said. "Be careful of what is in your heart." The backs of his hands prickled. She reminded him suddenly of old Otha the healer, mumbling into her pots.

"Come on!" said Sorren. Turning from the well, they followed her to the refectory. Ryke looked back as he went through the door.

Chayatha still stood by the well, watching them. He was glad it was too dark to see her eyes.

The folk in the kitchen had prepared food for them: cheese, dried meat, dried and fresh fruit, full waterskins. Maranth talked to Simmela in a corner, hands flying. Amaranth was there, solemn, silent. Ryke wondered if she was frightened at being left alone. He heard the sound of horses and glanced into the street. Dikta was leading a string of seven horses, saddled and bridled. Ryke recognized Errel's chestnut stallion fretting at the end of the line. Amaranth dived into her father's arms. He held her, talking softly, stroking her hair. Ryke went toward the horses, waterskin in hand. His riding clothes made him feel as if he were wearing a shell. He took the grey gelding's reins from Dikta. Hadril came from the refectory. His face brimmed with excitement. Ryke mounted. The chestnut wheeled in a circle. Errel cuffed it, and it snorted with surprise.

"Son of a mongrel donkey," he said to it.

Van and Maranth came into the street. Their riding leathers were stained and patched and looked as if they had not been worn in a long time. They mounted. "Let's go," said Van. He turned his horse—a dun stallion—toward the path. They went up. Ryke looked back once to the dark and dreaming fields. A hawk falling for the kill was the only sign of life.

t h i r t e e n

Van led. The valley dropped swiftly behind them. It was chilly in the heights. At evening the fog streamed over the peaks. Ryke was glad of the wool against his skin.

They rode the first day through a wearisome maze of rocks. They halted in a sandy channel that looked as if it had been carved by some long-dry, ancient river. Errel found a dead tree. He pulled it from its niche. Ryke found a natural firepit and built a fire. They huddled round it. The dry wood burned swiftly. The fog lowered like a hand.

Maranth was shivering despite the heavy wool of her cloak. She said, "Is it going to be like this all the w-w-way north?"

"Not all the way," said Errel. "It'll grow warmer when we leave the high places."

"Good," said Maranth.

Ryke ached. He wondered if anything lived in the rocks. They looked as if someone had built them in layers, starting from the bottom and working to the top. They were all different colors. He tried to make himself sleepy by counting the striations. He lost count twice and had to start over. Sorren poked at the fire with a stick. She said, "There's a saying in the north: It's colder in the mountains because they reach closer to the night."

Maranth pulled her cloak tightly round her shoulders. Norres rose. She disappeared in the general direction of the horses. When she returned her arms were piled with fur. She had brought the fur cloaks out of the packs. "Sleep on these," she said. "You'll be warm."

"Put one under you and one over you," Sorren said.

Maranth rubbed her face into the long dark fur. "Ah." She started to spread the cloaks out, and stopped. "Won't you want them?"

Sorren shook her head. "I'm not cold. I was born in the north."

Ryke rubbed his arms. He was cold. He watched Sorren and Norres roll together in one wool cloak. A mountain cat screamed, somewhere in the rocks. Hadril shivered. "It's all right," he said to reassure the boy. "They won't come near the fire." As if to taunt him, the cat screamed again. The horses whickered unhappily. Ryke glanced at Errel. "It's been a long winter," he said. The prince nodded. His bow lay beside him, unstrung, but ready to hand.

"Let's sleep," he said. "If it comes any closer the horses will warn us." He wrapped his cloak loosely around himself. "Go to sleep," he said to Hadril. The boy ducked his head under his hood and stretched his legs to the heat. The fire drove the fog back, so they lay in a clear space, but over them the peaks were covered. Ryke had a sudden vision of the cat, drawn by the heat and the smell of the living, padding soundlessly toward them.

Pulling the cloak tighter, he told himself not to be an idiot. He would not lie awake and imagine disaster like a witless child. He stared at the rock layers. That one was red, and that one the pink of fish flesh, newly hooked from the river, and that one pale yellow, like the belly of a frog . . .

He woke to a great noise. A horse was keening. A woman screamed, a yell of command or of warning, a cat snarled—he sprang away, fighting free of the wool cloak which had somehow entangled itself around his ankles. In the grey predawn light he saw the chestnut rearing, fighting the rope that held him tied to a stake, and a tawny missile which could only be the cat. It had found them after all. "Don't move!" Van roared at Norres, who was scrambling toward the horses. The bow twanged. The chestnut galloped down the trail, having snapped the rope—but the cat fell heavily to the ground, an arrow through its chest. It twitched and then lay still. Ryke was closest to it. He took a cautious step. It did not move. Its ears (which were notched and scarred) did not turn. He walked around it. Blood leaked from the wound in its chest and from its open mouth. It was gaunt with the winter's famine, and rank.

Hadril said softly, "It *was* hungry. It looks starved."

Errel said, coming up behind him, "Good thing it was or else my arrow might not have killed it." He put a foot on the dead cat to brace himself, and yanked the arrow out. He held it up. The blunt point and half the shaft were smeared with hair and blood. "None of my shafts have heads. I didn't have time to put them on. I didn't think I'd be hunting anything bigger than an early woodchuck or a rabbit." He looked calmly about for a tuft of grass on which to wipe the shaft.

Ryke went back to where he had been sleeping. He picked the cloak up from where he'd thrown it. His hands shook. The whole thing had happened so swiftly he'd had no time to react. Norres was soothing the terrified horses. Hadril, who had gone to catch the stallion, came pounding back up the path. "He won't come," he reported.

"Leave him," said Norres. "He'll follow us, and he'll come when he gets hungry. There's not enough grass around here for him. You'll have to double up," she said to Errel.

"No matter."

"You can ride with me," said Maranth. "I'm lightest."

"No," Norres said. "Someone should double with Ryke. His grey's steady and it can take the weight."

Sorren, crouched on the ground rolling a fur cloak, grinned at Errel. "I'll double with Ryke, brother. You take my horse."

Ryke saw Van's eyebrows go up. The dancer said nothing. But

as they led the horses from the pickets he murmured, "Brother? That says a lot."

Sorren smiled at him blandly. "Does it?"

Hadril circled around the body of the cat. "Shouldn't we take some meat?" he said, nudging it with the toe of his boot.

Norres said, "I doubt you could get a horse to carry it."

Errel took the rein of Sorren's brown mare. Ryke leaned down to help her swing behind him. She grinned and grasped his elbow. The grey barely moved beneath the extra burden. "Scoot forward," she said. He moved up the grey's neck a handsbreadth. She pressed against him. Her hair tickled his neck. "All right."

Errel said, "It's probably diseased and too stringy to chew." He mounted the mare. "Leave it. Something will eat it."

Maranth said, "It seems wasteful." The cloud around them was growing lighter. Van was already on the trail. She shrugged, and clucked to her horse. Norres went next, then Errel, then Hadril. Ryke and Sorren went last, so as not to hold the others up when the gelding slowed. Behind them, the chestnut whickered. Ryke heard its hooves click against the echoing rock.

By midday, they were out of the foothills. The clouds had lifted, and the sky was—not blue, but an odd color—a light pastel lavender, like the flower. Van brought out a map like the one he had unrolled on the floor of the cottage, but rougher and smaller, to explain where they were. Ryke's thighs still ached, but the rest of him was no longer sore. He asked Van where Chayatha's village was on the map. "I haven't got it marked," Van said. "But I'd guess it's there." He thumbed the scroll. "We're about two days west of it." He put the map in his pack. They sat on a small rise. West and south of them rose the red hills. North, it was grey. East lay a flat dark shadow; Ryke thought perhaps it was forest.

Patches of green decorated the steppe: dwarf pines. A stain of smoke coiled the air, looking brown against the strange hue of the sky. "That must be a village," said Errel. "Let's go there."

Sorren jerked a thumb toward the chestnut stallion. "You think you can catch that beast now?" The chestnut eyed them, and pawed at the hard ground.

"I'll get him," Norres said. Rising, she walked toward the horse, talking softly. Its tail went up like a flag. It took two stiff-legged steps back from her, poised to run, eyes bright as a colt's, but she continued to talk to it, and after a while its tail dropped and it permitted her to take gentle hold of its lead rope.

Errel brought the saddle and bridle to it. "Thank you," he said, catching at the rope. "Ho, you miserable monster. Hold still." He rubbed its nose and then eased the bit into its mouth.

The smoke turned out to be not a village but an isolated farm. The farmhouse and barn were attached. They were stone, grey and old. The plowed fields glistened as if they harbored bits of cut coal; the stony soil, sliced by the plow, took on a gleaming iridescent edge. As they approached the farm a dog came baying round the back of the barn, tongue lolling. But it halted a respectful distance from the horses' hooves.

A woman walked around the side of the house.

She was pale, stooped, and silent. "Here, Grip," she called. The dog ran to her. Her gown and her hood were brown wool, and like a good northern wife, she wore her hair in one long braid. "Greetings," she said, in the even accents of the north. She let her hood drop. She looked young, which meant, Ryke thought, that she was nearly a child. "Be you going to the town?"

Sorren answered. "Aye," she said—the hard northern word, so different from the melodious southern *Ai*. "May we refill our water-skins at your well?" She pointed to the farmhouse, where a well's peaked roof lifted in the yard near a coop. The woman pursed her lips and then nodded. Ryke and Hadril dismounted.

The dog rumbled, the hair on his neck risen with menace. "Shut up," the woman said. Four of the seven skins were empty. Hadril stared at the lonely buildings. As they neared the well, a shutter creaked. From within the farmhouse, an old face looked out. Ryke could not tell if its owner was man or woman. They heard the harried baaing of sheep.

"I hear sheep, I smell sheep, but I don't see sheep," said the boy. He tasted the water. "It's good."

"The sheep must be in the barn."

Filled, the skins were heavy; they dragged at Ryke's arms. As they returned to the knot of horses on the road, Ryke heard the shutter swing closed behind them. As he passed Sorren and the woman he heard the wife say, "Dead? Be you sure?"

"I saw it," said Sorren.

The woman clapped her hands and ran like a deer for the barn.

"What did you tell her?" said Maranth.

Sorren said, "That wildcat was living off the sheep. It killed three of their dogs. They heard it two nights ago and locked the sheep up. Her man went out hunting it. She's been waiting for him to come back. I told her we killed it and that it looked starved; for sure it had not eaten anything so big as a man."

Ryke laced the waterskin to the gelding's back. "Look!" said Hadril. They turned to see the sheep, freed, race like a white river to the steppe, followed by the barking dog.

They passed more farms. It had been raining; in places the plowed fields looked like squares of chopped black mud. The four northerners and Van rode with their hoods down, but Maranth and Hadril complained of the cold, and kept their hoods up. Where the land was unplowed it was green, not the heavy bright green of summer but a light evanescent spring green. Ryke sat the grey, contented. This was the way spring should look. Toward late afternoon, they reached a village. It had a smithy, a tanner, a butcher's, and a tiny cleared square of a Yard. Two boys within it hit at each other with wooden swords. Van went immediately to the gate of the Yard to watch.

The village headman came to talk to them. He kept eyeing Maranth. Politely he asked who they were and where they were going. It was clear they were not traders since they had no carts. He explained that the village had no inn, but there was a barn traditionally kept empty for the traders, with stalls for the horses and a firepit outside it and a wide sleeping loft . . . "Thank you," Errel said. They brought the horses to the barn and rubbed them down with straw.

Maranth said, "Why was the man staring at me, damn it? I behaved like a good northern woman and said nothing."

Errel laughed. "He's probably never seen anyone, especially a woman, so dark."

"How far is Pel Keep?" asked Van.

"Three days' ride across the steppe," Errel said. Ryke grinned into the gelding's mane. It wasn't far.

The barn was musty. Norres found a scuttle of firebricks, and they built a fire in the pit. Van asked what the bricks were made of. Ryke said, "Peat and dung." Sorren begged a basin from a house. She filled it with water, and they all dipped their faces and their hands and lastly their feet into it. The sky turned peach and rose. Ryke propped his head on his hands, staring north, pretending to find the smudge of the northern mountains against the bare horizon.

The wind shifted. Smoke blew into his face. He coughed, and sat. Sorren handed him a piece of venison jerky, tough as bark.

Van said, "I wish this place had beds."

Maranth chuckled. "I remember when we left Kendra-on-the-Delta. We rode four days straight across the Asech country to Shanan, and I was so weary you had to tie me to my horse." She reached out, barefoot, and kicked Van in the ribs. "My love, you've grown soft."

Van grimaced. "Have I?" He turned to Errel. "How did you tell the headman that we would repay the village for this hospitality?"

Errel said, "We don't turn travelers away in the north."

Van rose, eyes gleaming. "Maybe not. But the red clan pays its debts. Stand up."

The Yard was too small to hold the dancers and their audience. The headman led them to the village square. Ryke leaned against the well. He felt like a guard with nothing to guard against. The dancers consulted and then took their boots off. Someone lit a torch. Errel's hair shimmered, brilliant as sunset. They made the circle. Even Hadril looked weary with the long ride, but then Van stamped, and the beat waked them, stiffened them, and brought them spinning and alive. By the standards of Vanima the dance was simple, but these folk had never seen it before, or heard the word chearas. The dancers stamped and whirled and tossed their heads and bent their supple bodies. Awed whispers of pleasure and astonishment, small sounds, filled the twilit square when they stopped.

They returned to the field outside the barn. The headman came to the fire. He blinked into the smoke. "That was wonderful," he said.

"Join us," said Errel, patting the earth.

"No," said the old man, "no. You must rest, you are tired. But I wanted to tell you—I wanted to say—I have not seen such a thing since I was a boy, smaller than my grandsons, and I saw the wild horse clans dancing in the steppe, in the sunlight." He tugged on his beard. "Tell me again what you call yourselves?"

"We are the red clan," Van said. "We are chearis—that means dancers—and all together we are a chearas."

"A southern thing. But you move like the wild horses." He left, walking with small careful steps.

Ryke went to the well. He was tired of the taste of leather. He wanted a drink of springwater. A village cur, scenting a stranger, growled at him from a doorway. He bent for a stone and it cowered, ears flat against its lean yellow skull. A pebble clicked behind him. He turned. A shadow fell into step with him. It flicked its hood back and turned into Norres.

He worked the bucket handle. She steadied the rope. Over the dipper her eyes watched him, grey as pewter. The village smells eddied about them: grease and fat and the strong vinegar scent of the pale village wine. Ryke knew what it would taste like. His mouth watered.

He let the bucket stand and hung the dipper on its hook. Around the well the dirt was mud; their feet squelched in the soft ground. "Are you in love with Sorren?" Norres said.

The west wind riffled his hair. The cold water had made him cold.

He started to pull up his hood. Norres' hand darted forward and touched his wrist. "Answer me," she said. "Don't hide."

He temporized. "I haven't touched her."

She laughed. "She wouldn't let you. I know that."

It was a stupid answer. It was not even what she had asked. "I love her, I think. I know she doesn't love me." His tongue felt thick. He did not think very often about loving people. He had never learned to use the word right.

Norres' right hand rested on her knife hilt. She measured him. "She trusts you, though," she said. "Ryke, if you hurt her, I swear I'll kill you."

His hands were chilled. He thrust them under his armpits. "I wouldn't hurt her," he said. Silently they walked back to the barn. The others had abandoned the fire. He climbed the ladder to the loft and immediately kicked someone. "Sorry," he said. "I can't see." He crawled over legs until he found an uninhabited patch of straw. A dog howled. He pictured it prowling round the guttering fire. He worked his boots off and thrust his feet into the warm hay. There was a tension in his throat. His eyes itched. He wondered what was wrong with him, and then felt the tears run under his eyelids. Shamed and startled, he bit at his forearm, tasting wool. It made him gag. He swallowed, holding back the sounds, hoping that no one in the cramped, closed loft could feel him cry.

The second day on the steppe, Ryke saw the northern mountains.

They were grey and small on the horizon. They looked like cloud, only no cloud ever hung so low and lay so still. The sky was pale blue, clear as crystal. He shivered with delight. The gelding trotted, feeling his mood. He reined it back. Between where they rode and where the mountains sprang, the land was flat as a lake. Pale green grass sprouted from the level soil. In wet places the grass grew thicker, leavened by the fat-headed rushes that the villagers called babies'-brooms.

By the third day they were close enough to Pel Keep to see it.

Against the dark mountains it rose like a fist. It was bigger than Tornor. From the foot of its outer walls to the top of its inner battlements, it was white, painted with limewash. It looked carved. The paint made it look all one piece. When they were near enough to see the guards on the battlement, a troop of horsemen trotted to meet them. The men were dressed for war in light mail and leather, helmets decorated with Sironen's badge, the triple spears, silver on black.

Van spoke to the guards. The troop captain did not know what a chearas was. Van said, "We entertain, like acrobats or jugglers."

"Where did you come from?"

"South," Van said. The soldiers eyed the three women. One made his horse rear to catch Sorren's attention. She ignored him. Ryke tried to see the prince's face, but the cloak hood shadowed it. He looked at the sleek strong horses the guards rode, at their well-kept arms, and felt a rush of pleasure. Out of men like this war could be born.

A scout escorted them to the castle wall. He spoke to the gate guards. Maranth was tight-lipped, staring at the great building. The sun reflected hotly off the white paint. Ryke smelled smoke, and the acrid scent of heating iron. The grey's muscles were bunched. His knees were tight on its sides. He relaxed, and patted its arching neck. "Easy." He looked up. Men with pikes looked down. He closed his eyes, imagining for a moment that this was Tornor.

The little gate opened. "Go in," said the scout. Ryke let the others go ahead of him. Their shadows moved, sharp-edged against the bright stone. Men with tall pikes stood silent guard on the wall round the inner court. Four bored soldiers played a dice game in the arch. Stableboys came running for the horses. A page motioned to them to follow him. Ryke heard the sound of wood on wood. There were men in the Yard. Smoke rose from the kitchen chimney. A man in a leather apron screamed out a window at two small boys.

The travelers left their belongings with the horses, except for Errel's bow. The prince carried that himself. They went through the second gate into the inner court. The barracks overflowed with men. The smell of weapon grease hung everywhere. A man lounging outside the barracks wall saw the women and yipped. A dozen soldiers stuck their heads out of the upstairs windows. "Hello, darling!"

The apartments in Pel Keep were just like the ones in Tornor, except that the tapestries were clean. There were fresh rushes on the floor and a vase of flowers on a table. The smells of herbs and flowers made Ryke's nose itch. Maranth rubbed the hanging cloths with one hand. "This is fine work," she said. Her voice was subdued. There were two large beds in the room. Ryke sat on one to take his boots off. Three servants dragged a tub of water through the door. Maranth waited till they left. She said, "Is Tornor like this? So dark, and everything made of stone?"

They washed their faces and hands and finally their feet. A servant girl entered to take the dirty towels, face avid with curiosity. Errel's red hair fascinated her. She looked him up and down. The page brought them a platter of cooked meats. The table held a brass ewer. Ryke sniffed it. It was filled with white wine. Ryke had not tasted wine in a month. He poured himself a cup. It was more bitter than he remembered it, and stronger. Hadril was staring at the pictures. There was a scene of a castle on the west wall, with Anhard foot soldiers attacking and men on horseback, swinging swords, beating them back. The northerners wore the badges of Pel Keep, carefully drawn. It should be Tornor, he thought. It will be Tornor.

He turned to talk to Sorren, but she was busy with Norres. Dogs barked in a flurry of excitement in the courtyard. A man shouted at them. Ryke wished that the chearas had been given a room that looked on the courtyard. He wanted to see what was happening. He sipped the wine.

Van said, "Ryke, don't just drink. Eat something." Ryke went to the platter. Shyly Hadril, standing by it, offered him a slice of rib.

Leaning close, the boy whispered, "Before we fight, will I be able to get a sword?"

"Certainly," Ryke said.

Someone knocked on the door and then opened it immediately.

It was a young man dressed in black and silver, with a stern, almost cruel face. His eyes rested on Errel for a long moment. It's the red hair, Ryke told himself, but his nerves quivered. "Welcome to Pel Keep," he said. He wore the Keep badge on the right breast of his tunic. "I am Arno, the lord's fourth watch commander. The lord has instructed me to ask you if you will entertain us before the evening meal."

Van said, "That's what we came for."

Arno left. Maranth paced around the room. "Stuffy child," she commented.

"We are going to dance, don't overeat," Van warned his chearis. He sat on the other bed, one arm around Maranth. Her hair, unconfined, curled round her face and shoulders. Sorren sat in a chair plumped with cushions. She knuckled her eyes. She saw Ryke looking at her and spread her hands.

"The flowers make me sleepy," she said.

The page came in, staggering under the weight of the packs. He removed the platter and returned to light candles. A knife swung on his left hip. It made Ryke think of Ler. He wondered how many men Sironen had, and if he had sent any of them to help Cloud Keep. He paced from one side of the room to the other. Sitting on the bed, Errel turned the ring on his hand. Ryke worked his shoulders to loosen them. Footsteps rushed by their door, and he half stood before he realized they had gone.

Hadril cracked his knuckles. "Please don't do that," said Norres. The smell of cooked lamb made Ryke's mouth water. He went back and forth again.

Sorren threw a cushion at him. "Sit still!"

He lay flat on the floor in the fragrant reeds and put the cushion under his head.

The walls of the Keep's great hall had been left dark. Torches flared in iron brackets, but their light went mostly upward toward the ceiling. Ryke, walking last, had the feeling that he was entering a cave. Men's voices boomed and echoed off the roof. There were five tables in the hall; six, counting the one on the dais. He glanced from side to side. Tall pale men lolled on the benches, arguing, talking, laughing. Dogs weaved around their sprawling legs.

Sironen sat at the raised table on a carved wooden chair. Over his head, on the black sparkling wall, were three gold spears. Ryke wondered if they had melted down coins to get the gold. It looked solid, not like leaf or plate. Sironen wore black and silver, like his men. His commanders sat on either side of him, and three women sat between them. The one on Sironen's left, Ryke guessed, was his lady. She wore a gown red as Errel's shirt, and her hair was piled elaborately on top of her head. Her face was white with powder. Ryke supposed she was beautiful. The other two women were younger and looked very like her. Sironen was older than Ryke's memory of him. His hair was grey. But he did not look the least enfeebled. His back was straight as the bole of an oak. He had a long red scar like a sword cut across his right cheek.

"So," he said, "you are going to provide us with some southern entertainment. Do it."

"My lord," said Van. Ryke stepped back. The chearas made their circle in the cleared space before the dais. Van stamped. He was wearing boots. The heels rang on the stone. The soldiers craned their heads to watch. A few left the tables. They clapped, picking up the beat. Van swung Maranth over his head. The men yelled. The dancers linked, turned, spun, leaped; Ryke's fingers tapped. The servants came crowding out of the kitchen corridor. The commanders grinned from the dais. The dancers' cheeks were flushed. They finished the dance with a shout, and the soldiers stood, beating their palms on the tables. A coin clattered on the floor, and another, and more, until there was a ragged carpet of silver coin at the dancers' feet. Sironen spoke to the servants. Two of them scurried in front of the table. They picked the coins off the slate and dumped them into a silver dish. One of them gave the dish to Van.

"Here," said Sironen. He tossed something over the table. It gleamed round and gold in the air. Van caught it neatly. The soldiers cheered and stamped. "Make places for them, you slugs." Eager hands reached out from the tables. "Bring them wine; that's thirsty work."

"Come on, man, have a seat," said a fat man in a brown shirt, beckoning to Ryke. "You came in with them." He pushed at the men on either side of him. They shifted to make space. "Hell, it makes me thirsty just to watch them move." He smiled at Ryke. "My name's Torib, who're you? You look like a northerner."

"Ryke," said Ryke.

"You talk like a northerner. Where're you from?"

"Near Tornor Keep," Ryke said.

"Huh." Torib reached out and caught a servant girl by her apron. "Sweetheart, I'm thirsty," he said plaintively. "Bring us some wine." He rubbed a hand on her hip as if she were a horse and pushed her from him. "Near Tornor? You know what's happened to Tornor?"

"I heard," Ryke said.

"Aye. They say that southern bastard's tried to keep it quiet, but the news got out. Where you been living in the south?"

Ryke did not want to answer questions. The answers would mostly be lies . . . "The mountains," he said vaguely. "Where were you born?"

"Half a day's ride from these very gates," said Torib. "Where's that damn girl? Ah, there she comes. My mother claimed she got me on a marsh demon, but she was a shepherd's daughter and liked to make herself important. Thank you, sweetheart," he said to the girl. She twitched herself away from his hands and slid a pitcher of wine and a host of mugs onto the table. "Near Tornor, huh. Were you ever a soldier? You look like a soldier." A servant put a plate of mutton in front of them.

Ryke swallowed. "I fought in the Anhard wars," he said.

"Did you now? Cheers." They bumped mugs. "Ah, that was one hell of a fight. You know, I was in the field when we killed that bastard chief of theirs. Saw Athor of Tornor drag him right off his horse." He went on to tell the story with sound effects and gestures, barely stopping between bites.

After the meal, they returned to their chamber. Sorren sat in the cushioned chair. "I had to slam one man in the teeth for pinching me," she said. "It's so long since I've been a woman in public, I forgot what it's like."

Ryke walked to the table. As he poured himself a mug of wine, Arno came in. "My father is very pleased with you," he said. "He wants to know if you will stay a few more days."

Van and Errel exchanged glances. Errel said, "That depends." Arno looked at him. His eyes narrowed. Ryke put the mug aside. Errel crossed the room and held something out to him. Ryke knew it was the ruby ring. "Will you give this to your lord and make sure that no other eyes see it?"

The watch commander frowned. "I am not accustomed to being a juggler's errand boy," he said.

Errel's voice was smooth as wax. "Please do as I ask, commander. It matters."

Arno strutted out. Sorren snorted from the chair. "That peacock. Just think; if I'd stayed a dutiful daughter in Tornor, I might have had him for a husband!" She pulled her scarf off—each of the chearis had taken, during the dance, to imitating Van by wearing the red bands in their hair: only Errel could not, his hair was too short—and smiled across the room at Norres.

A servant brought in an iron dish on a tripod. It was filled with chunks of coal. He struck tinder to light it. Maranth stretched out her hands to the flames. She said, "My fingers are frozen."

Norres cocked her head. "Listen," she said. They heard the sound of boots in the hall. "More than one," she warned. Arno came in. The servant shrank toward the door. The watch commander wore a sword. So did the two soldiers at his back. They wore helmets and light armor. Ryke knelt, pretending to fiddle with his boot tie, feeling for the Anhard skinning-knife.

Arno said to Errel, "The lord Sironen wants to see you."

"I thought he might," Errel said calmly. "Do you mind if I bring two friends, commander? I dislike going anywhere alone. It's a custom of mine."

f o u r t e e n

The scent of flowers nearly overwhelmed them as they went through the halls.

A woman's voice called, bright and rich. They turned a corner and came upon her suddenly: a tall bony woman in a red gown, her vivid face covered with paint. Three maids followed her: one laden with dishes and vases, the others with sheaves of fresh reeds and flowers strewing petals underfoot and soaking through their aprons. The maids flattened into the wall to let the men pass, but the lady did not. She looked them up and down. She had light brown eyes. They were not large but they gazed out with an uncommon strength, reminding Ryke suddenly of Chayatha. Under that look, Arno grew several years younger. "Excuse us, lady," he said.

"Such formal speech to talk to your mother," she commented. He flushed. She picked a snowdrop petal from his shoulder. "Tell your father to look at those livestock lists if he wishes to supply his army," she said. "Where are you taking these men?"

"To the lord's chamber," Arno said. Ryke pinched his nose against the smell of the flowers. One of the maids smiled at him. Sironen's lady nodded to Errel and Van.

"You are welcome to the castle," she said. "You dance well, very well."

Sironen's chamber was big, still, and stark. A meager fire burned in a toothy grate. It shone on a bed whose mattress looked no thicker than those in a barracks, save that it was not stuffed with straw. Sironen sat in a cushionless chair. Across his lap he held a naked sword. The walls were dark and hung with weapons: swords, pikes, javelins, some of Anhard make, others clearly not. A brindle mastiff slumbered by the fire, as close to the warmth as it could get. Skin fell in folds around its massive, elderly jaws. Arno went ahead of them into the room. The soldiers stayed outside, standing stiffy on either side of the door.

Sironen's voice was harsh in close quarters. "I wished to see the one with the ring," he said.

Arno started to speak. Errel forestalled him. He said, "My lord, I hope you are not angry. I insisted that Van and Ryke come with me."

"You insisted?" said the old man. He glowered across the comfortless room. Ryke wondered if his lady ever slept with him. If she did, it wasn't here. There was no softness or grace in this chamber. "Who are you to insist?"

Errel pointed to the ring, where it rested in Sironen's upturned palm. "I am the man who owns that ring," he said.

"The man who owns this ring is dead."

"My father is dead, my lord. But I am not dead, I assure you," Errel said.

The scar on Sironen's face flushed scarlet. "Do you claim to be Errel of Tornor?"

"I am Errel of Tornor," said the prince. "Who else would have that ring?"

"And who are they?" demanded the old lord, staring at Van and Ryke.

"They are enemies of Col Istor," said Errel.

Sironen's right hand closed around the worked bronze and silver hilt of his sword. His voice rasped. "Forgive me if I doubt you. A month ago Col Istor accused Berent One-Eye of harboring his enemies, and attacked him. I sent one hundred men to Berent's aid under the command of Ter, my eldest son. He is dead. So are Berent and his sons. I am suspicious of strangers who come to my gates naming themselves enemies of Col Istor."

"I would be too," said Errel. "I am sorry, my lord. I remember Ter. He was much my elder." Ryke did not remember Ter at all. So many dead, he thought. Is this how we are meant to spend our lives? We fought Anhard—now we fight each other. He leaned on the wall. He wished Sironen would ask them to sit. The dark room made him nervous: the unadorned walls and the glint of light on metal made him think of a cell.

Sironen said, "You speak like a man of rank, at least."

Arno spoke. "I don't believe you. I knew Errel of Tornor. His hair was blond."

"So am I still blond," Errel said. "Have you never heard of henna?" By the fire the mastiff groaned. Its legs twitched. It was dreaming of the hunt.

"Let me see the color of your hair," said Sironen.

Errel walked to the old lord's side. Kneeling, he dropped his head, baring his neck like a man waiting for the axe. Sironen pushed his fingers through the red locks to expose the blond roots. "He is blond," said the lord. "That part is true." His hand fell away from Errel's head. The prince rose. "If you are Errel of Tornor," Sironen said, "prove it to me by telling me something of your father that a stranger would not know."

Errel said, "What shall I tell you, my lord? That Athor had a hot temper or that he loved dogs? Any fool who served him half a month would know that." He glanced at Arno. His mouth curved upward in a way Ryke knew. "I'll give you proof. Nine years ago, when the green clan came to Tornor to arrange the Anhard truce, you also came, with your sons. Ter stayed with you, but Arno and I were bored with the talk. We wandered off. One morning we fought, as children do, over a trifle, I don't remember what, perhaps Arno does. He won, so he might. We came back to the hall covered with dung from the stableyard." Ryke smiled. He knew the story was true because he had been on duty outside the stable that day. He had separated the combatants.

Sironen looked at his son. "Is it so?"

Grudgingly Arno said, "Yes, sir."

Sironen fingered the sword. "Then I suppose I must believe you." Rising, he slid the blade into its sheath. He held out the ring. Errel took it. Deliberately the old man reseated himself. "Wine," he said to Arno. The commander moved into the shadows behind the chair. He returned with a silver goblet in each hand. He gave one to his father and the second to Errel. Sironen raised the cup. "Welcome, my lord of Tornor," he said.

Errel said, "You do not sound overjoyed to see me, my lord."

"Oh, I am pleased that you are alive. But I confess I am curious to know where you have been this past month, and why you now reappear in the company of jugglers—and southerners." He curled his mouth around the word as if it had a sour taste.

"Where I have been is my concern, my lord," said Errel. "But let me introduce my friends. This is Ryke, who escaped with me from Tornor, and without whose help I would undoubtedly have died there." Ryke bowed. "And this is Van. He brings us a way to defeat Col Istor."

Sironen looked grimly at Van. "Do you indeed?" The scar puckered at the corner of his mouth. "Then you must have wine as well. Serve them." Coolly Arno poured wine into two more goblets. If he minded being told to do page duty, he didn't show it. Ryke waved away the wine. He saw a shape along the wall that looked like a stool. He went toward it. It was. He brought it to Errel.

"Thank you," said the prince.

The dog woke with a snuffle. It lifted its head, yawning, and curled itself into an even tighter ball. Sironen gazed at it with something like tenderness. Then his face hardened. "Since the death of my son," he said evenly, "I have thought much on how to kill that damned southerner. I have not yet found a way. He stays behind the walls of that castle. As far as we can tell he has three hundred men, all of them seasoned to war. I have four hundred. But I will not spend them trying to break stone. An army needs space in which to fight. Have you a means to lure the usurper from his stronghold?"

"No," Errel said, "but we have a means to open its gates. The chearas—the dancers you saw tonight—will travel to Tornor. At the same time you will move your army to Cloud Keep. You will take it and secure it, so no warning can go from it to Tornor to tell Col Istor you are coming. When that's done, you will go to Tornor. The dancers will open the gates from inside to let the army in."

Arno said, "Col Istor left a hundred men at Cloud Keep."

"You have more," said Van.

"If one of them gets free—"

Sironen interrupted his son. "That would be the task of the army, would it not? To make sure no one got free." His lips parted in a swift feral grin. "I like it. It is the sort of plan Ter would think of. How much time will you need?"

At his back, Arno's thin face twisted.

"Eight days," Errel said.

"Give me a day to hold a council. I must consult my commanders."

Women's voices weaved laughter through the bright cold corridors. Ryke wondered how his sister fared. A pulse beat in his neck. Soon he would see her again.

"I will give you war gear," Sironen said.

"I won't need it," said Errel. "I go to Tornor with the chearas. Ryke will ride with you. He knows armies. I am a hunter. My weapon is the bow."

"Dangerous for you."

"Not really," Errel said. He ran his palms over his hair. "Col would recognize Errel the Jester, his captive. He won't know Errel the dancer with hair the color of a copper beech."

*   *   *

Ryke did not attend Sironen's council. Errel went to part of it. When
he returned to the chamber he said little, except to report that the
commanders were agreed. Maranth said, "Good. I don't like this
place."

"You'll like Tornor even less," Norres said.

Sorren brushed her hair back from her face. "When do we
leave?"

That evening Errel went to the smithy, to forge broadheads for
his arrows. With the Keep's smith watching critically, he hammered
out the heavy metal heads and wired them to the shafts himself. The
chearis left the next day. Ryke went with Sironen and the commanders
to see them off. It was cold, barely morning. The sky was dark. The
travelers wore furs. They looked a lonely company. Ryke laid his
cheek against Errel's. The prince had given him quiver, bow, and
bowcase to take care of. "Eight days," Errel murmured. His breath
was warm on Ryke's ear.

"I'll be there."

Sorren took his place. Her cheeks were apple red. She put both
arms around Ryke and hugged hard. "See you." Behind her, Hadril
was having trouble silencing his chattering teeth. Norres stood with
the horses, her lean face grim. Sironen embraced Errel and raised a
hand to the others in farewell and encouragement. Guards opened the
postern gate. The chearas rode out. For a brief moment they were
visible on the lightening eastern sky as silhouettes, and then the sullen
darkness swelled and swallowed them.

The inner courtyard filled with beasts, carts, and men, as Sironen's
army made ready to go to Cloud Keep. Smithy smells—grease, hot
iron, steam, and the sweat of horses—overhung the Yard and barracks
like a cloud. Every pore of the huge whitewashed building bristled
with light. Ryke snatched a twist of bread from a platter. It was warm
and tasted of poppy. His stomach rumbled. He slowed, letting the lord
and the commanders get far ahead of him. It made him nervous to
be among them without Errel.

It felt strange to be wearing a sword again. Sironen had given it to him. It balanced beautifully; it was Tezeran work, much finer than the one he'd left in Tornor. He went looking for Torib. He had attached himself to the fat man. He had been unsurprised to learn that Torib was watch second to the commander of the third watch.

"Ho," said Torib. He was supervising the loading of the horses. "You ready to go?"

"I'm ready."

"Where's your horse?"

The grey was in the stable. It had been well cared for. Its coat was sleek; its hooves trimmed and oiled. Ryke saddled and bridled it and led it out. A servant walked by, barely able to see over a shapeless sack of millet or wheat or oats . . . The horse stretched its neck. Ryke pulled it back. "Behave," he told it. "You're already too fat." In a dark corner of the Yard a girl and a young soldier kissed, hands moving desperately on each other's bodies. Ryke watched them dispassionately. He had said his good-byes.

At noon they left for Cloud Keep. Sironen sent a vanguard ahead, a squadron of grim silent men on swift horses, with orders to chase the woodcutters and shepherds to their huts. "What about the folk who aren't peat-spaders and shepherds?" Ryke asked.

Torib, at his elbow, drew an expressive thumb across his ample throat. "We don't want no warning going ahead of us," he said.

The land jumbled. The road left the flat and curved up. It was fringed by pale green moss and rock. Once Ryke glimpsed Sironen framed in a far curve of the path. The lord rode a tall black horse.

It was impossible for four hundred men to make camp on the road. The order came snaking from the rider on the black horse: *Keep going. Walk.* The men slipped from their steeds. The fog blew past them. Ryke leaned on the grey gelding, sharing its warmth, breathing its breath. Still they walked. The warning came back: *Trail steepens. Stay alert.* A cat yowled in the crags. The horses shuddered. Torib slipped and fell flat. His horse, stumbling, kicked him. He swore. "You all right?" said Ryke. The second grunted and heaved himself up.

At noon they came to the steppe. They camped. *No fires*, said the voices. They were too far from Cloud Keep to be seen from its walls, but Sironen took no chances. They ate cold food. The vanguard returned and was replaced. The horses, fed and watered, rolled in the pale new grass, they were so pleased to be out of the rocks. Ryke slept. The first thing he'd done after feeding the grey was take his boots off. When he woke, his feet still tingled spasmodically.

They came to Cloud Keep in darkness.

It seemed to Ryke that they had been riding forever in the night. Sironen had set a brutal pace. They had stopped briefly, and then only because the horses needed rest. A dark regular bulge of rock northeast of them had to be the Keep. Torib had ridden forward for orders. Now he came back. "We go west," he said. "In a line. Stay together and keep your tongues between your teeth!"

The vanguard had done its work. The steppe had never been so silent and vast. Ryke squinted. The moon had set . . . It was near dawn. In the riding and riding he had lost track. He felt the gelding heave a great sigh between his legs. It was tired, tireder than he was. He smelled a familiar smell; it caught at the back of his throat. In the night someone had cornered a stray sheep. His mouth watered and he grinned in the darkness.

They were still quite far from the castle. The sky was streaked with light. The shape of men and horses grew clearer. Ryke saw what Sironen was doing. He was sending the army all around Cloud Keep in a huge half circle, cutting off the Keep from the steppe and from the roads, driving whoever might be caught in the circle back toward the castle. Torib's watch was part of the west wing. A turkey flew out of nowhere and fluttered almost between Ryke's horse's legs. The grey pranced and whinnied. Ryke gentled it. "Easy," he whispered fiercely. "Be still. Be easy."

It seemed to take a long time for the army to position itself around the castle. Couriers trotted from one wing to the other. The men dismounted to rest their horses and accustom their legs to earth. Ryke watched the blob in the north where Cloud Keep was. Occasionally he saw torches glowing on the walls: they looked like minute bobbling lights. But there were no signs of alarm, no flares or noises. He unpacked his waterskin and took a mouthful of water. It took several sips before he could taste it; his mouth was very dry.

"Mount up." His nerves were listening. They had him on the grey's back before his ears told him what he'd heard. His bladder ached and his stomach clenched like a fist. He ignored it and urged the horse forward. He could see the men on either side of him now. Torib was grinning, his long brown hair streaming back from his round face. Ryke felt for his shield. He hated it; it cumbered him, but he would need it if there were any bowmen within the castle walls. There might not be, he thought, reminding himself that they would be southerners. He leaned over the grey's neck. A pebble popped up and struck his cheek.

It hurt. He wiped it away. It left a smear on his glove. First blood. He could see the closing ring. Men shouted on the dark walls. Torches blossomed. Still Sironen's men were silent. Their horses galloped— Ryke swallowed. They were almost within arrow range.

But Sironen had bowmen too. The ring closed and they moved after it, shooting over the heads of their own men at the southern heads looking over the walls. "Dismount!" Ryke grabbed for his shield and sword. He heard a humming sound and jerked his shield up. So the southerners *had* learned something from the north. An arrow bounced off the tough leather, and another.

He heard the regular thudding sound of a ram. As he ran he wondered if Sironen had had it brought all the way from Pel Keep and if so how the men had carried it across the rocks . . . That was impossible. They must have cut it while he slept. "Here!" Instinctively Ryke put his hands in front of his face. Wood smacked into his hands. It was a ladder. Grunting with effort, the men lifted the ladders against the sky and propped them on the stone of the outer wall. Torib grinned. "Wish me luck," he called. "There's only a hundred of 'em; they can't be everywhere!" He climbed. Ryke gripped the ladder's side. Men followed him, awkward on the rungs. The arrows had stopped. Ryke lowered his aching shield arm. Someone pushed him from behind. He went up the ladder. A man with a scraggly black beard sprang yelling to meet him at the top, waving a pike, and Ryke drew his sword and held it out. The southerner ran right onto it. His mouth gaped in surprise. Ryke yanked the sword free and hit him with the flat of it. He staggered away. A yell rose from beyond the wall. The sound of the ram had stopped. Ryke held his shield up against his own side's arrows and scurried along the top of the battlement. A great exaltation filled him. He swung his sword in a wide arc. He was invulnerable. Nothing could hurt him. Below him in the ward, Torib was yelling. Grinning, Ryke looked for a stair.

The southerners fought like demons. But there were not enough of them for it to make a difference to the battle's end. Sironen ordered them chained and herded, under guard, into the outer ward. They looked a dispirited lot. Ryke scanned them for familiar faces but saw no one he knew. He was oddly glad of it.

He was not hurt. The battle lust had left him; he was tired. His arms ached. Torib had taken a shallow cut along his head, but that was all. "Bled like a pig!" he said in self-description. "Nearly killed me later—I couldn't see a thing. Blood all over my eyes!"

"Didn't keep you from finding the way to the women!" said someone.

Torib grinned. "I find my women by the smell."

"Was she willing?"

"After a month of these damned southerners, you know she was," declared the fat man. He started to scratch his head and pulled his hand back in a hurry from the bandage. "But you know what I say—if you can't leave 'em laughing, you can always leave 'em crying." The men guffawed at this wit. The laughter mingled with the cawing of the crows. They perched on the merlons, staring at the bodies of the dead, turning their sleek heads to look out of first one eye and then the other. Sironen's men roamed the corridors, looking for wine, food, and women. A few of them slept on or under the benches of the great hall. The wine and blood smells made Ryke's stomach leap. He raised a hand to Torib.

"I'll be back."

"Don't get lost!"

Ryke smiled with his face and went out of the castle to find his horse.

Someone had given orders; the horses were staked and grazing by the eastern wall. What dead there were had been piled together with cloaks thrown over them to protect them from the voracious birds. The cloaks were weighted with stones. Ryke checked the grey over and made sure his pack was untouched and that Errel's bow was safe in its case. It was. The sky was bright and clear. The dust from the ride had settled. Col Istor's pennants hung from the walls. Sironen's men had not gotten around to tearing them down. Some of the horses bore southern war gear—round unpeaked helmets and short-bladed swords—but generally there had been little looting. There was wailing in the women's quarters. But from this distance it almost looked as if nothing had happened.

He returned to the castle.

Sironen and his commanders were standing in the outer ward. The archers were picking up their arrows. The blood smell had thickened. Ryke stopped to catch his breath in the stench and heard the wet dreadful sound of someone breathing blood. He glanced at the gate, expecting to see litterbearers. No one was there. "Excuse me," said an archer. Ryke stepped aside. He saw Sironen walking away in the middle of his men, and the line of corpses. Ryke's tired mind balked. What reason could Sironen have for chaining corpses? he thought, and then saw that the blood running from the bodies was bright and fresh. He remembered the old lord's feral grin. Of course Sironen did not want to leave his soldiers to guard southern captives. He needed all the men he could take with him to Tornor. It was simpler to cut their throats.

Dizzied, Ryke put out a hand. Time reeled backward. He shivered under an indifferent sky, and the corpses were his friends, the chains bound his own bloody wrists . . . He fought himself to sense. He was in Cloud Keep, he was on the victor's side of this war. He was not in Tornor.

The dead eyes stared at him, mocking his horror. He told himself not to be a fool. But his skin was clammy with sweat and he could not stop the sickness shaking him. He ran for the gate. Under the disinterested gaze of the grazing horses he knelt, retching himself weak into a thorny tangle of brush.

Six nights later, he knelt outside the walls of Tornor.

His knees hurt. He crouched in a pool of mud. His back hurt from stooping, and the cloth of his pants legs was soaked through.

He ran his hands along the quiver and bowcase to make sure they were still dry. A three-quarter moon gleamed over his shoulder. Behind him, Sironen's squadrons breathed. He could almost imagine that he heard them. But when he listened there was no sound. He was alone. Nothing disturbed the predawn silence, not a footfall, not a whinny nor the jangle of a shank. He couldn't believe that four hundred men could stay so still.

He numbered the gates in his mind. The west postern gatehouse. He touched it with one gloved hand. The east postern gatehouse. The two inner postern doors. The outer gate with its guardhouse which led into the outer ward. The inner gatehouse, barred by the portcullis. The door to the tower. How many gates could six people open before they were discovered? His legs trembled. He stood slowly to ease them. He leaned against the postern gate, willing it to open. Nothing happened. He lowered himself into the mud.

He heard the click of metal on wood. It could be a guard, he reminded himself, a pike striking a stone wall . . . The postern gate opened. He froze. Errel looked out. His teeth flashed in the darkness, and he beckoned. Rising quickly, Ryke slid forward. His boots slipped on the wet ground. He staggered and nearly fell.

Errel seized his arm and pulled him inside the gatehouse. The little hut stank of wine, vomit, and wet wool. Ryke felt light-headed with relief. For six days (two days at Cloud Keep, four days coming across the hills) he had been envisioning Errel caught, imprisoned, dead. He gripped the prince hard. Errel's face was rough with hair;

as part of his disguise, Ryke guessed, he had let his beard grow. "All's well?" he said. He had to clear his throat before he could talk.

"Yes. We danced tonight and the night before. He likes us."

There could be only one *he* in Tornor. "Damn him." Ryke's eyes grew accustomed to the gatehouse darkness, and he saw the guards slumped on the floor, a pair of dice like white eyes at their feet. "Dead?"

"No." Errel mimed a blow on the head. "Did you bring my bow?" Ryke handed him the bow and quiver, heavy with arrows. "Thanks. I gather Sironen took Cloud Keep."

"Yes," Ryke said. He knew that Errel expected him to say more. He did not want to talk about it.

"Later," said the prince. "Come on, we have to get the main inner gate. Do you remember how to raise the portcullis?"

"Yes," Ryke said. He knew he sounded short. He felt Errel look at him. He could not say, *Give me time to believe that I am truly here*. He ran his fingers over the oaken beam of the gatehouse. *Give me time to know that I am in Tornor*.

Errel patted his lips to signal silence. They went out the back door of the gatehouse. There was a wan patch of moonlight between the inner and outer walls. The way to the inner ward was pitch-black and smelled of horse. Ryke kept thinking they were at the end of it. A dog barked, and his nerves jumped at the sound. Suddenly he was pinned to the stone. Light flashed on a knife blade. A hard forearm jammed in imminent threat against his throat.

Errel said, "It's us."

The knife disappeared. "Sorry," said a deep voice. Van let him go. "Your timing is perfect. Did you bring my army?"

"It's outside," Ryke said.

"The postern gates are open," Van said. "We're ready to open the main one. Maranth?"

A hand lifted in the shadow. Ryke heard a soft husky chuckle. Ryke bit the inside of his cheek. There were usually four men on duty in the inner gatehouse. He knew Maranth was fast but he did not think she could take them alone. He drew breath to speak. Errel touched his shoulder. "Watch." Ryke exhaled slowly. Maranth stepped into the waning moonlight. She wore the soft bloused trousers that looked at first like skirts.

She sauntered across the ward as if she were in Vanima. The gatehouse was blocky and imposing, with arrow slits for windows. Even the doors facing inward were reinforced with iron straps. Maranth rapped on the door. "Hello." Her voice lilted into the swelling dawn. The peephole shutter rasped. "I can't sleep. I need someone to talk to, and my friends are all snoring silly. May I sit with you?" She pushed her heavy hair back with a sensual gesture. Her hips swayed. "I brought some wine." She brought a leather wineskin from the folds of her shirt. The door unlatched. Two men looked out. She backed from the door, soundlessly beckoning. As if charmed, three men detached themselves from the gatehouse. Two reached for Maranth. The third prudently captured the wineskin from her hand.

Van said, "Yai!"

Norres, Sorren, and Hadril rose like wolves from the shadows. Maranth had both hands locked around one guard's throat. The others barely had time to look surprised. Sorren and Norres caught them as they fell. Hadril went into the gatehouse. "Come on!" said Van. He sprinted across the ward to the gatehouse. Ryke went after him. A light burned in the musty space. Over it, Hadril's face was set and pale. There was blood on his face. Behind him a man lay twisted on a bunk. "Are you hurt?" Van said. The youth shook his head. "Did you kill him?"

"I had to," said Hadril.

"Now you know what it feels like," said Van. He struck the boy lightly across the face. Hadril blinked. "Get hold of yourself."

A voice shouted from the battlement. "What's going on over there?" It sounded like Held. Ryke wondered who Col had appointed to take over his watch. Vargo, maybe. Sorren slithered into the gatehouse and closed the door behind her. Ryke heard the thud of the latch.

"Quick," said Errel. Ryke groped for the ladder to the winch house. His glove caught on a nail and tore.

He mounted the ladder. At the last rung he looked down and saw the dead man on the bunk. The helmet had rolled from his head. His face was unnaturally white; white as new milk. His glazed eyes were wide in terror. His mouth was open but the sound he'd tried to make had died with him. Hadril's dagger had sliced him under the chin, and his throat cords had been severed by the stroke. A familiar sickness curled Ryke's gut. He tightened his hands and pushed up.

In the winch house he hesitated. The dimensions of the room were different than he recalled. He turned in a circle and barked a shin on the pulley. Running his hands along the machine, he found the spindle wheel. He tried to turn it. It groaned but would not move. Of course, he thought, it's locked.

He heard ragged barking, and yells. The sounds seemed to be heading toward the gatehouse. "Hurry!" cried a voice beneath him. Ryke unlocked the spindle. He pushed the wheel. It was tight.

A slender form surged up the ladder. "What are you waiting for?" said Sorren. She fit her hands over his. Together they pushed. The portcullis lifted. The noise was hideous, loud enough to wake the dead. When it stopped, Ryke could hear the ram drumming against the outer door. He heard the cracks, like stones falling from a great height, as the iron straps burst.

Sironen led his army through the shattered gate.

f i f t e e n

It was an ugly fight.

Sironen drove Col's men back into the barracks, ringed the barracks with his soldiers, and then set fire to the structure. The stone walls would not burn, but the beams and crosspieces flared and fell, trapping the southerners in a maze of timber. The stones grew hot as an oven. To prevent the flames from jumping to the kitchens the old lord kept a squad of men standing near with buckets.

Terrified horses screamed in the stable stalls. The men who had been on watch raced along the battlements, stalked by Pel Keep's soldiers. Ryke slid down the winch house ladder, Sorren behind him. There had been fighting in the gatehouse; more dead men lolled on the bunks. Errel and the chearis had vanished. Sorren started for the door. Ryke held her arm. "Wait." He hunted through the death-crammed room till he found a loose sword.

Stray arrows littered the inner court. A man writhed on the ground in the gatehouse doorway, eyes wild with pain, holding a huge rent in his belly. He had two smashed hands. Ryke stepped over his legs. Sorren stopped. He saw her sword lift for the killing stroke. Smoke stung Ryke's eyes and nose. He looked for Sironen's banner and saw it in front of the great hall. "Come," he said to Sorren.

A Pel Keep soldier ran by, leading a string of horses. One of them had a bleeding gash on its rump. A woman in a grey gown scuttled toward the gate, blond hair flying. Everyone in the castle seemed to be shouting. He heard a crash from the barracks and a cheer from Sironen's men. A small knot of soldiers, so grimed that Ryke could not see their badges, were fighting furiously in the middle of the Yard.

A black-haired man raced across the ward toward the tower stairs. It was Held. Ryke yelled wordlessly at him but the man did not seem to hear him. He looked unwounded. "Later for you," Ryke called.

Metal clashed on metal. A southerner had jumped out of nowhere and attacked Sorren. Calmly the woman stood her ground, parrying his swings, letting him wear himself out. His armor was loose. It flapped like curtains. He swung two-handed. Ryke recognized the swing; it was Ephrem. Sorren dropped. The stroke whined in the air over her head. She leaped up and laid her sword with a surgeon's precision through Ephrem's ribs, angling upward for his heart.

He went down. The blade stuck in his chest. She put her foot on the body and jerked it free. Sironen's banner still waved over the hall. Ryke pointed at it. Sorren wiped her sword and ran ahead of him.

The sound of metal on metal was so loud it made Ryke's ears hurt. The big room hummed. Men seethed in long lines, hacking at each other with swords and axes, stabbing with spears and bright knives . . . Death, they called. He gripped his sword. He smelled blood, and the smoke from the fires. His belly hurt. He did not want to go in there.

An axe sheared past his ear and he leaped away, swinging blindly in the direction it had come from. Flesh split under the sword. A man howled. Another man wearing Col's red and black badge rushed him, cursing and crying. He was in it; he could not get away. He planted his feet. He was in Tornor, he would not die here. He tensed his shoulders and sucked in great breaths of smoke-stained air, making a bright whirling circle of his sword.

He felt someone brace against his back. The press of battle sucked him in. Halfway across the room, a deep voice said in his ear, "Where is Col Istor?"

Hatred soared in him. That was what he had come to Tornor for, to kill Col and all his men, to free the land of him and all his works and ways and progeny . . . "In the watchtower."

"How do we get there?" said Van.

Ryke bared his teeth. "Across the ward." There was only one stair to the tower. No doubt Sironen would have it guarded—he pictured Col pacing in fury around the tiny room like a cornered rat. "Let's go." He blinked the seat from his eyes. Van nodded. They edged toward the doors, back to back. Suddenly the room shivered, as if the floor had buckled. A wedge of men battered their way into the hall, tearing toward Sironen. The point of the wedge was Col. His men roared. Ryke saw Held behind his chief, spear in hand. Ryke lunged, trying to get to him to kill him.

Van swore and fell.

Back exposed, Ryke swung his sword two-handed. His lungs burned. He gulped air. He straddled Van. He could not stoop to see if the cheari was still alive. He couldn't leave him to get to Col. Something bit his left side. The blood smell made him stagger. He stepped on something soft. He hoped it wasn't Van. His head spun and buzzed. He wanted to lie down in the softness and sleep.

He felt the pain again in his side and knew he had been cut. It was his own blood he smelled. Raging, he lifted his head toward the light. He was almost close enough to Col to touch him. He heard Sironen yelling orders. He snarled at the man in black and silver who stepped in front of him. "Get out of my way!" He had to kill Col. He had promised to do it. The spears struck out. The soldier in front of him kneeled over.

Suddenly Held flung up one hand and fell like a dropped stone. An arrow stuck out of him. The trim white feathers glinted in the light. A second man fell. Ryke looked over his shoulder. Errel stood on a table. His face was smeared with soot. He was holding his great bow. He lifted it and shot. Another southerner fell. Errel picked Col's men away from him, one by one. For a moment there was near silence in the hall. In the quiet, Ryke heard the released joyful leaping of the thawed Rurian.

Shading his eyes with one broad hand, Col gazed across the room at Errel. His lips moved. Errel shot two shafts in succession. One went into Col's belly, the other into his neck. The southerner grimaced. Blood ran down his mail, coating it with red. He folded over slowly on top of his men.

Van had taken a pike thrust through the large muscle of his left leg. The cut on Ryke's side was shallow. He wadded up a piece of cloth and stuck it against the wound under his leathers. His ears buzzed. He crouched. Van was sitting, pulling the cloth from his wound, swearing. "Help me up," he said to Ryke.

"Better to wait for the surgeon."

"Damn you." Van tried to lift himself and fell back.

"I can't help you up," Ryke said. "I'm hurt."

"Then reach me a pike," said the cheari. Ryke wished he would shut up. Sironen was roaring at a troop of men and he wanted to hear what he was saying. Something about the stables. Perhaps they had not got all the horses out of them. Perhaps they had burned. He held himself stiff. If he leaned he would touch the dead. Sunlight moved slowly downward over the dusty walls, brightening the faded colors of the tapestries.

Maranth waded through the carnage. She carried a waterskin. She held it first to Van's lips, then to Ryke's. Her hands had blood on them. "Are you hurt?" Van said.

"No." She crossed her legs. "Sit still," she said, laying a hand across her husband's forehead.

"Are the others—"

"Safe," she said. Van sighed. He closed his right hand over hers.

The surgeon was plump and imperturbable. He made Ryke unlace his mail and his shirt. "That's not bad. Drink this." He pushed a flask into Ryke's right hand. "Hold that arm still." The drink was wine laced with honey. Ryke gagged. "Careful. Don't get sick." Ryke felt something cold on his side.

"What's that?"

"A poultice to help the cut heal. Lift the other arm too, please." The surgeon wound strips of linen around Ryke's ribs as he sat with both arms over his head. "Thank you. You can put them down." He turned to Van. "What's this, hmm?" He clicked his tongue. In his shiny black and silver he reminded Ryke of a beetle clicking its wings. Ryke rubbed his mouth to keep from laughing. They teach them how to make that sound, he thought, when they take them as apprentices.

The surgeon made appreciative professional noises as he worked on Van's leg. He bathed it with hot water. Van's mouth twisted but he did not speak. Maranth stroked his hair. "It's a clean thrust," said the fat man. "You're lucky. You'll walk on it."

Van said, "I'm a dancer."

"Dance on it, too, if you give it time to heal. If you walk too soon you'll open it. It's bled enough. Leave it be or it'll fester."

Over his head Maranth said, "Don't worry. If I have to, I'll tie him to a chair."

Ryke stood. The poultice numbed the pain of his side, and the bandage made him itch. He looked for his sword, found it, and slid it into the sheath. "I'll see you later," he said to the chearis.

Maranth said, "We'll be right here." Van said nothing. His breathing was faster than usual, and there was little color in his face. Ryke went out of the hall. A soldier limped by him, his left boot hanging in strips.

Crows wheeled in lazy circles over the castle. Smoke drifted upward from the ruined barracks. Most of the walls had fallen in. Men with buckets made a line from the well to one corner of the building where the ashes still smoldered. The wind shifted. Ryke smelled the sweet odor of burning meat.

He went to the watchtower stairs. Two silver-and-black-clad soldiers sat on the bottom step. "Sorry. No one goes up there."

"I'm not a looter."

"Prince's orders."

Ryke wondered which prince had ordered it, Errel or Sironen. He retreated. Useless to tell these men that he had wanted to look, not take.

He pulled off the leather breastplate. It was making him sweat. The sword dragged at his waist. He took it off and leaned it against the wall. He didn't need it. The wind shifted again, blowing from the west. He heard weeping. Warily he pushed open the red door to the apartments.

His foot struck something metal as he went in. He squinted down the dark hall. The thing glinted. He lowered himself carefully and picked it up. It was a woman's brooch in the shape of a daisy. He thought it was silver. He turned it in his fingers and let it drop.

No guards had been posted here. The rooms had been ransacked. Lengths of silk and velvet trained across the floor, mud-stained. Deep within the building he heard a man's voice. A door hung off its hinges. He looked in. A woman sat in the center of what had been a curtained bed. The curtains lay in heaps on the floor. The woman's breasts were bare. Her pale hair straggled across her face. Her eyes were swollen but she was not crying now. Ryke swallowed. The buzz had started in his head again. "I won't hurt you," he said. She stared at him stonily. "I'm looking for my sister, Becke." She seemed not to hear him. Finally she licked her lips.

"Fourth door," she said.

"Thank you," Ryke said. He went back into the hall. He counted four doors. Behind the third he heard small shrill pulses of noise; he couldn't tell if they were giggles or shrieks.

He opened the door of the fourth room. The blood smell made his nostrils curl. He took a step into it. Under the stench of death, he smelled the light mingled fragrances of honeysuckle and jasmine. The room was smashed, ugly. Becke lay in the bed, one arm outflung as if she were asleep. They had tucked a cover around her. Her hair trailed outside it. Her eyes looked past him. The brown locks reached to her knees. He hadn't known her hair had grown that long. From the outline of her body under the blue silks he could see what they had done to her. He wondered if the Pel Keep soldiers had known she was Col Istor's woman, his property, and killed her because of it. The other was unimportant. It happened to all women. In war you could not even call it rape.

He came out of the apartments and was face to face with Errel.

For a moment he did not know him. He started to walk around this red-haired stranger. He saw the bow and quiver and stopped. "Ryke." The prince touched his shoulder. "Are you hurt?"

"My side. It's not bad."

A soldier in black and silver ran to Errel. "My lord."

"What is it?" said the prince.

"My lord Sironen wishes you to know they still hold the stables. He asks, *Do you wish them burned out?*"

"On no account!" said Errel sharply. "Tell him I'm coming." He gripped Ryke's arm. "Come with me." He was wearing the ruby ring on his left hand. There was a trace of soot on one side of his face, and his left eyebrow looked singed.

Gam and some men of his watch had barricaded themselves inside the stables. Sironen paced in front of the doors. The scar on his cheek throbbed redly. His men sat like hungry cats at all the doors and windows. Errel walked to Sironen. They spoke. The men watched, waiting to be told what to do. A few held torches.

"No," said Errel. He shook his head emphatically. He strode in front of the shut doors and raised his voice. "You men! Col Istor is dead. The forces of Pel Keep hold this castle. If you come out and surrender you will be left unharmed. Otherwise, we'll starve you out."

The soldiers muttered. Clearly they wished to burn the holdouts. The wind skittered straws along the court. Errel glared at them, his eyes icy. The mutterings subsided. There was a babble of argument on the other side of the doors. Gam called, "Who do we surrender to?"

Errel answered. "To the lord of Tornor."

It took the men inside a long time to drag the sacks and bales away from the stable doors. Gam came out. He wore a round northern helmet and a striped horse blanket for a cape. His beard was straggly. "If I'm killed," he said, "the others will close the doors again."

Errel stepped toward him. "Throw down your weapons."

Gam stared. "Oho," he said. "I see. I know you. The jester."

Errel smiled grimly. "The cheari."

"Here." The horse commander laid his sword and knife at Errel's feet. He knelt in the sunlight, palms in the dust.

"Get up," Errel said. The old man stood. He was very bowlegged. "You can go."

The soldiers growled. Gam tugged at his beard. "You're freeing us?"

"You think I want you cluttering up the castle?" said Errel. "The gate is that way. You may leave. Take your men with you."

Gam gaped at him, incredulous. "Without a horse?"

Sironen laughed, a flat bark. The soldiers began to howl. Gam stumped back to the stable, disgust plain on every line of his face. In the midst of mirth the southerners came out of the stable, weapons dragging in the dirt. Bewildered, they gazed at their overcome conquerors. Wiping their eyes, the Pel Keep soldiers closed around them.

After the bodies had been dragged outside the walls and pyres lit, Sironen sent his men to bivouac in the field under the command of the watch seconds. Errel, Ryke, the chearis, Sironen and his commanders, and Gam and his men stayed inside the Keep. Sironen had convinced Errel to make prisoners of the surviving southerners. "If they go outside these walls," the old lord said, with his wolfish smile, "my men will kill them." Errel told the southerners this. Then he ordered them to work. They shuffled from the well to the apartments bearing mops and buckets, guarded by a few bored soldiers. Sironen's men had thoughtfully spared the kitchen staff. As the noise of battle died away, they crept from storerooms, pantry, scullery.

Most of them knew Errel. The southerners looked wary. The northerners flung themselves at his feet. A few were weeping. He sent them back to the kitchen. "Evad, wait." The scullion so named turned back, twisting his apron in his hands. "You can ride, can't you?" The boy nodded. "Ride to the village. Tell Sterret what's happened and ask him to come here and see me. Tomorrow will be soon enough."

"You'd best send a trooper with him," said Sironen.

"No, he'll do it." Errel smiled at the boy. Athor smiled at his soldiers like that, Ryke thought, and they loved him. "Sterret's his uncle. Won't you?"

"Yes, my lord." He flushed with pride.

"Take one of the slower horses," Errel said dryly. The boy bowed and loped to where the horses were tethered grazing outside the wall. Errel leaned on the table with both elbows, resting his chin in his hands. He had found clean clothes somewhere. They were too big for him. Ryke wondered if they were Col's. The tunic was purple. Col had a purple tunic. His eyes blurred and he rubbed them. He was very tired.

Sironen and his commanders talked about the hundred southerners still at Zilia Keep. A servant girl brought a jug of wine from the kitchen, and they passed it round the table as if they had not just fought a war. The setting sun turned the Anhard weapons on the walls scarlet. The chearis sat a little apart from the men, listening, not talking. Hadril had his head down in his arms. Sorren's head lay on Norres' shoulder.

"Excuse me, my lords." Errel and Sironen both looked up. It was Torib. He stood in front of the table, one massive hand crooked around the thin shoulder of a small boy. "Thought you might want to see this. He says he's the son of Berent One-Eye." The boy was thinner than Ryke remembered him. His tunic was ragged and filthy. But his hair was pale and spiky, and his eyes were pale blue, pale as marshfire . . . Errel stretched a hand to him.

"Come here." The child moved jerkily toward him. Errel nodded. "I remember you. Do you know me?"

"You changed your hair," said the child.

"Yes," Errel said. "It's confusing at first, isn't it?" Ler nodded. "Were you frightened when the fighting started?"

"Yes. But I was with *him*. He told me to go to the kitchen and hide in the pots, and not come out until the noise stopped. So I did."

"You were right to do that," Errel said. "Are you hungry?"

"Yes, sir."

"Take him back to the kitchen," Errel said, "and feed him." Torib bowed. He reached for Ler and pulled the boy to him.

Sironen said, "Aren't you watch second? What are you doing away from bivouac?"

Torib's moon face creased in a bland smile. "Talking with the kitchen maids, my lord," he said, "about supplies." He bowed again and went toward the kitchen, still holding the boy. Ler walked stiffly, hands flat against his sides, his prior grace spoiled.

So Col had not killed the boy after all. Errel had been right. On the battlements Col's banners flapped like laundry on a line. But Becke was dead. Ryke's thoughts scuttled from that one like frogs from a snake. His mother would have to know. He pressed the heel of his hand against his eyes. He would have to tell her; no one else could.

A servant brought out a platter of meat, steaming and brown, the sauce still bubbling. The men jostled forward, reaching with the tips of their knives.

Lune, Sironen's senior commander, said, "Perhaps we should send out a call for the green clan to deal with those men in Zilia Keep." He waved his morsel of pig in front of his face to cool it.

The others chafed him. "Tired of fighting?"

"What do you think, my lord?" Lune leaned toward Errel. The meat dripped juice on the table.

The prince looked up. "That will be your decision to make," he said. "Not mine."

Sironen said, "What?"

Errel clasped his hands in front of him on the wood. "I am not staying at Tornor."

A black dog stole slowly from the kitchen into the hall. Sironen's commanders looked at their lord, and then at each other. Arno said, "What did we fight this war for, then?"

"To rid yourselves of Col Istor," said the prince. "You would have had to fight him sooner or later."

Sironen thrust his jaw out. "You are lord of Tornor."

Errel said, "Not if I give it up."

"To whom?" said Arno. Sorren's head lifted from Norres' shoulder. Errel turned the ring on his finger around and around.

"My father had another child," he said.

Sironen barked. He laid his hands flat on the table. "Athor was a man. He probably sired a dozen. What of it?"

Ryke shivered. The sweat was pouring off him. "A child fit to rule," Errel said. "A child who is more of a warrior than I."

He had their attention. "Who?" demanded Arno.

Errel looked at the chearis. Sorren sat bolt upright. All the color had gone from her face. Beside her, Norres was as motionless as if she had been carved from stone. Her eyes were brilliant with tears. "Sister, will you take it?" Sorren nodded. Errel leaned the length of the table and dropped the ring into her palm.

Sironen's commanders cried out. At the perimeter of the ward, the captive southerners turned to look, leaning on their brooms and mops the way they were used to leaning on their swords. Arno stood. The silver on his badges glittered. He put his hands on his hips. "How can a woman rule a Keep?"

Sorren tilted her head to one side. She said, "You have seen me fight."

He flapped a contemptuous hand. "You can fight. Wolves fight. Dogs fight. Can you lead?"

It was a fair question, Ryke thought. Sorren's right hand fisted on the ring. "I have been a messenger," she said, "a member of the green clan. Ask my brother, he will tell you." The heads turned to him; Errel nodded. "Who are you to challenge me if the green clan takes me in?"

Lune pursed his lips.

Arno scowled. He seemed suddenly very young. "Women are to

fuck and to bear men's children," he said doggedly. "They are not supposed to command."

Sorren rose. Her eyes were smoky. "Little boy," she said, "I will nail your ears to your head for that." She stepped over the bench and glided toward him. He stared at her in astonishment and then realized that she was serious. He fell into a defensive crouch, feeling for the long knife at his belt. Their boots thudded on the stone floor. They circled. Sorren's hands were empty. Her face was taut and watchful. Arno drew his knife from the sheath. He held it clumsily, blade straight, all of his fingers wrapped tight around the bronze hilt. He struck at Sorren. She weaved away from the blade, dancing to his back with compelling grace. Van grunted approval. Arno whirled to find her, furious. She smiled sweetly at him and held up her hands as if to say, *I can beat you bare-handed, boy.* He sliced backhanded at her, a swordsman's stroke. She spun with the slash, leaped behind him, and brought him down on his back, her knee in his spine, his right arm stretched out across her other thigh. She bent his arm back. His hand opened. The knife rolled from his fingers. She picked it up. Her left arm tucked itself deeper into his throat. She drew his head back. His body arched. His heels scraped the stone. His left hand, strengthless, clawed at the choke. She let him go. He rolled onto his face, gasping. She stood, breathing hard. She walked to the table and put the ring onto the first finger of her left hand. "Tornor is mine," she said.

The next day, Sterret came to the Keep. He looked no different. The tip of his cane went *tock, tock* on the ground. He was so unchanged that it made Ryke realize for the first time how little time had passed since he and Errel had left Tornor. It was less than a month and a half. Yet in that time they had gone from winter to summer to winter again, juggling between north and south—and now it was spring in Tornor. The birds were nesting in the parapets, and in the grasses the horses pranced like colts. It seemed ironic. He had longed for this spring in Vanima.

He met Sterret beside the smashed gates. One of the soldiers took the old man's horse. "Good day," he said, as if they were standing at the gate of his house. Ryke thought, Evad must have told him I survived. "Your mother greets you."

Ryke had to ask. "Is she well?"

Sterret was looking at the wreck of the barracks. "Yes," he answered absently. "Quite well." No doubt he was totting up in his mind the wood the Keep would need for rebuilding. "Is the prince well?"

"Yes," Ryke said. His collar was crooked. He twitched it straight. He pointed toward the great hall. "We go there." He shortened his stride to fit Sterret's pace. He was not going to tell the old headman that Errel was no longer prince, no longer lord of Tornor.

Sorren and Errel sat on a bench beneath the shining length of a pike. The head of the pike, below the blade, was shaped like the jaws of a dragon. He brought Sterret to them. He bowed to them both. He could not help it that his eyes went first to Errel. "My lady," he said formally, "may I present Sterret, headman of Tornor village." Sorren rose. Errel did not. Ryke left Sterret looking from one to the other of them in growing bewilderment.

He sat in the sunlight. He could hear Gam's voice across the ward, swearing at the stableboys. He told himself he would soon get used to southern faces wearing Tornor's badge. Sironen had offered to leave a small garrison of men at the Keep. "Torib here has volunteered to be acting commander until you wish to name other men."

Sorren's eyes had rested on Torib's unctuous smiling face. "Has that old man left yet?" she said. "The horsemaster?"

"You would hire southerners?" said Torib. "My lady, only consider—" He stopped at the look on her face.

"He fights for pay, does he not?" she said. "If he can fight for Col Istor, he can fight for me." Sironen directed one of his men to find Gam and bring him to them. He came, still carrying a mop, bandy-legged and stooped. She folded her arms across her breasts and stared at him. He licked his lips. "Old man," she said, "my name is Sorren. I am Athor's daughter and Errel's sister and this castle and its trust are now mine. I need commanders. Will you be one of them?"

His jaw dropped. His teeth were big and yellow, like a mule's. "Why should you want me?"

"You never did me any harm," she had said, "and you know horses."

He had bowed awkwardly. The strings of the mop wet his feet. "At your service, my lady."

"Ryke." The soft voice cut like a knife across his memories. He jumped. She stood in front of him. She moved so quietly he hadn't heard her. He rose. He did not know what to call her. "I don't want to disturb you," she said.

"You don't disturb me," he said.

"May I sit?"

The question struck him as funny. There was no place in Tornor she could not sit. The very stones were hers. "Please," he said. She folded down beside him, hair falling in a bright wing across her cheek, knees to her chin. She wore a silk tunic with pale green flowers embroidered on it, and men's breeches, and the red band of a cheari on her head. She brushed her hair back.

"This is a nice spot you picked."

"Yes."

She gazed over the inner ward. The black dog trotted across it. Ryke wondered if it were the black wolfhound. He whistled softly. It turned its head but did not come. It went purposefully toward the apartments. "I'm glad it's over," she said. She gestured at the battered Keep. "So much hatred to fill one small space . . ."

"Is it over?" Ryke said.

Her face tightened. "It is for me." She sat up. "Ryke, I have something to ask of you." He waited. "This is hard to ask. I need strong men around me. Others will feel like that puppy Arno. They will doubt my ability to hold the Keep."

She wanted him as commander. He ran his hands over the warm gritty stones and waited for her to say it.

"Gam will be one watch commander. The lord Sironen has very kindly offered me any of his seconds—at my own choosing—to be second watch commander. It will not be Torib, you may be sure of that." She grinned. "Norres will be my third." He looked up quickly. She held his eyes for one long moment. "She has promised me that she will stay in Tornor at least a year." Only the control in her voice displayed the depth of emotion that had prompted that promise. Ryke wondered if Norres would be man or woman to the men she commanded. Maybe she would turn back into a ghya. "Van will send me a Yardmaster from Vanima. I can make do with three watch commanders. Van tells me such a routine is common in the south."

"But I thought—" he checked it. His back was tense. He stretched to ease it. "What do you want of me?"

A black-haired kitchenmaid walked out of the kitchen door toward the postern gate. A beheaded chicken dangled from one hand, held casually by its legs. She was singing. The tune came faintly to Ryke's ears, borne on the fickle wind. He found himself fitting the words to it. *I am a stranger in an outland country . . .*

"I want you to go to Cloud Keep," she said. "I want you to be regent for the boy Ler. He needs someone strong, and I need someone strong and loyal, both between me and Pel Keep. I don't entirely trust Sironen. You will have to levy troops from the villages and farms, and so will I, and they will all be too old or too green, but you will manage. The first thing we must do is call for the green clan to secure a peace among all the Keeps."

The woman went into the alley between the inner and outer ward. Ryke wondered if the chicken were for Torib. He brushed the stones again. He guessed that this had been one of the terms of Norres' promise, that Sorren ask him to leave . . . He could refuse. "I have to talk to Errel," he said.

Sorren's voice was warm. "Of course."

As he passed the apartment door Norres came through it. She stood, hand on the bolt. She did not speak, and he could not think of anything to say to her. The black wolfhound came out. She closed the door behind it. He went on. He found Errel with Hadril and Van on the tower steps, like cats lazing in the sunlight. Van sat on the lowest step, leg stretched out on a cloth. His chest was bare. His cheeks were pebbly with a day's beard. Hadril sat on the second and Errel on the third step up. He wore the red band of the cheari around his arm. "Ho," said Van. "Come sit."

"I thought Maranth was going to tie you to a chair."

"I'm healing well. Besides, we compromised. She swore not to yell at her and I swore not to yell at her and I swore I'd hop." He poked Hadril's leg. "Move down one, chelito." Hadril complied. Now the second step was vacant. Ryke went between Hadril and Van and sat on it.

He was terribly aware of Errel lolling on the step above him. A door banged in the apartments. Maranth strolled out. She had washed her hair; it radiated from her head in all directions. Ryke moved up one step. Hadril moved up. Maranth took his place next to Van. She narrowed her eyes dramatically at her husband. "I hopped," he protested.

She relented. "I won't yell." She leaned into his side. Their bodies fit—Ryke felt a stab of pain. It had nothing to do with the cut on his side. He had never found anyone to lean on like that.

He said over Hadril's shoulder, "What are you going to do now?"

Van said, "Wait for this damned hole to close." He put his arm around Maranth's waist.

"And then?"

"Go back to the valley, of course." He sounded surprised at the question. "What did you think I would do?"

The linen around Ryke's ribs itched. He would have to get the surgeon to change it. "You could go south," he said. "The Keeps would speak for you. You could challenge the edict of exile. You could go home."

As he said it, he wondered if Van would be angry to have his true identity spoken of so lightly. Hadril might not know it. The big southerner twisted around. He didn't look angry. He said, "You mis-understand. I *am* going home."

Hadril took his shirt off. His bare shoulder rubbed Ryke's knee. "Are you going back, too?" Ryke said.

"Yes," said the boy. He laid his shirt across his knees to fold it. "I don't like it in the north, it's too cold, and I hate wars." His voice shook passionately. His vehemence made Ryke feel suddenly old.

His mouth was dry. He moistened it. "Prince—"

Errel's head turned toward him. "You should not call me that," he said gently.

"Are you going too?"

"Yes," Errel said. He leaned his elbows on his knees. Their shoulders touched.

"Why?"

Errel said, "You know why, Ryke. I'm like Hadril. I was happy in Vanima. I'm not happy fighting wars." The breeze shifted, and Ryke smelled his scent, that unique odor that every human being carries with him from birth and does not change and is different for everyone. Ryke had breathed it, in their shared bed, many times. Errel had shaved, and the line of his jaw was smooth and polished. His skin was more gold than Sorren's. His hair just touched his shirt. His eyes were a deeper blue than hers. It was the likeness to Errel that Ryke loved in Sorren. His eyes blurred. He wondered if there were any way for him to explain that to Norres.

He said, "Sorren's asked me to go to Cloud Keep as regent for Ler."

The chearis were silent. Errel said in his formal tones, "She could not find an ally or a friend more loyal." In his own voice he said, "I would like you to do that."

Hadril, head bowed, was busy picking a sliver out of his palm. Van and Maranth were absorbed in each other. Chayatha told me, Ryke thought. *Be careful of what is in your heart.* He had had his heart's desire—and lost it. He had not been careful enough.

He had thought she was making magic. An ant crawled over his forearm, a bit of grass in its jaws. He flicked it off. Two soldiers wandered out of the gatehouse. One of them pointed at the Yard.

Through the thick castle walls, Ryke heard the ancient music of the river as it curved close to the Keep, swollen with melting snow from the heights. He pictured it weaving among the rocks. It has no choices to make, he thought. The rocks make them. He listened to the limpid sounds. Maybe the river would tell him what to do. It seemed to be speaking, but the words were in a language he didn't know.

He pleaded in the only way he could. "I could go with you to Vanima."

"You are not a cheari."

His throat ached. "No."

"You swore an oath to my father," Errel said. "I release you from it."

Ryke looked north, over the castle wall. The mountains' sharp edges cut the sky, shredding the clouds into white ribbons. They passed over his head, going south. You cannot release me, he thought.

"Thank you, my prince."

He rose. The others made way for him. He stepped with care between their legs. Sorren was waiting for him inside the hall.

He went to give her his assent.